The Secret Rose

by

LAURA LANDON

PRAIRIE MUSE PUBLISHING

©2016

This is a work of fiction. Names, characters, places, and incidents either are the product of the author's imagination or are used fictitiously. Any resemblance to actual persons living or dead is entirely coincidental.

Dedicated

With much appreciation
to my readers

AUGUST 1862

In the space of one infinitesimal heartbeat, Abigail Langdon's perfect world shattered beyond recognition.

She stared at the entangled lovers on the bed and clamped her hands over her mouth to stifle a scream. Her mouth opened as the cacophony of clashing explosions collided inside her head. But all that spilled into the tepid air—rife with the sweet smell of human passion—was one small, pathetic gasp. And a strangled moan barely loud enough to be heard.

"Abigail!" the female called out.

"Bloody hell!" the man swore.

Abigail lifted her skirts and ran down the long hall. Disgust and revulsion churned in her stomach, threatening to make her ill. Tears stung her eyes as she raced down the winding staircase that would take her to the entrance hall below.

He would come after her. He would try to make her understand.

She took the last two steps in one unladylike leap.

He could rot in hell before she would accept what he

had done.

She ran through her father's study, wishing her father was home and the servants had not all gone to bed. She wished someone would be there to help her. She couldn't bear it if he touched her.

"Abigail!"

She raced through the double French doors and onto the stone terrace. Her skirt caught on a wrought iron bench and ripped when she yanked it free. Her world spun around her as she sped down the cobbled path, ignoring the sharp pebbles that cut through her soft slippers.

She veered to the right, oblivious of the flowering rhododendron branches that whipped around her face. The cupid fountain bubbled softly, a stark contrast to the terror building inside her. But even the loud thundering of her heart couldn't drown out his nearness as booted steps raced toward her.

"Abigail. Dammit! Stop!"

His voice echoed so loudly in her ears, she swore she could feel his warm breath against the back of her neck. She wanted to turn around to see how near he was, but knew she would lose precious time doing something so foolish.

She clutched her hand to the stitch in her side and forced one foot in front of the other as she circled the fountain. She'd taken barely one step off the main path before his large muscled fingers clamped around her upper arm. He jerked her to a halt and spun her toward him, pulling her against his chest with such force the air rushed from her lungs.

"Dammit, Abigail. Listen to me."

She swallowed past the bile in her throat, trying not to look at the wrinkled clothes he'd thrown on in haste. His white lawn shirt gaped open halfway down his chest. His shirttail hung loosely over breeches that were barely fastened. She turned her face away, too repulsed to absorb any more.

"You have to forget what you just saw."

She struggled to free herself from his grasp, but he would not release her. She struggled harder. "Take your hands off me. You make me ill."

"No. Not until you listen to me." He placed his fingers beneath her chin and forced her to look at him. "What happened was regrettable. But it meant nothing."

She tried to pull away from him. "Nothing? How can you say it meant nothing?"

"Don't be such a silly twit. Things like this happen all the time. Someday you'll be thankful they do."

She turned her head in disgust. "Get away from me. I never want to see you again."

He pressed a finger against her lips to silence her, then cupped his hand to her cheek. "You don't mean that. We are well suited to each other, destined to marry."

His tone had softened, sounding like the Stephen she was used to hearing.

She found the courage to look at him. A painful jolt surged through her. She, too, had believed they were well suited. She'd been attracted to him from the moment she'd seen him, had imagined herself in love with him. Her knight in shining armor. The man she would marry.

"You've ruined everything," she whispered, struggling to maintain her dignity. "I don't ever want to see you again."

"You don't mean that." He tightened his grip on her shoulders. "Nothing has changed."

She shook her head. "Everything has changed. I could never marry you now."

"Of course you will marry me. We are betrothed."

He caressed her cheek with his manicured fingers.

His touch was distasteful. His nearness left her feeling dirty. She slapped his hand away.

"Don't touch me."

"Don't talk like that, sweetheart."

Abigail stared at him, the blinders suddenly gone, transforming the sensitive, endearing hero she thought she loved into a weak, self-indulged failure. "How could you? I believed you when you said you loved me."

"Of course I love you. You are the woman I'm going to marry. The future Countess of Burnhaven."

His words sickened her. "Do you really think I would marry you after what I saw?"

"Yes." There was panic written in his features, desperation in his eyes. Without warning, he brought his lips down to cover hers.

His kiss was hard, demanding, nothing like the tender way he'd kissed her before. Abigail twisted her head to free herself, then swiped her mouth with the back of her hand. "Find yourself someone else to marry, Stephen. I would rather give myself away on the street than ever let you touch me."

"No!" he yelled, his single word an uncompromising demand, his voice harsh with emotion. "You will marry me!"

She twisted the engagement ring from her finger, poised to throw it back at him.

He grabbed her wrist and forced the ring back where it had been. "You will not ruin me. I need your dowry. I am bankrupt without it!"

Abigail's world stopped. She stared at him in shocked disbelief, unable to take in what he'd said. His words of love had meant nothing. It was her dowry he wanted, her father's wealth.

The rigid expression on his face changed in a heart's

beat, turning softer, more controlled.

"Sweetheart, listen to me." He lowered his head and kissed her softly on the cheek. His breath smelled strongly of brandy.

"All that is left is to sign the marriage contract and we will be married as planned. Better yet," He cupped her cheeks in the palms of his hands. "I see no reason to wait. I will talk to your father in the morning, and we will have the wedding in two weeks. The sooner we marry, the better."

"There is no way I would ever marry you now," she argued defiantly.

The look in his eyes changed. Darkened. "There is one way."

He grabbed her, his fingers digging into the flesh at her shoulders. His lips dragged wet kisses across her face, at her temple, down her neck. Then he kissed her full on the mouth.

Abigail pulled back, trying to release herself from his grasp. Stephen had never kissed her like this before. Her heart thundered in her head, her breathing ragged and short. The whimpering sound she heard must have come from her, or the angels were weeping in her stead.

"Please understand, dearest," he said, touching her, stroking his hands up and down her arms. "I am so sorry—so very, very sorry—but I have to make you mine. I cannot chance losing you."

He kissed her again, muffling the scream that rose from deep within her. His hands skimmed over her body, touching her in places she did not want to be touched, holding her like she did not want to be held.

Hot scalding tears welled in her eyes, spilling down her cheeks, falling to the ground.

He pushed her back until her legs touched the

fountain, and she could go no further. Then he forced her to the ground.

"No. Please, don't." Her voice sounded barely more than a fragile whisper, her words unanswered pleas.

He pulled at her gown.

Cool air struck her flesh. Panic built within her until she couldn't breathe. She pushed against him, fighting to stop him, struggling to be free. Her hands slapped at him. In desperation, she scraped her fingernails down the side of his face, making long bloody scratches on his cheeks.

He pulled back to wipe away the blood. "It will do you no good to fight, my darling. I no longer have a choice. I have to make you mine."

Abigail shook her head from side to side, fighting his heavy weight atop her. When she screamed again, he clamped his hand over her mouth, stifling her pleas for help.

"Sweetheart, please. It's all right. You are almost my wife."

He rained more kisses over her face, her neck, then lower, over her exposed flesh. She was powerless against him, his sheer size and muscled strength an insurmountable enemy. Abigail's arms flailed at her side.

Her hand struck against something hard—something jagged and heavy. She wrapped her fingers around the large rock that had come loose from the fountain and lifted it, as if it were a lifeline to save her.

Chapter 1

JANUARY 1864

Ethan John Cambridge, second son of the late Earl of Burnhaven, took the stone steps leading to his brother's London town house two at a time and strode through the open door. Suppressing a sigh of frustration, he threw his soft kid gloves into his top hat and dropped the black satin-lined cape from his shoulders into Hargrove's waiting arms.

Bloody hell. He didn't think this night would ever end. Spending time with his mother required more patience and control of his temper than he had left at the end of a long day. He swept his fingers through his dark hair, then slipped a finger into the knot of his cravat and gave it a hard tug.

With his usual precision and aplomb, the butler set Ethan's hat on the round table in the middle of the foyer and turned to ask the same question he did each time Ethan returned from dinner with his mother.

"And how did you enjoy your evening with the countess, sir?"

Ethan undid the last button on his tailcoat and

stripped it off. Hargrove caught it before it fell. "Wonderful," Ethan lied, working loose the three buttons of his silver brocade waistcoat. "Just. Wonderful."

Hargrove gave a soft, undignified snort, indicating Ethan's lie was not lost on him. Nothing was lost on the butler. Ethan wondered if Stephen had ever even noticed the man who ran his household with an efficiency Ethan found staggering.

That deficit in his brother's character angered Ethan even more. That, added to the fact that this was the second time in the last eighteen months Ethan had been forced to return to London to play the temporary earl brought his blood to a boil.

For the thousandth time, Ethan wondered what had happened. The Stephen he'd grown up with would never have nearly bankrupted what had been passed down to him. Or walked away from the responsibilities that went with being the Earl of Burnhaven without a look back. The son next in line to inherit the Burnhaven earldom would never have cared more for gambling, womanizing, and drinking, than doing the responsible thing and marrying the woman to whom he was betrothed. The woman whose massive dowry would have solved all their problems. Yet he had.

Without a word as to where he was going, or why, Stephen had mysteriously disappeared nearly two years ago and hadn't been heard from since.

Ethan rubbed his throbbing temple. *Bloody hell. Where could Stephen be?* Didn't he realize how close he was to losing everything?

Ethan pulled his mind back to the multitude of details he had to take care of yet tonight. "I am expecting some papers from the steward at Penhurst Manor. Have they arrived yet?"

"A messenger brought them a few minutes ago. I put

them in the study, sir."

Ethan nodded as he paused to sift through the cards and messages left on the silver tray on the hall table. A dozen or more invitations to an endless round of dinners, balls, and soirées. How he hated participating in such frivolities. They were the exact reason he'd left London five years ago. The reason he'd never intended to return.

Bloody hell. If Stephen were here right now, he'd beat him within an inch of his life. How dare he disappear with only a note saying he needed time to see the world before he settled down with a wife. How dare he leave with his affairs in such a precarious state.

Anger simmered to a slow boil. Ethan could not afford to spend much more time in London. He had a plantation of his own to run and a fleet of ships whose cargo needed checking. He didn't have time to keep Stephen's holdings afloat, too.

Hargrove turned from placing Ethan's garments in the closet. "A message also came from East Sussex that requires your attention."

Ethan looked at the butler with raised eyebrows, waiting to hear the evaluation he knew was coming.

"I would say an answer can wait until morning, sir. There is, however, a letter that came by special messenger that appears quite urgent. I put it on your desk. It would seem it cannot wait."

"Anything else?"

"Perhaps that is enough for tonight, sir," Hargrove suggested in his most conciliatory tone. "There are a few more minor details—personal cards and social invitations," he said, glancing at the tray, "but I will go through them and present those I deem most important in the morning."

Ethan nodded, then flipped the card he held in his

hand back onto the silver tray before walking to what was beginning to feel more and more like his own study and less like Stephen's. For a few hours at least, he would put the pressures behind him. And he would try to put behind him the anger he felt toward his brother.

He walked to the small oval table on the far side of the room and pulled the stopper from one of Stephen's expensive cut crystal decanters. After pouring a generous amount of the amber liquid into a glass, he raised it to his lips. The first long swallow burned on its way down his throat. He welcomed the feeling.

"One of these times, Mac, you're not going to make it past Hargrove," Ethan said without turning.

Ethan heard a hearty laugh and turned to face his friend and fellow sea captain Malcolm MacDonnell. The big Scot sat in the dark on the other side of the room in one of the burgundy leather wing chairs angled before the blazing fireplace. An empty brandy glass dangled from his fingers.

"Your wily butler nearly discovered me tonight," he said, holding out his glass to be filled. "I'm going to have to remember to oil the hinges on that window before I return. Hiding in your closet while your protector checked for intruders was damned uncomfortable."

"It would not hurt for you to come in through the front door like everyone else."

A long pause stretched between them. "I think I'm being followed."

Ethan stopped filling Mac's glass, then breathed a deep sigh. Mac's warning was not welcome. Not now. Ethan still had too much to do.

Ethan shrugged his shoulders, then continued filling Mac's glass. The broad-shouldered Scot had sailed the seas with him since the day Ethan had boarded one of his father's trader ships bound for China. He was more a brother to him than Stephen had ever been. "I guess I'll just have to take more care," Ethan said.

"I think it may require more than that." Mac stretched his long, muscular legs out and studied Ethan with a look of concern.

"Perhaps it will give me an excuse to beg off from a few of my more unpleasant obligations."

Mac sighed. "Another enjoyable evening with the countess, eh?" he said, sitting back in his chair.

Ethan sat in a chair opposite Mac and threw another swallow to the back of this throat. "She can't see his faults, Mac. Even after all these months, she still seems more eager to cut out her tongue than say something negative about her firstborn."

"She's his mother. Mothers have a tendency to turn a blind eye to their children's mistakes."

"That's fine to a point, but Stephen has lost nearly everything that was left him. He is far from the bloody saint she thinks he is. And what's worse, there's a bitterness growing in her that's frightening. She's more convinced each day it's the girl's fault he left."

Mac pinned Ethan with a hard look. "What do you think?"

"Don't forget, it was my luck to be in London when Stephen decided to take off. I was the one who had to take his note to his betrothed and explain that Stephen had left her practically standing at the altar."

"Have you seen the girl since?" Mac asked, resting his elbows on the arms of the chair and propping his chin atop his steepled fingers.

Ethan shook his head. "Not since the day I was issued the invitation to travel to their country estate so her father could tell me that because Stephen had abandoned her so abruptly, his daughter was calling off the betrothal."

"Surely you don't blame her for crying off, do you?"

"No. I just wish I knew why Stephen left like he did."

"I cannot imagine it, either," Mac said, sitting forward. "He had everything to gain from the marriage. The girl seemed perfect. An eighteen-year-old beauty. The picture of youth and innocence with a dowry that was the envy of every eligible bachelor in England."

Ethan lifted the glass to his lips again and fought the fury smoldering inside him. "My mother believes that the girl's innocence and naïveté when Stephen courted her was nothing but an act." He walked toward the fireplace and stared at the flames. He saw the face of the girl betrothed to his brother, as pale as it had been the day he'd broken the news to her. "Mother is convinced she was only playing the part of the enamored fiancée. The shocked look in her eyes and the drawn expression on her face seemed a superb performance."

"Do you think it's possible?"

Ethan looked up. "If the way she nearly collapsed in my arms was not real, the girl should be on stage. When I had to reach to hold her, there was no doubt she was overcome by shock."

Mac crossed his legs in a relaxed pose and leaned back in his chair. "Stephen must have known when he left she would cry off. He must have known that leaving like he did would cause every gossipmonger's tongue to wag. I'm surprised there was not more of a scandal."

Ethan watched the flames dance in the blazing fireplace. Mac had never been known for mincing words. His directness hit home. "Damn him to hell, Mac. I can understand his wanting to leave for a little while. But not without a word to anyone, and not for eighteen bloody months! He needed the girl's dowry to stay afloat. What did he think would happen if he left?"

"Perhaps your mother is right and he didn't want to marry. Or perhaps the girl intended to cry off, and Stephen didn't have the courage to stay and face the consequences."

Ethan fisted his hand and brought it down on the arm of the chair. "No. I think the girl truly loved Stephen and was devastated when he left. That, followed by her own mother's death not even a year after Stephen's abandonment has been very difficult for her. Evidently she rarely goes out in public."

"Perhaps she entertains in the country?"

Ethan shook his head. "Mother has made a point of watching the girl's every move. She never entertains, and in the eighteen months since Stephen's been gone, she's left Fallen Oaks, the estate where she lives, only to help her father with his shipping interests. It's as if she's determined to remain a spinster if she cannot marry Stephen."

"Have you seen her father, Baron Langdon, lately?" Mac asked.

"No, why?"

"He commissioned William and James Hall, of Aberdeen fame, to build one of the new clipper ships."

Ethan's head rose. "Have you seen it?"

"Aye. She sailed into London just this morning. The *Abigail Rose*. She's far and away the most beautiful ship I have ever seen. I hear clippers like her can average fifteen knots a day and can make the run from China to London in about one hundred ten days."

Ethan rose and walked to Stephen's desk. He lowered himself onto the soft leather chair and picked up the important letter Hargrove had placed on the desk. He absently fingered his name written on the front, then stopped. "Was Langdon there for its docking?"

"Nay. Word has it he took ill nearly two months ago

and has been confined to Fallen Oaks. His captain, James Parker, was there. Everyone knows Captain Parker runs Langdon Shipping as efficiently as Langdon."

Ethan turned the letter over in his hands. "There's a hefty profit to be made with the tea runs to China, as long as the Americans are occupied with their war."

"And Langdon's ships are bound to be passed down to his daughter."

"As if that might benefit Stephen any longer."

"Perhaps if Stephen were to fall on his knees and beg her forgiveness, she would take him back. The fact that she hasn't put herself back on the marriage mart must mean something. Perhaps she fancied herself so in love with Stephen that she couldn't fathom the notion of keeping her place in Society without him. Perhaps if he were to ask, she would still marry him."

Ethan threw his head back on his shoulders and gave a bitter laugh. "That would be the perfect answer, except I do not have a bridegroom to fall on his knees and beg her to take him back. Nor do I have enough capital of my own to cover Stephen's vast debts."

Mac's expression turned serious. "You cannot stay here forever, Ethan. It's only a matter of time until Stafford finds you. He has runners looking for you. I think that's who followed me tonight."

Ethan shrugged his shoulders. "England is a long way from the colonies. Perhaps he won't think to look for me here."

Mac shook his head. "He's searched for you in every port from India to Australia. What makes you think he won't look for you in England?"

Ethan swept his fingers through his hair. "I cannot leave with matters the way they are. I have to find some way to hold off the creditors until Stephen comes back.

I still have three ships at my disposal, and I intend to get tea commissions for all three of them."

"Then you will na want to see these." Mac leaned forward and handed Ethan the papers he'd brought.

Ethan read the papers slowly, panic welling inside him at every word. When he finished, he crumpled the pages and threw them into the fire.

"You need a clipper to stay in the running for the tea trade, Ethan. The buyers are only contracting with those who can guarantee the fastest delivery from China. They want the freshest China tea that is harvested in May and June."

"We will take what we can get," Ethan spat out, every word as bitter as gall. *Damn Stephen and his irresponsible behavior.* Ethan didn't want to care, but he did. That had always been the problem. He had always cared too much. He had looked up to Stephen—had idolized and loved him his whole life. How could Stephen have done something so irresponsible?

Ethan rubbed the tense muscles at his shoulders. "There has to be another answer."

"Your ships are nearly ready to set sail now," Mac said, his enthusiasm hinting at an optimism Ethan knew was not really there. "With everyone else concentrating on the tea trade, there are other goods in demand, like Australian wool. We will garner the lion's share of that."

"And pray it will be enough," Ethan finished. He took another swallow of the brandy in his glass and turned over Hargrove's important letter. "I tried to hint to my mother that her purse is not as deep as it was before Stephen left, but she still spends money as if Queen Victoria prints it special just for her." He threw the letter on the desk in frustration. "What could have happened to make Stephen leave like he did when he knew—"

Ethan's eyes focused on the seal, the Langdon seal. A sudden jolt punched him in the chest. He snatched up the letter and turned it over. The writing was a small, shaky scribble, definitely not in a feminine hand. It was not from her.

He broke the seal and opened the missive, scanning the words quickly the first time, studying them intently the second.

Cambridge—

I fear I may have waited too long to write you. My health fails me more each day, and I do not want to face my Maker before I atone for my greatest sin. You must know the truth.

Be assured, I alone am responsible for the tragedy. My daughter Abigail is completely blameless. But unless I confess what happened, she will be the one left to suffer the consequences.

Even though Abigail had no part in it, she does have something of the greatest importance that belongs to your brother, Lord Burnhaven. I know she will never give this up willingly, but she must. For her own sake, and any hope for her future, there is no other way. I only pray in time she can find it in her heart to forgive me for what she will see as my ultimate betrayal.

Do not tarry long or it will be too late for me to help you.

Langdon

Ethan stared at the letter in his hands and let his mind conjure anything that Stephen could have left with the girl. Nothing he could imagine seemed important enough to match the desperation he detected in Langdon's words. Perhaps there was a diary, or a book of Stephen's personal thoughts their mother would cherish.

The air caught in Ethan's chest. Could it be the fortune in Burnhaven jewels that Stephen claimed had been stolen? Could he have given them to her, and Langdon knew, whether out of bitterness, or spite, or the remembrance of a cherished love that had been lost, she'd never part with them?

Ethan folded the letter and leaned back in his chair. He breathed a deep sigh of relief.

All he had to do was get the stones back and his problems would be solved.

. . .

Fallen Oaks stood in the distance. A winding lane lined with mammoth oaks led to the massive country estate. Withered leaves lay crushed and scattered on the ground, discarded by winter's stark hand.

Langdon's manor house reached upward in towering majesty, its sturdy strength the guardian of an immense domain, the rugged stone structure a formidable yet welcoming refuge.

Ethan spurred his mount cautiously down the lane, careful to avoid the craggy ruts, hard from last night's freeze.

Thick black smoke curled from the roof, its warmth beckoning him inside.

He both dreaded and anticipated his meeting with

Langdon and the girl. Dreaded because he'd hoped never to set eyes on either of them again. Anticipated because they held in their grasp the fortune that would wipe away Stephen's debts.

A cold wind whipped around him, and Ethan lifted the collar of his greatcoat, then stuffed his hands deeper into the coat's generous folds. He didn't remember it ever being this cold, even in the dead of winter. It seemed the weather had decided to correlate a foreboding prediction with the reception he would receive.

Ethan stiffened his spine in resolve. He didn't give a bloody damn how precious Stephen's gift of the stones was to her or how reluctant she was to give them up. She was no longer Stephen's betrothed, and Ethan needed the jewels far more than she did. He'd be damned if he'd leave without them.

Ethan dug his heels into his steed's sides and made his way closer to the manor house. A dozen or more carriages lined the lane, their middle-of-the-day presence an unsettling premonition. A light mist was falling, its wetness turning to icy shards that pelted him about the face. He lowered his head to shield himself from its sting and crossed the circle of cobblestones, then raised his gaze.

The drapes in every window were pulled shut, the downstairs windows covered in black. Black satin draped the door frame in formidable forewarning.

He was too late. Edward Langdon was gone.

Ethan dropped to the ground and handed his reins to a young lad who'd run to take his horse. He hesitated once, then he walked toward the huge black wreath that rustled ominously above the entrance. An uneasy feeling swept over him.

Before he reached the portal, the front door swung open. A tall man with a generous sprinkling of gray in his hair stood as an indomitable sentinel. He wore a finely tailored suit and an air of authority that indicated he considered Ethan's late arrival an intrusion. He gave Ethan a harsh glance, then his look narrowed, turning cold and serious.

Ethan knew the moment the loyal butler remembered him from his youthful visits.

A fresh gust of wind whipped his coat around his legs as Ethan waited to be admitted.

A look of deliberation passed over the man's face as if he debated whether or not to let this late and clearly unwelcome guest enter. Finally, he stepped back and let Ethan step inside before closing the door.

Without a word, the butler led the way through the front part of the house, out the double doors that took them across a terrace, then through the brown, ice-covered garden, to a small chapel. They walked down the narrow aisle, and Ethan barely had time to notice the stained-glass windows before they exited the warmth of a church just vacated, to step into the stark, frigid outside air.

They walked down a cobblestone path until they reached a small fenced-off area. Dozens of marble headstones marked the graves of the Langdons already buried there.

The somber-faced butler stopped, indicating with a less-than-subtle gesture that Ethan should stand at an obscure place in the back.

Ethan ignored his warning and walked forward, focusing on the front of the small throng of mourners gathered around the freshly dug grave. There he found her.

She barely resembled the young girl he remembered from before. Gone was her look of youthful innocence. Her boldness seemed a gallant effort to withstand and conquer this latest hardship thrown at her. There was a bravery to her stance as she stood at her father's open grave. With her chin held high, her spine rigid and straight, her shoulders squared with regal pride, she portrayed a single-minded self-reliance.

Yards of dull black cloth draped across her slender form, cloaking her in shrouds of formidable resolve. Yet each drab fold seemed to add to her strength and self-confidence, and transform her into an image safe-guarded with an intractable resolve.

She shouldered her burden alone. No one stood close to her—no family to support her, no friends to comfort her. Only a small crowd of neighbors and tenants and household staff who had come to pay their last respects.

The minister read the familiar quotation from the Bible, committing Langdon's flesh to the earth with words rife with dust and ashes.

Ethan made his way to the front, ignoring the eye-brows that lifted as he passed. There was no reason for him to be here. She and Stephen were no longer betrothed. From her rigid stance, she did not expect anyone to stand beside her.

He took another step toward her.

A dry, brittle twig snapped beneath his booted foot, and she turned her head. Huge, sad green eyes, as deep as the most brilliant emeralds God had ever fash-ioned into stone, looked up at him.

Recognition, though not immediate, was, when it came, jarring. A flash of awareness overtook her face—the sudden fear he glimpsed hidden so quickly he nearly missed it. It was as if she possessed the ability to camouflage her vulnerability by turning it to indifference.

She lifted her shoulders. With her gaze still locked

with his, she held steady, then slowly turned her icy glare away. She stood in rigid defiance, as if daring him to intrude where he was not welcome.

Ethan moved to stand beside her.

Her reaction was the same as before, when he'd gone to tell her that Stephen had left. She drew within herself, closing herself off from the world around her.

And from him.

Chapter 2

Abigail reached deep inside herself to find every last shred of courage she possessed so she could endure just one more minute of this day. She was hard-pressed to find the strength she needed. She'd lost so much.

She allowed herself to cast a quick glance in Ethan Cambridge's direction. He occupied a vacant corner of the room as if he owned not only the area where he stood, but the entire room.

Something about the harsh expression on his face, and the narrowed look in his eyes as he assessed his surroundings, caused the people Abigail had known her entire life to avoid coming into contact with him. Even Reverend Smythe's wife, who went out of her way to greet any stranger, kept her distance, realizing there was something to fear about him. And Abigail was afraid. She was afraid because she realized that she could lose everything.

He leaned against the far wall and silently watched the guests as they came forward to offer their condolences. Just as he watched her.

His presence filled the room like a commanding

sentinel, his stillness far more intimidating than if he'd muscled his way through the small crowd of mourners.

Piercing blue eyes evaluated her as his broad shoulders braced for battle, his muscled arms crossed over his chest in readiness. The closed look on his face remained steadfastly unreadable.

He was as dark as Stephen had been blond. As menacing as Stephen had been congenial. As mysterious as Stephen had been endearing. She would trust Ethan Cambridge even less than she had learned she could trust Stephen.

Abigail turned her face. His penetrating eyes sent waves of trepidation racing through her. A cold chill wracked her body. She recognized it for what it was. Fear.

The room spun around her as her mind screamed a denial, and she focused her attention on the small group of people who had come to bid her father farewell. The gathering seemed to move in slow motion, as if their reason for being here wasn't real, but was a nightmare from which she would soon awaken.

She shivered and clutched her hands around her arms for just one second before pulling them away and clasping them together in her lap. She could not let anyone know how close she was to giving in to her grief. And her fear.

One by one her father's friends and acquaintances finished the light lunch her servants had laid out, and wished her well before leaving.

"Our most sincere sympathies, Miss Langdon," George Peacroft said, twisting the corners of a perfectly pressed handkerchief. "If there's aught me and the missus can do, ye only have ta let us know. Yer father was a right fine master, and we'll sorely miss him."

Abigail lifted her head and tried to smile. "Thank

you, George. Thank you, Emma. Father would have appreciated that you came. And don't worry. Please tell the other tenants that nothing will change. Things will be run as they've always been. With everyone's help, everything will go smoothly."

A broad smile crossed George's lips. "You can count on us, miss."

Abigail stood to walk the visitors to the door and swayed as the room moved beneath her feet. She couldn't recall the last time she'd eaten. Or the last time she'd slept. Her father had been ill for so long she couldn't remember when she'd had even a moment to herself. Especially this last week.

She reached out her hand to steady herself against the end of the sofa. Strong arms clamped around her waist to anchor her.

She looked up. A deep frown creased Ethan Cambridge's forehead. His full lips pressed to an unsmiling straight line. When he tightened his grip around her waist, the unease she felt surged to a new level.

"Please leave," she whispered, her voice soft yet firm. "I don't want you here. Any association between our two families was severed long ago."

He made no move, as if her words did not affect him.

Every eye in the room focused on them, and in a commanding tone of voice, he tilted his head and announced just loud enough to be heard, "I think it is time to bid your remaining guests farewell so you can rest."

As if his command had been a royal decree, the last of the stragglers made their way to the door.

A wave of resolve crept through her. She was not the confused eighteen-year-old she'd been that night eighteen months ago when her world had crashed down around her. She was nearly twenty. How dare he step in as if he owned her. She was nothing to him, as he was nothing to her.

Abigail stiffened her shoulders and twisted out of his arms, praying her legs would support her as she walked across the room.

She thanked the remaining guests for coming, while ignoring Ethan's towering presence which hovered a few feet away from her. Twice she'd had to hold on to the extended hand of one of her guests until the room stopped spinning, but she quickly stiffened her back when she saw him move toward her. She would not show such weakness. She would not allow him to help her.

The door closed behind the last of the guests, and Abigail resisted the urge to lean her forehead against the cool wood while the earth rotated back into place.

Why had he come? He had to know how uncomfortable it was to have him here, but in a possessive show that indicated he didn't care, he offered her his arm and ushered her back into the parlor. Her butler hovered nearby.

"Your name," he demanded when the butler stepped near.

"Palmsworth, sir."

"Palmsworth," he said, his voice more a command than a request. "Perhaps you might bring Miss Langdon a tray with something more nourishing than those little sandwiches and cakes. And a cup of fresh tea."

Palmsworth hesitated a moment, then nodded but didn't leave.

"There is no need to watch me like I'm about to do your mistress harm, Palmsworth. I have no intention of being the cause of another burial at Fallen Oaks."

"Bring the tea, Palmsworth," she said with as much force as she could.

When Palmsworth left, Ethan Cambridge led her through the parlor. He ushered her to the long sofa in the center of the room with the practiced ease of a man accustomed to being in control.

"I am perfectly capable of taking care of myself," Abigail protested. She tried valiantly to keep her voice from sounding like it was ready to give out on her.

"You aren't strong enough to carry your fancy lace handkerchief to the other side of the room without assistance, let alone the little flesh that's left on your body. When was the last time you ate?"

Without waiting for an answer, he walked to the fireplace and placed another log on the dying embers. When he was assured the fire was again blazing, he moved one of the large wing chairs nearer the heat. "Come, sit by the fire."

"Why are you here?"

He ignored her and moved a small table nearby for the tray of food Palmsworth had been ordered to bring.

"Why have you come?" she said a little louder.

He halted with his back to her and turned around slowly. The vivid azure depths of his startling blue eyes stopped her short.

"You have my sympathies. I didn't know about your father."

"Would you have had the courtesy to stay away if you had?"

The look he gave her told her it wouldn't have mattered, but Palmsworth entered the room, silencing him for the moment. A servant followed with a tray, and Cambridge stepped back while the servant set down the food and poured two cups of tea. "Thank you, Palmsworth. That will be all."

Palmsworth turned a questioning glance to Abigail, and she answered with a nod.

Although she would love to, there was no use putting off hearing what Ethan Cambridge had come here to say. Unlike Stephen, Ethan Cambridge didn't seem the type to be dissuaded.

"If you need me, mistress, you have only to call. I will be near."

Abigail forced a smile to her lips. "Thank you, Palmsworth. I could not have managed this day without you."

Palmsworth gave Cambridge a lengthy look of warning, then left the room.

"Come over by the fire and eat," he ordered. His voice was soft, but contained a threat.

"The soup will stay warm enough." She stood to face him. "We'll talk first. If you didn't know about my father, then you had another reason for coming. What was it?"

He braced one hand against the casing at the side of the window and stood in statuesque rigidity, staring at the snow-covered trees and bushes. His broad shoulders strained the fabric of his finely tailored suit, making his size and the breadth of his shoulders appear even more massive. The deep claret of his jacket enhanced the golden bronze of his skin, giving it an even richer hue.

Hair a thunderous mahogany lay in thick waves. The length in back touched the top of his white collar, the front combed to one side instead of in the fashionable part down the center. One dark lock fell errantly against his forehead, giving him a fierce, roguish look.

Everything about the man gave him a foreboding mystery.

There'd been a tough texture to his palms when he'd taken her hand. The calluses she'd felt told her he earned a living doing something other than sitting behind a desk or playing cards at his clubs.

Stephen's hands had been soft, the look in Stephen's eyes gentle, until...

Abigail focused on the scene he watched outside the windows. Snow had started to fall in huge flakes, the kind that blanketed the ground quickly and made the earth seem clean and new. She thought of her father lying beneath the snow, and the breath caught in her throat. "I want you to leave, Mr. Cambridge. I would like to be alone."

His shoulders lifted as he took a deep breath, then he turned and pinned her with the concentration of a swordsman ready to lunge.

"You have something that belongs to my brother, Miss Langdon. I am here to get it."

His words struck her with the force of a deadly blow.

He knew.

Abigail clenched her hands around the back cushions of the chair and took one labored gasp after another.

"Get out," she rasped. "Get out of my house and leave me alone."

"I'm afraid I can't. I'm sorry I have upset you, and I regret coming here on the day of your father's funeral, but I will not leave until I have what belongs to my brother."

She shook her head. "I have no idea what you're talking about."

"Yes, you do."

Abigail took one threatening step toward him. "Out! Get out!" She pointed a trembling finger toward the door.

He came toward her. Even his footsteps sounded harsh and angry. He clamped his hands around her shoulders and glared into her eyes. "You have no right to keep what legally belongs to Stephen's family, Miss Langdon. Surely you realize we cannot let you have something so valuable?"

She shook her head, frantic to have him gone. Frantic to protect the only thing in the world she had left. *How could he have found out? Who could have told him?*

"I don't have anything that belongs to Stephen, or to you. Anything I have now belongs only to me."

"That's not true." He dropped his hands and reached into his pocket and pulled out a letter. A letter that bore her father's seal.

"Here. You can read this for yourself."

Abigail's hands trembled violently as she reached for the letter. She unfolded the paper with the greatest trepidation, already knowing what her father had done. Before he'd died, her father had begged her to take her gift and give it back to Stephen's family, but she could not. She would rather die than do a thing so unthinkable.

She glared at the words written in her father's hand and railed silently at the renegade tear that rolled down her cheek.

She took a step away from him and sat in the nearest chair. "I will not give you anything."

"And I cannot let you keep it. If it is a fight you want—"

He stopped, a hint of regret filtering through the look on his face.

The room was suddenly stifling, the air suddenly too heavy to breathe. How could her father have done such a thing? How could he have invited Stephen's brother back into their lives? Didn't he know what could happen if Cambridge found out what she had? Didn't he know what would happen if Cambridge found out what she'd done?

She lifted her chin. Blood pounded in her head,

roaring against her ears with alarming ferocity. "Please go," she said.

A dangerous silence stretched between them. It sent tremors of dread pulsing through her. She felt his eyes boring into her back. Felt his dominance trapping her in his clutches. Realized the threat he was to her. Somehow she knew Ethan Cambridge was a master at being ruthless, where Stephen had only been adept at deceit. And this man would move heaven and earth to take her treasure away from her. This man would do whatever he must to see that justice was served.

"Did you love him-so much you cannot bear to part with anything he gave you? Or is it your hatred for him that drives you to keep what is not yours?"

She stiffened. His words hit her like a wall of freezing water. She lowered her gaze, unable to face his penetrating eyes.

"Did you care that much for Stephen, or did you care only for the title he could give you? Are you that greedy to keep such a treasure to yourself, regardless of how much its loss will mean to his family? Especially to Stephen's mother?"

She bolted to her feet. "How dare you accuse me of taking anything from you or your family. Your family has taken more from me than anyone should have to give up. Stephen—"

If the repercussion to telling the truth had not been so devastating, she would have gained a sense of self-satisfaction in telling him. But he could never know what had happened. If he wanted to think she missed Stephen that much, let him.

She twisted away and clutched her hand to her forehead when the room swayed beneath her feet. From the corner of her eye, she saw him reach for her. "Leave me be," she intoned, swinging her arm out to keep him away. She would not let him touch her. She would not let him help her. There was no one left to help her.

She wiped her damp palms on her black bombazine skirt and leaned against the corner of the small writing desk.

"Excuse me, mistress," Palmsworth interrupted from the doorway, "but Mr. Sydney Craddock is here."

Abigail looked up as her father's longtime solicitor entered the room.

"I'm so sorry I'm late, Miss Langdon," Sydney said, rushing into the room. "I meant to be here hours ago, but my carriage lost a wheel and I—" Sydney's attention suddenly focused on Abigail's guest, and his words died on his tongue. "Mr. Cambridge," he exclaimed in surprise. "I had no idea. What a pleasure, sir."

"Sydney," Cambridge greeted with a curt nod.

"I did not expect you to be here, but of course you would, seeing as how your brother was once betrothed to Miss Langdon."

"I have asked Mr. Cambridge to leave, but he has refused. Any connection our families had in the past was severed long ago."

Abigail prided herself on the shocked look on Sydney's face and watched as the solicitor stuttered to cover her rudeness.

"Surely you are glad to have someone of Mr. Cambridge's vast knowledge and experience with you at such a time. I have come with your father's will, and I am sure you will feel more comfortable with someone so astute to help you. There are some very delicate matters involved with the estate and the shipping interests. Far more than you can be expected to understand, especially at a time like this."

Abigail bristled. "No," she said, her voice an unladylike growl that contained more hysteria than composure. "I do not want—"

Ethan held up a hand that stopped her words, then turned his attention to Sydney. "Is it necessary for Miss Langdon to go over this now? Perhaps it would be best if she could wait until tomorrow to hear her father's will. I think she has been through enough for one day."

"Well, I—"

Cambridge stood at his chair, a gesture that indicated the subject was closed. "Why don't you and I seek shelter for the night at the Journeyman's Inn? We shall come again in the morning when Miss Langdon has had time to rest."

"No," Abigail argued. "I don't need your help." She gave Cambridge a look she prayed held more ferocity than fear.

"That may be so, Miss Langdon, but our business is far from concluded. Unless I failed to make myself clear, you know I have no intention of leaving here empty-handed. Sydney," Cambridge said, moving toward the door, "I have some business I would like to discuss with you. Perhaps over dinner?"

The solicitor bobbed his head in eager anticipation. "We will return in the morning, Miss Langdon." Sydney looked over his shoulder as they turned to leave. "And I am so pleased the earl's brother is here to see you through this trying time. How fortunate for you."

Abigail clutched her fists to the cushions on the sofa and gripped tightly until she heard the closing of the front door. Cambridge wanted what she could not give him.

Cold, gnarled fingers wrapped around her heart, squeezing the very life from inside her. She paced the room, desperation welling within her, then she raced across the foyer, toward the door.

"Palmsworth!"

"Yes, mistress."

"Have the carriage brought round," she ordered, "and get my cloak."

"Ah, no, mistress. 'Tis the dead of winter outside and too late to go there."

"It's not too late." She grabbed her cloak from Palmsworth's hands and put it around her shoulders, then pushed one hand inside a fur muff. "Did you hear him? He knows."

"Stay here where it's warm, my lady. You can go in the morning. I'll take you myself."

"No! Bring the carriage."

Abigail wrapped a thick woolen scarf around her neck and headed for the door.

"Wait, mistress. I'll have Bundy ready the carriage, and Stella will fetch some blankets and warm some bricks to put inside and up above. You should stay warm, at least on the way over."

Abigail nodded, then paced the floor, waiting for Bundy to come with the carriage. She would run away if Cambridge forced her to, but she would not let him have what was hers. It was all she had left.

Chapter 3

The sound of muffled voices at the front door swept through the entryway and into the morning room where Abigail stood. A strange peacefulness came over her. A feeling of completion. She was glad they were here, glad to have this over with. The waiting was always worse. Now she would know what threat Stephen's brother intended. And she would know how to fight him.

Their heavy footsteps clapped against the marble in the foyer, pounding as hollow as a bell tolling the message of doom. Let him threaten as he would. She would never give up what was hers. Never.

She looked at the snow-covered ground, her back rigid and straight, her chin held high. She was on the brink of exhaustion, last night no more restful than the night before or the one before that. But she had no choice but to be strong. She was alone now. The reality of her isolation never more daunting than at this moment.

There was a knock, and Palmsworth opened the door.

She turned and focused on the man who was her

greatest threat.

He looked much the same as he had yesterday, his dark suit cut to perfection, his pristine white shirt freshly pressed and his silk cravat perfectly knotted. He'd combed his mahogany hair back from his face, its casual style accentuating high cheekbones and the stern line of his thick brows. He looked even more dangerous than before.

"Mr. Cambridge and Mr. Craddock to see you, Miss Langdon," Palmsworth announced from the doorway.

"Thank you, Palmsworth. Please bring tea and the muffins Cook has prepared."

"Yes, Miss Langdon."

Abigail stepped to where three chairs sat in a semicircle around the fire. "Won't you sit down," she said, pointing to the two chairs facing each other on the right and left of the blazing hearth. She stood before the chair in the middle, furthest from the heat.

She ignored the smile that crossed Cambridge's face, as if he realized she'd intentionally placed her guests opposite each other so neither he nor Sydney Craddock could face her.

"Please, let me express my profound sympathy, Miss Langdon," Sydney gushed, wiping the sweat already forming on his brow from the blazing heat in the fireplace. "I told Mr. Cambridge on the way how pleased I was that he was here to look out for your interests."

"And I," she said, pouring the tea Palmsworth had set on the table in front of her, "thought I'd made myself clear yesterday before you left. I am perfectly capable of looking out for my own interests and do not need Mr. Cambridge's assistance."

Willing her hands not to tremble, she poured Mr. Craddock's tea and handed it to him. She kept an amiable smile on her face. When she finished, she poured a second cup.

Ethan Cambridge accepted the tea with a slight nod. "Consider your objection duly noted and appreciated, Miss Langdon."

She sat in the chair between them and placed her hands in her lap. She didn't trust herself to hold a cup of tea. "Perhaps we should begin, Mr. Craddock. I'm sure you can understand my need to have things settled."

"Of course. Of course." He fumbled with the papers in the leather folder on his lap.

Abigail took the cup the solicitor tried to balance on one knee and placed it on the table before it could fall to the floor. She didn't turn to look at Mr. Cambridge. She knew he was studying her, taking in her every move.

"Very well," Sydney said, lifting out a small stack of legal documents. "This is your father's will. I discussed its contents with him shortly after your blessed mother passed away. He was quite distraught, but wanted to make sure everything was in order so you would be protected."

Abigail felt the air grow cold around her. Didn't her father realize that nothing could protect her? The man sitting next to her would never let what she'd done go unpunished.

Ethan Cambridge propped his right ankle atop his left knee and relaxed in the chair with his fingers steepled beneath his chin. "Did Baron Langdon mention from what—or from whom—he was protecting his daughter?"

"No, Mr. Cambridge," Sydney stuttered. "I'm sure he only meant to protect her from anyone wishing to take advantage."

"Go on, Mr. Craddock," Abigail said.

"Let's see," Sydney continued, obviously flustered.

"First of all, your father made a generous yearly provision for a number of your staff: Mrs. Finey, the cook; the gardener, Jeremy; Bundy and Grover and Percy in the stables; and Mattie, your mother's nursemaid, as well as your own, I believe." He turned the first page. "There is also a large yearly bonus awarded his long-time friend, Captain James Parker, with the stipulation that he be given a permanent post aboard your father's new clipper ship, the *Abigail Rose*."

Sydney looked in her direction to get her approval, and Abigail nodded.

"Next, your father bequeathed the sum of ten thousand pounds to his butler, William Palmsworth. Far more than I thought was necessary," Sydney Craddock said with a click of his tongue. "I tried to explain to your father that you might object to giving a household steward such a huge amount, even if the man had been with you for a very long time, but he was quite adamant and certain you would agree with his decision. I hope—"

Abigail lifted her chin. Her sudden movement stopped the solicitor's words. "Go on, Mr. Craddock."

"Now, we come to your father's London properties and his shipping interests. They will all go to you, Miss Langdon, until your marriage. Then they will, of course, transfer to your husband. This includes your London town house on Old Province Drive and your father's fleet of three ships, including the new clipper, the *Abigail Rose*."

"And what about Fallen Oaks?" she asked anxiously.

Mr. Craddock looked at her dumbstruck. "Fallen Oaks is not yours, Miss Langdon. I thought you knew."

"Not mine?" she uttered, her voice barely able to choke out the words. "But Fallen Oaks isn't entailed. What did Father do with it?"

"I'm afraid your father left Fallen Oaks to a distant cousin, which is...let me see..." He nervously thumbed through his papers until he found the right spot. "Fallen Oaks, as well as your father's title, will now pass to your father's deceased second cousin's oldest son, Rodney."

Abigail felt the room spin around her. Her father had never told her. She'd thought it would be hers.

"But it isn't entailed," she repeated.

"No, Miss Langdon," Sydney stuttered. "But your father thought it important that it pass down to the new Baron Langdon. I think he did not want you to seclude yourself in the country."

"No," she whispered, standing on legs that threatened not to hold her. Surely her father hadn't done this. She couldn't lose the estate.

"All is not lost, Miss Langdon," Mr. Craddock said, trying to console her. "You have the ships and your town house in London."

A wave of panic chilled her to the bone, a fear as great as any she had ever known. "I will not give up Fallen Oaks. I cannot."

Abigail frantically paced the floor, then spun around to face Sydney. "Is there any way we can change such a stipulation?"

"No, Miss Langdon. I'm afraid what's done is done."

She clenched her hands in tight fists. "It can't be. There must be something we can do."

"Miss Langdon," the solicitor said, running his finger around his too-tight collar. "I hesitate to mention this, but perhaps it is in your best interest to be rid of Fallen Oaks. It has not been profitable for many years. It is only because of your father's immense and very lucrative shipping interests that he was able to give away such generous gifts in his will."

Abigail's mind raced in dizzying circles. There had to be something she could do. She couldn't lose Fallen Oaks. She couldn't. Everything that was important to her was here. And she would not be separated from it.

She shot the solicitor a frantic glance. "Can the estate be sold?"

Mr. Craddock stuttered nervously. "Well, uh...Yes. There is nothing preventing your cousin from selling Fallen Oaks."

Ethan Cambridge's eyebrows shot up, but Abigail ignored his questioning look.

She pressed her sweating palms against her skirt. "Have you spoken to my cousin yet, Mr. Craddock? Does he know what Father left him in the will?"

Sydney fumbled with the papers on his lap. "No. I wanted to go over the details of your father's will with you first."

"Do you know where my cousin resides, Mr. Craddock?"

"Your cousin owns an estate in Northumberland. But at present I believe he resides in London."

"Is there anything that would prevent *me* from purchasing Fallen Oaks?"

"Uh...uh...I'm afraid that would not be advisable, Miss Langdon."

"I didn't ask if it was advisable, Mr. Craddock. I asked if it was possible."

"Well...yes. Of course it's possible. But I'm afraid you will find it difficult."

"Why? What makes it so difficult?"

"Money, Miss Langdon. Although your father left you the ships and the promise of a more than adequate yearly income, he did not leave you enough cash to pay what your cousin would undoubtedly demand for his newly-acquired country estate."

"What about the ships? Could I find a buyer for the ships and pay for Fallen Oaks with the money from the sale of the ships?"

For the first time since Mr. Craddock had started the reading of her father's will, Ethan Cambridge made his presence known. "Such a move would be foolhardy, Miss Langdon."

Abigail glared at him, then turned away. She refused to listen to his opinion. "Might I sell the ships, Mr. Craddock?"

"Well...uh," he stammered, casting Cambridge a look that pleaded for help. "It isn't that you *cannot* sell the ships, Miss Langdon, it's that you—"

"Yes, it is," Cambridge interrupted. "You cannot sell the ships. I will not let you."

She spun on him. "You have nothing to say about it, Mr. Cambridge."

"Perhaps not, but may I suggest that were your father still alive, he would never approve of such a move."

"Well, my father is not here to approve or disapprove of anything I do."

For long, tense moments they faced each other, each daring the other to make the first move.

Cambridge released a deep sigh, then raked his fingers through his hair. "Please, Miss Langdon, let's discuss this calmly before you make any rash decisions."

He held out his hand, indicating he wanted her to sit, but Abigail waved him away. He raised his hands in surrender, then backed up and let her step in front of him. Before he sat, he slid his chair to face hers. Their knees almost touched.

"Miss Langdon," he said, leaning forward, positioning himself only inches away from her. "Let me explain the problems you would have if you traded your father's fleet of ships in exchange for Fallen Oaks. Although your estate is beautiful, your residence here in the country is not large enough, nor profitable enough, to support you for long. You need the income from your father's ships to keep Fallen Oaks in the black. The ships are all your father left you that is of any real value. In time, the sale of their cargoes will make you a wealthy woman. If you give up your ships, it will only be a matter of a few years and you will lose Fallen Oaks, too, and have nothing to ensure you are an enviable marriage prospect."

She couldn't keep the bitterness out of her voice. "Are you referring to my dowry, Mr. Cambridge? Are you insinuating that without a handsome dowry, I would no longer be of value to another suitor as devoted and considerate as Stephen? Well, Mr. Cambridge," she said with all the rancor she'd held back for eighteen months. "I am not an enviable prospect now. Your brother saw to that."

He blanched as if she'd struck him. Her words had accomplished everything she'd intended.

"Mr. Craddock," she said, giving Ethan Cambridge her back. "I would like a message sent to the new Baron Langdon, requesting a meeting at his earliest convenience. Please inform him of my desire to forfeit all or part of Langdon Shipping in exchange for Fallen Oaks."

Abigail walked across the room and opened the door. "Now if you gentlemen will excuse me, I am suddenly feeling unwell."

She waited for them to leave.

"Miss Langdon—"

"Good day, Mr. Cambridge." She cut him off before he could say more, then turned to the solicitor. "I look forward to hearing from you, Mr. Craddock, as soon as you speak with my cousin."

"Yes, of course," Craddock stuttered, then shuffled out the door.

Abigail ignored the thunderous look in Ethan Cambridge's glare and shut the door behind them both.

When she was finally alone, she clutched her hand to her stomach and fought the urge to be ill. She had just made the decision to give up her ships, the part of her father's legacy she loved more than anything. Yet what choice did she have? She could either lose the ships or the convent on Fallen Oaks.

Abigail swiped away a tear that dared to fall from her eyes. She had no choice at all but to sell.

. . .

Ethan sat in Stephen's London town house study, alone and in the dark except for the dwindling fire in the grate. In an uncharacteristic show of temper, he threw his half-full whiskey glass into the fire and watched the flames shoot brilliant oranges and blues and yellows.

Damn the woman's independent nature, and damn Stephen for whatever he'd done to her. What had he been thinking, walking out on a girl he was engaged to marry with no more thought to her feelings than his selfish excuse that he needed to see the world? And where the hell was he? Ethan had sent runners looking for his brother for nearly a year, and they couldn't find a trace of him anywhere.

Ethan fought the fear that turned his stomach every time he thought of the tragic possibilities. What could have happened for him to leave like he did, without even a note or a message in all those months to explain where he was and tell them he was safe?

Ethan bolted from his chair and paced the room. *Bloody hell!* How could Stephen have abandoned the girl like he had? If anyone needed advice, she did. She was willing to give up a clipper ship! One of the most profitable ships on the sea. He did not even want to contemplate the benefit such a vessel could provide for her future. For his.

Ethan braced his arms against the mantel and stared into the flames. The remains of a half-burned log crashed into the smoldering embers, scattering a brilliant shower of blinding sparks. For a moment he saw her pale face staring in disbelief when Sydney Craddock informed her she would lose Fallen Oaks. He knew at that moment she was closer to losing control than she'd been in the two days he'd been with her.

His conscience nagged uncomfortably. She was right when she'd said he had no right to interfere. She was not betrothed to Stephen any longer. He saw how she reacted each time Stephen's name was mentioned, as if her feelings for him were still so raw she could not hide the hurt caused by something as innocent as the mention of his name.

Ethan lowered his head between his outstretched arms. It had been eighteen bloody months. What could possibly be important enough to keep Stephen from returning?

A noise at the front entrance pushed Ethan from his thoughts. A moment later Hargrove knocked softly, then opened the door, carrying with him a large candelabra, each branch glowing brightly.

"Mr. Sydney Craddock to see you," he said, placing the candles on a table and lighting the sconces on the wall. "He insists you are expecting him."

"Yes, Hargrove. Show him in."

Hargrove opened the door wider and let in a very agitated Sydney Craddock.

"Will there be anything else, sir?" Hargrove asked before leaving.

"No, that will be all, Hargrove." Ethan turned his attention to the solicitor. "Won't you have a seat, Sydney?"

"Yes. Thank you."

The solicitor sat in the chair nearest the big oak desk that had been Ethan's father's, and now was Stephen's. Many were the times Ethan had sat in that same chair and listened to his father's harsh lectures, heard the disappointment in his voice. Many were the times Ethan had been forced to suffer through glorious tales of Stephen's brilliant accomplishments, while Ethan had been reprimanded for one misdemeanor or another: his unruly behavior at one of his mother's social functions, his inability to conform, his failure to meet his parents' expectations, his independent nature. From little on, Stephen had always been the perfect son. Ethan had never quite been able to measure up.

"What have you learned, Sydney?"

"I did just as you asked, Mr. Cambridge. I met with the newly titled Baron Langdon."

Ethan was intrigued. "What kind of person did you find him to be?"

Sydney looked around as if he were telling tales out of school. "I fear my informants were correct in their assessment of Baron Langdon. If his behavior tonight is the norm, it is obvious he is given to strong drink and has a weakness for the gaming tables. I had heard these rumors before our meeting, but as we talked, I saw firsthand how fond he was of his liquor and taking any bet that was offered. I left him at Manny's, and venture he will be there for quite some time yet tonight. He was losing heavily."

"Did you talk to him as I instructed?"

"Yes, Mr. Cambridge. I informed him he was now the proud owner of his deceased father's second cousin's country estate just outside London."

"What was his reaction?"

"At first, he was quite pleased, until I explained what all would be involved. As you expressed, I described the large manor house in infinite detail, making sure he understood the vast amount of money it would take to maintain its upkeep."

"Did you tell him about the pact the late Baron Langdon had made with his tenants concerning the yearly provisions he guaranteed?"

"Yes. He found this quite distressing. He could not understand any owner caring so much about the condition in which his tenants lived. He expressed his opinion that such a promise was a flagrant waste of money."

"And did you explain to him about his responsibility to the convent?"

"Yes. That was my last point. I fear by the time I left, he did not look on his newfound acquisition as a gift, but more as a liability." Sydney fumbled with the leather folder still clutched in his hands. "I'm not sure what you are planning, Mr. Cambridge, but—"

Ethan held up a staying hand. "That's for the best, Sydney." Ethan breathed a deep sigh, then stood behind his desk while the solicitor fidgeted, then finally took the hint that their discussion was at an end.

"If I can be of service to you in any other way..."

"Yes, Sydney. Thank you."

Hargrove appeared to show Sydney Craddock out.

Ethan listened for the front door to close, then shut

his eyes and took a deep breath. He was about to take the biggest gamble of his life.

"Will there be anything else, sir?" Hargrove said when Sydney Craddock was gone.

"Yes, Hargrove. Have my carriage brought round. I am going out."

Chapter 4

"Did a message come while I was out?" Abigail asked, taking Palmsworth's outstretched hand to dismount the carriage. Huge snowflakes fell as she walked to the front entrance.

"No, miss," Palmsworth said, closing the door behind them, then taking her cloak to hang it to dry. "No message came today."

Abigail stopped short. "It's been two weeks. Surely it can't have taken this long for Mr. Craddock to give my cousin a message."

"Perhaps wait a day or two longer. If you haven't heard by the end of the week, I think it might be best to pen a letter of your own, expressing your desire to meet with your cousin."

"What if he does not want to sell?"

"He will, miss."

A shiver shook her body. She had to have the deed to Fallen Oaks. "Why, Palmsworth? Why did things happen like they did? If only Father hadn't spent so much time away from home. Perhaps the events that night wouldn't have happened." The words slipped out before she had time to take them back.

"Oh, miss. You know there's no use crying over spilt milk."

Abigail fisted her hands at her side, then made her way to the morning room. Palmsworth followed.

"Are you sure it's best to give up the ships, miss?" the butler asked.

His voice could not conceal his concern. Just as her voice could not conceal her conviction. "What choice do I have, Palmsworth? I cannot lose Fallen Oaks. I cannot lose the convent. No. I have no choice but to do everything possible to keep Fallen Oaks. The money will come from somewhere."

"Living the life of a recluse in the country is not what your father would have wanted for you."

"It is too late, Palmsworth. It is the only life he or Stephen left for me."

Abigail breathed a deep sigh, then walked over to the flaming fire to ward off the chill. Thankfully, Palmsworth turned the conversation in a different direction.

"How did you find everything at the convent?" he asked, adding another log to the fire.

A smile lit Abigail's face. But one always did when she thought of the convent. Her words tumbled over themselves as she related everything about her visit.

She stopped abruptly. "Oh, Palmsworth. What if Ethan Cambridge finds out what I did?"

"Don't upset yourself with fears of things that will not happen. After your meeting with your cousin, you will undoubtedly never see Mr. Ethan Cambridge again."

She gave Palmsworth a halfhearted smile before he left the room. It quickly faded as her mind went back to her conversation with Ethan Cambridge the day of her father's funeral. Thanks to her father's letter, he knew she had something of Stephen's. It didn't matter if he knew what it was or not, he'd never give up until he had it.

Abigail stood by the fire, warming her hands that had grown cold from her trip to the convent. Time was of the utmost importance now. She had to have possession of Fallen Oaks before Cambridge came back.

"Miss Langdon," Palmsworth said from the doorway. "There is a rider coming up the lane."

"Is it my cousin?" she asked, clenching her hands together nervously.

"I don't know. He's still too far away to recognize."

"Oh, yes, it must be. Show him right in, then have some tea and sandwiches brought in. Everything must be perfect."

"Yes, miss."

Abigail sat in the corner of the sofa and smoothed the creases from her black bombazine skirt. She waited as patiently as her pounding heart would allow. She must handle this as if she were an expert negotiator. Perhaps there was even a chance she could keep one of the ships. Perhaps even the clipper.

A loud knock at the front door made her heart skip a beat. He was finally here.

Voices echoed in the entryway, and the blood pounded in her ears as she rehearsed the right words to say. She would do whatever it took to save Fallen Oaks. And the convent.

The voices grew louder, and heavy footsteps pounded on the marble floor.

"Miss Langdon, you have a visitor," Palmsworth announced from the doorway.

Abigail heard the warning in Palmsworth's voice and turned. She focused on the tall, broad-shouldered force that consumed every inch of the open doorway.

Ethan Cambridge stood there, his gaze riveting.

"I told Mr. Cambridge you were not receiving guests, but he insisted," Palmsworth continued.

Cambridge took a threatening step forward. "As you can see, Miss Langdon, I refused to take no for an answer. After I had ridden all this way in such inclement weather, you can hardly expect me to turn around without first making use of your warm fire and your stables to rest my weary horse."

He entered the room as if to lay claim to it. "May I?" he said, pointing to the fire. Without waiting for an answer, he walked over to the flames and held out his hands, rubbing them before the heat.

"I am not up to receiving visitors, Mr. Cambridge."

He turned, arching his thick, dark brows in surprise. "Perhaps just for a moment?"

"I prefer to be alone, sir, so—"

He took a deliberate step toward her, holding up his hand to silence her. "You and I have some unfinished business, Miss Langdon. I do not intend to leave until we have our differences resolved."

"I would appreciate it if you would gather your coat and gloves and mount your horse before he is made too comfortable in the stables. There is little chance we will ever resolve our differences. Nothing you can say will change my mind about selling my ships."

With slow deliberation, he walked across the room and stood with his hand on the door. "Thank you, Palmsworth," he said. "That will be all." He closed the door, leaving her butler in the hall.

"Mr. Cambridge—"

"Miss Langdon, please." He held out his hand. "It will do neither of us any good if you continue to build this wall of hostility between us. Please." He pointed to the sofa, "Sit down."

She studied the rigid look on his face. He seemed too confident, too self-assured. Too controlling. The first niggling of fear raced through her.

He poured two cups of tea a servant had brought in and handed one to her. She didn't want to notice how the room shifted once he entered it. Or how her breath caught in her chest when their eyes met for the briefest of seconds. But it was hard to deny the way he masterfully consumed every part of the room. Stephen had never had that ability. He had not been as manipulative or as high-handed or as huge a threat as the man standing before her.

She was glad when he sat in the chair opposite her. To have him stand, his massive height towering over her, was too disconcerting. He rested his cup on his knee, his pose casual and relaxed. She had to look away from him.

"I didn't have the chance the other day to apologize for arriving in the midst of your father's funeral service. Please believe me when I say that I truly did not know he had died, or I would have waited to come to you."

Abigail lifted her chin, not certain she could believe him. "It would not have mattered. My answer would have been the same."

He leveled his gaze on her, the dark, shadowed look in his eyes intense, the flat line of his thick, foreboding brows frightening. "Have you any idea, Miss Langdon, the enormous responsibility that has fallen upon your shoulders now that your father is gone?"

"Yes, Mr. Cambridge. I understand better than you think."

"Your father's holdings are massive, his shipping interests vast."

She struggled to bring a confident smile to her lips. "And you think I am incapable of running them?"

"I think your capability is not the question. Your gender is. As is your age."

Abigail stiffened.

"Has Stephen written you since he left?" Cambridge asked, his voice filled with more than a hint of concern.

Her heart leaped to her throat. "No."

"Don't you find that odd?"

She shook her head. "Not in the least. We are no longer betrothed."

"A fact of which I am not sure Stephen is even aware."

She turned her face from him, unable to form any words.

"He has not written our mother, either," he continued. "Not even a note on her birthday. Don't you find that strange?"

"Not considering your brother's lack of concern over anything or anyone other than himself."

Her words had shocked him. *Good.* "How well did you know your brother, Mr. Cambridge?"

Cambridge took a sip of his tea. "Obviously not as well as I thought." He placed the saucer back on his knee. "Did he say anything at all before he left that might explain why he felt the need to leave?"

"He said nothing."

Her heart pounded in her chest like a team of runaway horses. She could not look at him.

"Do you know what I think?" His voice was soft, his tone threatening. "I think you know what happened to make Stephen leave so unexpectedly but you refuse to tell me. What is it, Miss Langdon?"

She turned on him. "Get out."

"Miss Langdon." He placed his cup on the table to his right and leaned forward in his chair. His penetrating gaze captured hers. "You have something in your possession that belongs to my brother."

Abigail shot from her chair. "I have nothing that belongs to your brother." She made her way to the other side of the room before she turned on him. If it was a fight he wanted, it was a fight he would get. "Stephen gave me nothing." She was unable to hide the anger or the bitterness from her voice. "I would give anything if he were here right now to tell you how little he left me, and how much he took."

He rose to face her. The fire in his eyes blazed with determination. "What you have may seem like nothing to you, but to me it is the difference between survival and losing everything."

"Then you will lose everything!"

He took a step toward her, the black look in his eyes as harsh as anything she'd ever seen. "I will not leave until I have it."

Her heart thundered. The blood raced through her head. He was a force with which to be reckoned. His dark brows angled in an unyielding line over eyes that brimmed fire. His high, chiseled cheekbones molded in rigid perfection. The solid set of his jaw clamped in warning. He was without a doubt the most frightening man she had ever met. The only man in all of England who could take away what she held most dear.

He turned on her with all the anger and hostility of a battle-ready soldier. "You cannot keep it. Surely you realize that."

She faced him with every ounce of strength she could find. "You have no right to it. None!"

He slapped his hand against his thigh. "Dammit, woman! The jewels are not yours. They belong to Stephen's family!"

The air left her body, sucked out of her lungs like a huge wave pulled from the shore. *Jewels.*

She sank down onto the nearest chair, and clamped

her hand over her mouth to stop the strangled cry that wanted to shatter into the gaping silence. One tear slipped down her cheek, and she swiped it away with frantic urgency. It was a tear of joy.

He thought Stephen had given her jewels.

Chapter 5

Ethan felt as helpless as a ship dead in the water. He stared at her, devastation pummeling to the pit of his stomach, each word a blow as debilitating as if she'd fired on him with a sixty-cannon warship.

She did not have the jewels.

He stared at the relief on her face. He'd been so sure Stephen had cherished the girl with the huge green eyes and hair of spun copper above all else in the world. He was so sure he had given her the Burnhaven jewels for safekeeping. How could anyone not give her everything he possessed?

But she did not have them. He could see it written on her face.

"You don't know what I'm talking about, do you?"

She shook her head, still taking in big gasps of air as if just surfacing from too long beneath the water.

"Then what were you so fearful I would take from you? What did Stephen give you that you refuse to give up?"

Her shoulders lifted. "Nothing of any consequence to you, Mr. Cambridge."

Ethan turned away from her and looked out the long, wide-paned parlor window. This time he didn't see the beauty in the giant flakes of snow that fell to the ground. "Damn him!" He pounded his fist against the window casing. "How did he think this would all end?"

"He expected my dowry to save him," she whispered.

He looked over his shoulder. His probing eyes locked with hers. The haunted look in her eyes matched the faraway sound of her voice.

How could Stephen have turned his back on such strength, on such uncommon beauty? Each time he looked at her, a heaviness settled deep in his chest. She was far better than Stephen deserved.

"Then why did he not stay to marry you? Why did he leave when he knew there would be nothing left when he returned?"

Her face paled even more, but when she opened her mouth to speak, her fragile jaw quivered. "Perhaps he could not bring himself to care for me."

A sharp pang twisted deep in his gut. It pained him to hear such unabashed honesty. "I am sure you are mistaken. He always spoke most appreciatively of you."

She smiled, a smile that said she knew things he would never know. Was the smile one that told how much she had loved Stephen? Still loved him? Or one that told him how much he'd hurt her?

Never had Ethan felt more anger toward his brother than he did at this moment. How could Stephen have left her so unprotected?

"Miss Langdon," he said, sitting in the chair beside her. "I know how difficult this is for you, but—"

She rose to her feet, her chin high, her back rigid and straight. Her small smile turned her features more fragile and delicate. "Do you? I think not."

With dignified grace, she gave him her back and

walked to the door. "I would like you to leave now. I do not have the jewels you thought Stephen had given me, nor do I have anything else that would be of any monetary value to you. I am afraid we have nothing more to say to one another." She opened the door as if ordering him to leave.

Ethan followed her to the door. He stood so close he could smell the clean scent of rose petals in which he imagined she'd bathed. "Have you changed your mind about selling the ships?"

He knew his size was intimidating. Scores of brave men had lost their courage when challenged by him. But not her. She held her ground, glaring at him with a look that defied the smallness of her stature.

"No. I am expecting my cousin at any moment. I intend to sell the ships in order to keep my home, Mr. Cambridge. And nothing you can say will change my mind."

"You are wrong, Miss Langdon. I know just the words to change your mind."

She shook her head. "Keeping Fallen Oaks is too important to me. I will do anything to keep it. Even sell the ships."

Ethan couldn't help it. He reached out his arm and closed the door, then braced his palm against the wood at the side of her head and pinned her against the wall.

A riot of burnt copper curls cascaded around her shoulders, brushing against his skin, burning him wherever they touched. Her eyes opened wide when he leaned closer. This was the first sign of fear he'd seen from her.

Without dropping his gaze from hers, he whispered in a voice just loud enough to be heard, soft enough to be menacing, "Fallen Oaks is not for sale."

Her eyes opened wider, and with a startled gasp she

twisted to the side, ducking under his arm. "You don't know that. My cousin is the only one who can make that decision."

"Fallen Oaks is not for sale, Miss Langdon. Not at any price."

She shook her head. "How do you know it is not?"

Ethan reached in his pocket and took out a folded piece of paper. "This is the deed to Fallen Oaks. It is mine."

"Yours! How did you get it?"

Ethan shrugged his shoulders. "Let us just say that your cousin was most eager to complete the sale of a property he had never seen and to which he wasn't especially partial."

"You stole my home from me?"

"I didn't steal it. I offered him what he considered a fair price, after he found out how much it would cost to repair Fallen Oaks and provide for the tenants and the convent."

Her mouth shaped a disbelieving O while her eyes blazed with anger. "How dare you! You knew how desperate I was to keep Fallen Oaks. You stole my home from me on purpose."

"No. I intended to bargain with you. Fallen Oaks for the jewels I thought you had."

She held deathly still, her eyes glaring with enough intensity to strike a lesser man dead. "Would to God I had never laid eyes on you. Or on your brother."

She spun away from him, her hands clenched at her side, her cheeks a brilliant crimson against the pale complexion of her face. Back and forth across the room she stormed, her fragile body a tinderbox ready to explode. "How else do you intend to plague me? Is it not enough that your brother left me ruined?"

"Stephen did not leave you ruined, Miss Langdon."

"You think not? Do you think I have not heard the speculation bantered about London as to what kind of creature I must be to make someone of Stephen's easygoing, amiable nature bolt rather than take me for a wife? Do you think I have not heard the rumors your mother spreads about me wherever she goes, defending Stephen with the most flattering lies and making me seem a truly abhorrent ogre? And now you have taken my home. Will you and your family not be satisfied until I am left with nothing?"

"Silence!" Ethan felt the fire blaze in his cheeks, and from the step she took backward, he knew that same fire flared in his eyes. "I won the deed to your home honestly. It is your cousin's fault he was not wise enough to quit before he lost everything."

"I hope that thought allows you to sleep well at night."

"I had no choice. I knew how desperate you were to keep Fallen Oaks. I thought I could bargain with you for the jewels if I had the deed."

"You thought I would keep jewels that did not belong to me? What kind of person do you think I am?"

"Desperate enough to sell your ships to keep Fallen Oaks, knowing that without the profits from their cargoes, you will be destitute in a matter of a few years."

"What do you care?"

Her words took him aback. "Damned if I know," he answered. "If Stephen would have done the honorable thing and stayed at your side, I would not have had to do it."

"But he did not."

"No. Tell me what happened the night he left. Did you have an argument? A fight? Did he leave because of something that happened? Because of something you said, or did?"

"Stop!"

Her anger stopped him. There was so much hidden here. So much she refused to reveal.

"I do not want to discuss Stephen. I only want to know how this will all end," she demanded, her cheeks still a fiery red.

"I don't know, Miss Langdon. Why don't you tell me what you see as the solution?"

She lifted her chin, the steely determination evident. When she was ready, she faced him, the indomitable look in her eyes giving evidence of her resolve.

"Mr. Cambridge," she said. "You were correct earlier when you said we each have what the other wants. You have the title to Fallen Oaks, which I want, and I have the title to my father's fleet of ships, which you want. May I suggest we reach an agreement?"

He raised his brows ever so slightly but said nothing.

She faced him with shoulders raised and chin lifted. "I propose my ships in exchange for Fallen Oaks."

Bloody hell. Did she realize what she was saying?

"And if I refuse your offer?"

She smiled as if she knew he would not. To save Stephen's inheritance, he could not.

She shrugged her shoulders. "Then I will use my dowry to find a husband and be content to take what I cherish with me and make a new home. You can keep Fallen Oaks, and whomever I marry will have my ships."

She was bluffing. If marriage had been her goal, she would have gone back into Society long ago.

Ethan stared at the determined look on her face. But what if she was serious?

A wave of unease washed over him. He would call her bluff. "You have this husband chosen?"

"Although your mother has worked quite diligently to ruin what little of my reputation Stephen left intact, I am confident I can find at least one man in England who would offer for me. Or at least who wants my ships as badly as you."

He caught and held her eyes, his eyebrows arching even higher, daring her to give him a name.

"The Earl of Longsbey came to speak with my father shortly before Father died, expressing a desire to wed me."

Ethan took a harsh breath. "He's an old man!"

"Perhaps I see that as a blessing. At least an old man will be content to stay home with a new wife."

Her remark hit home. He knew his resolve wavered, if only for a moment, and wondered if she noticed.

He had to stop her from going any further. "Let's say I accept your offer and give you Fallen Oaks in exchange for your ships. What do you intend to do when you run out of operating capital and no longer have a fleet of ships to help with the expenses? What do you intend to use for a dowry if I own your ships?"

"That will be my concern."

"You will be destitute and alone."

"I am alone now."

She stared at him, the concentrated glare in her emerald-green eyes as penetrating as a rapier. Ethan swore she could see right through him.

"What is so bloody important here that you would give up everything to keep it?"

"That is my concern, and only mine."

Ethan looked around. It was a wonderful home, roomy and well kept, brimming with a welcoming feeling he envied. But the house could not hold such importance that she would want to give up the ships to keep it. If she did indeed have the jewels, she might have had a chance at survival. But he believed her when she declared she knew nothing of them. There had to be something more.

"I extend my offer for the final time, Mr. Cambridge. Fallen Oaks in exchange for my ships."

Ethan stared at the hopeful expression on her face and had to turn away. An exchange would be the easy answer—for him. He would have what he needed to save the Burnhaven inheritance for Stephen. And Abigail Langdon would have Fallen Oaks. And in the end she would lose everything.

But he was desperate for her ships, especially the *Abigail Rose*. If he did not accept her offer, there was no chance he could get a contract for a shipment of China tea. There was no way he could hold off Stephen's creditors past spring. A cold shiver raced up and down his spine. He would have lost it all. He would have failed.

He thought of all the reasons he should hand over the deed to Fallen Oaks and take her ships.

And all the reasons he could not.

He tried to reject the only option that would benefit them both, but something deep inside him would not let him dismiss it. He could not take her ships and leave her unprotected. Lesser men had been forced to do more to save their inheritance. This sacrifice would not be too great if he could save what his father had worked so hard to build.

Ethan turned slowly to face her, unable to mask his resolve. He had made up his mind. He would not go back on his decision now. "I have decided to accept your offer, Miss Langdon."

"You will give me the deed for Fallen Oaks in exchange for the ships?"

"No. I will agree to marry you."

Chapter 6

Abigail felt the floor ripple beneath her feet. She opened her mouth to say something, to tell him she would never accept his offer of marriage, but no words would come.

A slow, lazy smile lifted the corners of his lips, his perfect white teeth forming a mocking expression against the darkened bronze of his skin. "What's the matter? Fallen Oaks is not worth such a sacrifice?"

"You cannot be serious," she whispered on a gasp.

"Oh, but I am. Completely serious."

"Why?"

"Why do I want to marry you?" He walked to the side-board and lifted a decanter and poured some brandy into a glass. "I don't."

"Then why? Nothing under God's heaven is demanding that we marry."

"Isn't it?" He lifted the glass to his mouth. "How do you expect me to sit by and watch you struggle to keep Fallen Oaks, while I get rich sailing your ships? And what are my chances of making one full run to China without finding out on my return that you are betrothed to the lecherous Earl of Longsbey, and he demands I turn over your ships to him as part of your dowry?"

"I will sign a note saying the ships are yours for as long as you want."

"What court in all of England do you suppose will uphold such a piece of paper?"

Her stomach flipped. Every nerve in her body screamed to tell him he was demanding too much. She shook her head back and forth in denial.

Her intense study of the man escalated as she watched for some sign that his words were a joke. But she saw no indication that he intended to take them back. Only deep regret that he'd had to make such an offer in the first place.

"Make up your mind, Abigail. Marry me, and Fallen Oaks will always be yours."

She turned away from the confident smile on his face. He was blackmailing her with everything she held dear. He knew she had no choice if she wanted to keep Fallen Oaks.

She pressed her forehead against the pane of glass overlooking the barren garden. She was more afraid than she'd ever been in her life.

Every reason she could not marry him flashed before her, each one more frightening than the last. How could she chance him finding out about Stephen? How could she chance him finding out that he'd married a murderer?

The earth shifted beneath her. She was in jeopardy of losing everything that was important to her. Fallen Oaks. The convent. And yet...she could lose more if she married him. She could lose her life.

She shook her head. The risk was too great. There was nothing she could do to save herself or Fallen

Oaks. No way she could ever marry him and expect he would never find out what she'd done.

The clock chimed the quarter hour, then the half, before she could force herself to speak. She said the only word she could. "No," she whispered, looking at the snow-covered ground beyond the frosty window-panes. "I will have to find another way."

There was a long silence. "That is your final decision?"

Her voice faltered the first time she tried to speak and sounded only a little stronger the second. "Yes."

"Very well. I will escort you to your town house in London myself yet this afternoon and have your belongings sent to you by the end of the week."

She spun around to face him. She couldn't find the air to speak. "You would force me out of my home today? You would make me leave without even a month, a week, or a day to say goodbye?"

"I see no reason to stay," he said, touching the back of the sofa as if testing the quality of what he now owned. "Believe me. Leaving today is for the best. The longer you wait, the harder it will be."

She was frantic. She had to get to the convent. "But I cannot leave today. There are matters that need taken care of. Matters that—"

He held up his hand to stop her. "Just leave a list before you go, and I will take care of everything for you."

Her heart pounded so hard she feared it would leap from her chest. He couldn't do this to her. She needed time. How could she get to the convent?

"You cannot do this, Mr. Cambridge. You cannot force me to leave without giving me time to even pack my belongings."

"I assure you, Miss Langdon, I am not doing this to be cruel, but Fallen Oaks is now mine. Since there is no longer the possibility of acquiring your ships to help pay Stephen's creditors, I will have to make other arrangements. Time is now of the essence. As I said before, my intent was not to purchase Fallen Oaks because I was in need of a country estate, but because I wanted it to barter for the jewels I thought you had. Since that is no longer a possibility, I will have to get back to the ships I do have as soon as possible. That doesn't leave me much time to board up the house, inform your tenants they will have to find other places to live, and close the convent."

Her mind screamed a thousand denials while she struggled to breathe. "You cannot close the convent. You cannot!"

"I'm sorry, Miss Langdon, but I cannot afford the upkeep on the convent without the income from the ships. I wish I could, but it is just not possible. I'm sure the good sisters will have no trouble finding another abbey in need of their excellent services."

She didn't think her legs would hold her. "And the tenants? You cannot expel them from their homes. They have no place to go."

"Don't worry," he said with a smile on his face. "They will each receive a generous stipend as reward for their loyal service."

She stared into his eyes and saw only the dark intent of a man used to getting what he wanted. A man intelligent enough, and cunning enough, to know what threats to make to control the futures of those around him. He knew she would never let him cause her tenants a hardship or close the convent. He knew and he didn't care.

"You think you will only gain from having the ships, Mr. Cambridge?"

"I know I will only lose if I do not have them."

"Then give me the deed to Fallen Oaks, and I will hand over ownership of the ships."

"If I made such an exchange with you, you would be the one to watch your tenants starve because you could not support them. And close the convent because you could not maintain it. And watch your estate fall to ruin around your pretty neck because you did not have the money for its upkeep." He filled his empty glass and took another swallow. "You can hate me today or yourself in the future. I would rather save us both such misery."

She closed her eyes and thought of the secrets she must always keep from him. "Are you sure you can face Society after taking as your wife the woman your brother discarded?"

"What Society thinks means nothing to me. Saving what Stephen is in jeopardy of losing is all that is important."

He stepped closer and glared at her with a look that held even more resolve. "My offer still stands. Marriage is your only option if you want to keep Fallen Oaks. Otherwise, I will call for a carriage to take you to London."

A violent shudder wracked her body. She had no choice.

She walked to the other side of the room and stared out the window as if an answer would magically appear. But there was no answer. No way to keep Fallen Oaks. No way to save the convent. She had no choice but to say the words she swore she would not.

She turned around and faced him squarely. "Very well, Mr. Cambridge. I will agree to marry you."

She wanted to take the words back as soon as she'd said them, but knew it was too late. She had to buy time, time to figure out another way to keep Fallen Oaks.

"You think you have won, but you have not." She didn't even try to keep the acid out of her words. "I will agree to marry you, but not without conditions."

He lifted his brows, waiting for her to speak.

"First, we will not marry until my year of mourning for my father is over." She took a step toward him, as if such a move would validate the rest of her demands. "Next, I will have it in writing that you will adequately provide for the convent and the tenants who live on Fallen Oaks from the profits made from the ships. You will never—" She paused and took one more step toward him. "You will never neglect the convent or the tenants or the manor house. And," she said, taking a deep breath, "I will have the deed to Fallen Oaks in my name as soon as possible, as you will have ownership of the ships. We will go to London to see Sydney Craddock immediately. He will draw up the papers."

He took a step toward her, the look in his eyes leveled at her. "Do you have any other demands?"

"No."

"Very well. Then here is my answer. We will not wait one year, but will marry in the spring. Since you have been in mourning for the past year due to your mother's death, I'm sure no one will object to a small, quiet affair in a few months' time. After all, you cannot be expected to remain alone and unprotected now that your father is gone."

She flashed him a hostile look, but he only smiled at her.

"Society has greatly underestimated you," he said with a good deal of humor in his voice. "They think you are like all other women, weak and incapable of taking care of yourself."

He paced the room, clasping his hands behind his back. The look on his face had turned even more serious. "The other demands are acceptable. You need never worry over the sisters in the convent or the tenants who work the land. I will always see to the needs of those for whom I am responsible. And, if it is important for you to have the deed to Fallen Oaks in your name, then you will have it.

"Of course, you realize what a marriage between us would mean?" The tone of his voice was flat, hollow. Resigned. "I have no title."

She stiffened. "You think I am only interested in gaining a title? I am not even interested in gaining a husband."

"How reassuring." He paused with his shoulder against the mantel, his arms crossed over his chest. "Not exactly the perfect beginning for a marriage."

"It was your demand to marry. Not mine."

"I only offered you a way to keep Fallen Oaks."

"And I only agreed because you gave me no choice." She turned her head. She refused to let herself think what it would mean to be married to Ethan Cambridge.

He pushed himself away from the fireplace and took a step toward her. "I did not threaten to destroy them. I just do not have the time to stay here and work Fallen Oaks as it needs to be worked. England is no longer my home. I am here only until Stephen returns."

"What if Stephen does not come back?"

"He will. When he recovers from whatever happened to make him leave, he will come back. Then I can go home. What I own is halfway across the ocean. A small spice plantation in the Caribbean and three cargo ships."

Ice water washed through her veins. "That is where you live?"

"Yes."

"And you would expect me to go with you?"

"I would expect you to be my wife."

"But now you have Fallen Oaks. Surely you would want to stay here, or at least allow me to."

He lifted his chin. The harsh glare in his eyes forced her to bear the full brunt of the power he wielded. "What is there about this place you cannot give up?"

"It is where I was raised."

"No," he said, shaking his head. "It's more than that. What is here that you cannot leave?"

She spun away from him. "It is my home. It's where I belong." She was determined to make him understand from the start that she would not leave.

He took another step closer to her. The clean smell of the outdoors and the scent of the soap in which he'd bathed filled her head. Confused her thoughts. She turned to face him with squared shoulders and lifted chin. A broad smile brightened his features, causing a riot of unfamiliar stirrings deep in the pit of her stomach.

"Perhaps, in time, it will be impossible for you to stay here without me?"

She tilted her head in defiance and prayed he would not come any closer. "You have my ships, Mr. Cambridge. Be content with the profits you can make from them. It will be the only benefit you receive from our marriage."

His thick brows arched high. "I think not." He cupped her cheek with his hand. "Our marriage will be a boon to both of us."

His touch sent a rush of fiery explosions racing to every part of her. Her traitorous body gave way to emotions she swore she would never let herself feel. Her heart ached to come alive, to be filled with something other than loneliness and bitterness and loss. But she couldn't allow it. She remembered the hurt, the pain of betrayal, the loss and emptiness. She would never hurt like that again.

Abigail pushed herself away from him. "It is a warning I give you now. Do not expect more. When you leave, I will not go with you."

The deep blue of his eyes turned even darker, the masked expression on his face even more obscure. "Do not think, Abigail, that every order you give will become a reality. So far, you have been the only one to make demands. That will soon change."

He locked his gaze with hers for a long moment, then turned away. "Palmsworth," he announced from the center of the room.

The butler appeared as if he had his hand on the door, waiting to be called.

"Bring your mistress's cloak and have a carriage brought round."

"Yes, sir."

Abigail rushed to object. "I don't—"

He ignored her protest and continued his instructions. "Miss Langdon and I are going out for a while and will be back in a few hours. Would you ask Cook to have dinner ready when we return? I missed lunch and am quite hungry."

"Yes, sir." Palmsworth started to back out of the room.

"Palmsworth," he ordered again. "Have Miss Langdon's maid begin packing. We will leave in the morning for London."

Palmsworth nodded once, then left. Abigail stood rooted to her spot and gaped after him.

Without giving her a chance to argue, he spun back to her. "The sun has come out, and it has turned into a beautiful winter's day. Before we leave for London, I should like to meet a few of the tenants and speak to your father's steward. I am sure he will manage well enough in our absence, but it is best we come to an understanding before we leave."

Abigail opened her mouth to speak, but he held out his hand to silence her.

"There is also the convent for which I am now responsible. I would like to see it."

Fingers of fear spiraled through her body, and she shook her head. "There is no need to go to the convent. Everything is already in place to see to its needs."

"That may be so. But I would still like to see it before we leave for London. It seems especially important to you, and I'd like to know why."

She paced the floor, searching for a way to change what was happening. There was none. "How long do you expect us to be in London?"

"A few weeks. Perhaps longer. There are banns to be read and announcements to be made. Although you will not be able to attend any social affairs due to your father's recent death, there are still small family gatherings at which we will be expected to make an appearance. You can hardly expect me to go to London to announce our impending marriage and proclaim myself the future owner of Langdon Shipping without you at my side to tell the world it is true, and show them how happy we are about our new state of affairs."

"I doubt your mother will be happy to hear our good news."

"I doubt she will, either, but she will either accept it or be content to spend the rest of her life in poverty."

Abigail felt the sting of his meaning. She knew why he had agreed to marry her. Because he wanted her ships, and he could not bring himself to hand over the deed to Fallen Oaks. It was his misplaced sense of honor that forced him to take care of Stephen's financial mess. It was an even more misplaced sense of principled integrity that forced him to take care of her.

She intended to use the few months he'd given her to show him she did not need him.

"The carriage is in front, sir," Palmsworth said, standing at the door with their heavy cloaks in his arms.

Ethan took hers and placed it around her shoulders. She tried to hold back the shiver that shook her body when he touched her, but she couldn't.

"Are you cold?"

"No." She wrapped the cloak tighter around her.

"Here," he said, handing her a thick fur muff, then putting on his own cloak. "This will help keep you warm."

Abigail wrapped a thick woolen muffler around her neck then slid her trembling hands into the muff. She wanted to tell him all the clothes in the world would not stop the chill that shook her body.

His hand rested lightly on her back as he led her from the house. The heat from his touch burned through the thick layers of clothing. Doubt and indecision ate away at her. She was left trembling from the inside out.

Didn't he know she had more to fear from him than from the cold and the wind? Didn't he know she would never trust him, no matter how desperately she wanted to? Putting her life in any man's hands was a lesson Stephen proved would destroy her. It was a lesson she would never forget.

She walked with him to the waiting carriage, the safety and surety of his nearness a false panacea to the trembling fear that would not go away. How could she ever feel safe with him? There were too many secrets to separate them.

She thought of the bargain she'd just struck with

him and knew she could never honor it. There was too much at stake. Too much she would lose. Let him think he could marry her for her ships. That is all he wanted anyway. Let him think all his problems had been solved. They had only just begun. She had survived far greater threats than Ethan Cambridge and his misplaced sense of honor and responsibility.

She would go through the motions, pretend to agree to his proposal, but in the end, it would not be as he thought. Sydney would draw up the papers. Once they were signed, she would have Fallen Oaks and he would have her ships. He would be the only one who thought there would be more.

One fact was for certain. She had no intention of ever becoming his wife.

Chapter 7

Ethan stood alone in the quiet of a world already gone to sleep and stared at the multitude of shining stars that twinkled in the clear winter sky. Here at Fallen Oaks, away from the rude London noises, and despite the day's earlier hard-fought battle, he felt strangely at peace. A huge moon shone radiant and full, reflecting its silver spires upon the blanket of pure white snow in a dazzling display of gleaming splendor. The vivid brilliance cast his room in a brightness more powerful than that of a hundred glowing candles.

Downstairs, the clock struck one, then two, and still sleep eluded him with a vengeance. What was there about her that caused such emotions to rage unguarded? What great secret did she hide?

Memories of the day he'd spent with the woman he would soon take as his wife refused to go away. Whatever she wanted to keep secret was not just hidden at Fallen Oaks, but was concealed behind the convent walls.

The minute their carriage pulled up to the large stone enclosure, her demeanor changed with alarming ferocity. She became as protective as a starving man guarding his last morsel of bread.

Did she think he would not care for the sisters as her father had before him? Oh, how he wanted to reach out to her and show her she had nothing to fear from him.

The startling realization of how he felt frightened him. Why did he feel so protective toward her? Why couldn't he just hand over the deed to Fallen Oaks and leave?

He ground his teeth. He knew damn well why. He couldn't give over the deed, knowing in a year's time she would be struggling to keep her family estate solvent. Or forced to wed someone as repulsive as Longsbey to save it. Without the ships, she would lack a dowry enticing enough to make an advantageous match, and would end up with someone who was not worthy of her.

He thought of himself. What made him think he was worthy of her? He wasn't titled. He had nothing to give her. Neither a safe home nor a secure future. Especially with Stafford's men so close to finding him. Such a selfish act would only put her in danger.

He snatched Edward Langdon's letter from the table and reread the words, words that had plagued him since the first time he'd read the dying man's plea.

Be assured, I alone am responsible for the tragedy. My daughter Abigail is completely blameless, but unless I confess what happened, she will be the one left to suffer for what happened.

It didn't make sense. What confession did he have to make?

Even though Abigail had no part in the tragedy, she does have something of the greatest importance that belongs to Stephen. I know she will never give it up willingly, but she must.

What did Abigail Langdon have to hide? If not the jewels, what did she have that she must give up?

Ethan's thoughts turned to Stephen, and he uttered a vile curse. Of all the irresponsible things his brother had ever done, leaving the young girl he could have had as his wife was the most unforgivable. Leaving her to face his mother's viperous tongue and Society's vicious gossip was beyond cruel. Leaving her to shoulder her mother's and father's deaths without anyone to stand at her side was worse yet. He knew it would take time for her to trust him with even a small part of her heart. He feared it might take forever.

A disturbing noise that shattered the peaceful silence of a house long ago gone to sleep rudely halted his contemplation. He listened, an unsettling confusion alerting his senses.

For a moment, the sound was nothing more than a childlike whimper, a small, pathetic moan not loud enough for him to be certain he'd actually heard it. But it grew louder. A cry for help. An agonizing plea of desperation. Then a scream of terror.

Ethan tore across the room, flinging open the door and racing down the hall. Her scream raged through the silence again, then settled to soft whimpers. He threw open the door to her room. She lay on the bed, her hair of fiery copper fanning out across the pillow, her hands fisted in terror at her side, her bedclothes twisted and bunched as if she waged the battle of her life. Then he looked at her face. Her features were frozen in the most frightened look he'd ever seen. A look no one so young and innocent should have reason to wear.

"Shh, Abby." He sat on the bed beside her and placed his hands on her shoulders.

She slapped at him, struggling to push his hands

from her.

"It's all right. It's only a dream. A dream."

"No!"

Her voice raged, ragged and raw. The desperation in her pleas tore at something deep inside him.

"Abby. Wake up. It's me. Ethan."

She threw her head from one side to the other. "No. Stephen!"

A heavy lump fell to the pit of his stomach when she called out his brother's name.

He pulled her into his arms, holding her tight, calming her struggles. "Wake up, Abby. You're all right now. I'm here."

Ethan rocked back and forth with her in his arms. He held her close and pushed the coppery strands from her face. Her eyes fluttered, then opened. Huge wet tears streamed down her cheeks, soaking into the white lawn shirt he still wore. Recognition dawned and she pulled away.

"No. It's all right," he comforted. "I won't hurt you."

Her chest heaved in and out as if she had just finished a long, hard battle. Her breaths came in painful, quick gasps.

Ethan rubbed his hand over her shoulders, soothing the tense muscles wound so tightly they quivered. "Shh. You're safe. It was only a dream."

She looked up at him, her huge green eyes brimming with indecision, then she gave in and sank against him.

He sat with her in his arms. The bright moonlight streamed through the window. The sleeping household remained as silent as before.

Eventually, her eyelids closed and her breathing calmed, even though the grip with which she clutched his shirt did not ease. Ethan did not move, but sat with her cradled in his arms.

As if a voice warned him they were not alone, he turned to the doorway. Palmsworth stood there, a look of concern on his face.

"She had a nightmare," Ethan whispered.

"I should have expected she would," Palmsworth answered, his words an admission. "Today was not easy for her."

"She has had these before?"

"Yes. Often."

Palmsworth's admission was damning.

Ethan looked down at her pale face, made even more translucent in the moonlight. *Bloody hell. What did Stephen do to her?*

Ethan took a deep breath and held her in his embrace. He studied her for a long time while she slept, and let the warmth that blanketed his heart consume him. "She will be all right now, Palmsworth. You may go back to bed. I'll wake you if she needs you."

"Very good, sir. I will send Stella in to sit with you and leave my door open in case you call."

Ethan nodded in understanding, then laid her down on the bed and straightened the covers.

Abigail Langdon had more than one secret she was hiding. He would not rest until he discovered each one of them. She'd suddenly become too important for him to ignore them.

He placed his hand against the soft, smooth skin of her cheek and watched as she slept peacefully in the warm downy covers. His fingertips tingled long after he'd pulled his hand away from her. In that one instant, he knew why he would marry her.

He could not bear the thought of her belonging to anyone else.

· · ·

Abigail was desperate to reach the convent. Ethan Cambridge was going to take her to London, and it would be weeks before she could return.

Abigail stared out into the frosty, overcast sky, silently wanting the driver to urge the horses to travel over the frozen ground at a faster pace, yet knowing going faster wasn't safe. Frigid air stung her cheeks as she leaned her head near the side window in search of her destination. The trip to the Convent of Mary the Immaculate had never taken so long.

She sat back against the seat and folded her hands in prayer. For the last two months and more she had done very little except pray, even though God had not once seen fit to answer her. And now He'd chosen to send her another cross to bear.

How many crosses would it take before she could no longer stand up under the weight? Where would she find the strength to fight Ethan Cambridge?

The carriage finally came to a halt near the convent doors, and before the driver had time to dismount, Abigail jumped to the ground. She raced to the thick oak door that barred the outside world from intruding on the peaceful serenity the sisters guarded with such care, and pounded on the wood using the large brass knocker.

The door didn't open immediately, and she pounded again, then again. She didn't give up until Sister Angela timidly peeked her head through the small opening.

"Miss Langdon? Is that you?" The soft-spoken nun pulled the door open a little wider.

"Yes, Sister Angela. Please, may I come in?"

"Of course. Of course."

Sister Angela opened the door and Abigail rushed inside. After a few words of greeting, she raced down the long, familiar corridor that took her to the stairs that led to a private chamber above.

"Is something wrong?" the sister said, following her.

"No," Abigail answered. "I just needed to come."

"But it is so early. The sisters have barely begun to sing the morning Lauds!"

"I know," Abigail answered. "But I just got word I have to leave for several days. I needed to come before I left."

"Of course," Sister Angela said.

Abigail's heart beat faster. She was almost there. It wouldn't be long now.

She ran up the stairs, then down another hallway, then stopped before the third door on the right and opened the door.

A small gasp caught in her throat as she raced across the room. "Hello, my precious," Abigail whispered, kneeling before the small babe who stood on two chubby legs that wobbled as she grasped a chair to hold herself upright.

The babe turned her head and squealed with delight. Then she let go of the chair and fell into Abigail's arms.

Abigail clutched the babe to her breast and held her tight. Tears she couldn't stop flowed down her cheeks as she sank to the floor and held the babe on her lap. Abigail pressed a kiss to the child's chubby cheek and brushed away a strand of the same burnt copper hair as her own.

"She wants so badly to walk, miss," Sister Angela said.

"Do you really, my Mary Rose? So soon?" Abigail lifted her in the air, and the babe gave a gleeful laugh.

"She does, and you should see her pull herself up on anything she can find," the sister said. "She gets the biggest grin on her face, as if she knows it's beyond her, but she's going to try anyway. Then she just plops down on her backside."

Abigail couldn't help but laugh.

"The other sisters and I always think she might cry, but instead, she just makes the most awkward attempt to pull herself up again. It won't be long before she'll be running across the room."

Abigail lowered Mary Rose into her arms and rocked her back and forth. The babe was growing so fast. Abigail gave her another squeeze, and Mary Rose wrapped her stout little arms around Abigail's neck and held tight.

This was the reason she could never lose Fallen Oaks. The reason she would do whatever it took to protect the convent.

She would never let Ethan Cambridge take her away.

Chapter 8

Ethan woke with a start, blinked twice, then closed his eyes again to the blinding sunlight shining through the window. It was late. The sun had risen far above the horizon. He considered the sleepless night he'd had and contemplated closing his eyes again. But he knew that wasn't an option. Not if they were to get to London before nightfall.

He listened for any sound that might come from her room down the hall but heard nothing. She was probably still asleep. Even though she'd eventually fallen to sleep, her night had been no more restful than his own. It would do her good to stay abed longer.

He threw back the covers and walked to the basin to wash. A servant had left a razor and a brush with a cup of soap on the square table before a large oval mirror. As Ethan slid the sharp-edged blade over his skin, he relived Abigail's nightmare, her cries for help. If his brother was responsible for those screams, he didn't want to think about what he'd do to Stephen.

Ethan washed, using the bayberry soap and the clean cloths that lay on the stand next to a pitcher of warm water. His chest tightened when he thought of the way she'd clung to him in her sleep.

He scrubbed his skin harder, hoping it would erase the effects of her touch. When he finished, he combed his hair and readied himself for the long trip they would make to London.

He checked the knot of his cravat a final time before walking down the stairs to eat a hearty breakfast. He would at least start the day with a full stomach.

"Good morning, Stella," he said, greeting the maid as she was exiting the breakfast room. Stella was Miss Langdon's maid and would be coming with them. "Is your mistress packed and ready to travel?"

Stella gave him a quick curtsy, then answered with a shy smile. "Yes, sir. George and Freddie are loading the trunks in the carriage right now. This is a hamper Cook packed in case we feel peckish while we're traveling."

"Good. Thank Cook for me."

Stella smiled. "I will."

"Is Miss Langdon still asleep?"

"Oh, no, Mr. Cambridge."

"She is up?"

A hint of red colored Stella's cheeks. "For hours, sir."

Ethan looked around, checking to see any sign that she'd already come down and broken her fast. There were no used plates or cups sitting on the table, and none of the breadstuff or dishes of eggs or kidneys on the sideboard had been touched. "Has your mistress already eaten?"

Stella looked at the floor and shuffled her feet nervously. "No, sir. Not yet."

"Good." Ethan was anxious to talk to her before they left. There were many details he wanted to discuss with her before they reached London, and not everything could wait until later.

Ethan picked up a plate and scooped a large helping of eggs and a warm muffin onto his plate. "Would you go upstairs and ask Miss Langdon to come down and join me for breakfast?"

"I..." Stella twisted the corners of her crisp white apron between her fingers. "I'm afraid I can't, sir."

Ethan lifted a brow. "Can't? Why not?"

The maid lowered her head, her cheeks turning a deep red.

"Is there something wrong with your mistress, Stella?"

"No, sir. Nothing is wrong."

"Then why can't she come down?"

The maid shuffled her feet again, then cleared her throat. "She's not here, sir," she whispered.

Ethan placed his plate on the corner of the sideboard and braced his hand against the top rung of the nearest chair. "What did you say?" he asked, certain he had misheard her.

"Miss Langdon has already gone out."

"Gone? Where?"

"I really can't say, sir."

Ethan stared at her, unable to believe what he was hearing. "Are you telling me she left the house? Alone?"

"Oh no, sir. She wouldn't go alone. Bundy took her."

"Where did they go?"

"Out," Abigail answered from the doorway.

Ethan turned to look at the woman whose nearness had kept him awake almost all night. The woman who was the catalyst for the turmoil that raged through his body.

She stood in the open doorway with her chin elevated, her shoulders raised in proud defiance, and her hands clasped calmly in front of her at her waist. She made the most elegant picture he had ever seen.

Even though she was clad in funereal black from head to toe, she could not have been more stunning had she been wearing a brightly colored gown in the latest London fashion.

A dark traveling cloak covered her simple mourner's weeds. She'd fastened the cloak beneath her chin with a large jeweled brooch, the emerald stones in the pin bringing out the brilliant green of her eyes in startling clarity. An overly plain bonnet of black felt sat upon her head, the wide, black velvet ties acting as a muffler, which she wound around her neck to keep her warm.

With slow, deliberate movements, she pulled the ties free and loosened the knot beneath her chin. Long curling strands of coppery tendrils came loose and framed her face in picturesque splendor. Stella rushed to take her bonnet and cloak.

A heavy weight settled low in his stomach, warming his insides like molten lava seeping into every crevice. How could Stephen have walked away from her?

Ethan focused on the rosy glow to her cheeks, made even more vibrant from traveling in the cold, then noticed her red-rimmed eyes still puffy and swollen. "Where have you been?"

She didn't flinch. "I had some business to take care of before we left."

"At this hour?" He couldn't keep the surprise from his voice.

"Yes. I was not sure when we would be back, and this could not wait."

She walked through the room to the sideboard filled with breakfast dishes. "I know there are certain details we must attend to when we reach London. Would you like to discuss some of those now?"

"If you don't mind."

"Of course not. I know we must meet with Sydney

to have the papers drawn up that will transfer Fallen Oaks to me and my ships to you. Once that is done, I will introduce you to Captain Parker and see that he is assigned a position, as my father stipulated in his will."

She returned to the table and sat in a chair opposite him. There was hardly enough food on her plate to keep a bird alive.

"I am certain we will have to face Society—and your mother—at one point or another to inform them of our plans and face their shock and insinuations. I have little choice but to...*enjoy* London—at least until our business is completed."

"Have you included wedding plans in the *business* that needs to be taken care of?"

She shrugged her shoulders. "If there is time."

"Your enthusiasm is...overwhelming. With the anticipation of so many enjoyable adventures, we are guaranteed to have a wonderful time in London."

"It is the way things must be. I know there is no way to avoid these pleasantries in order to be permitted to return to Fallen Oaks."

"Where you intend to hide away for the rest of your life?"

"Where I intend to live my life in peace and solitude."

"And what about me?"

"You are welcome to...visit any time you are in England."

Ethan flashed her a hard look, intending to show her his displeasure. She was sorely mistaken if that's the way she thought their marriage would be.

She picked up her fork and slid some eggs around on her plate.

"How are you feeling?" he asked.

Her fork halted in midair, her trembling noticeable.

She lowered her eyelids. "I'm fine. I—I'm sorry I disturbed your sleep last night."

Ethan took a sip of the coffee Palmsworth had just refilled, then placed his cup back on its saucer. "Do you want to talk about it?"

"No."

"I'll not let you shut me out forever, Abby."

She lifted her chin and stared at him. "I don't know what you mean."

"You know bloody well what I mean, and I won't allow it. You're building a wall between us. It's impossible to start a marriage with something of such magnitude in the way."

She shoved a small piece of meat from one side of her plate to the other as she ignored answering him.

Ethan leaned back in his chair and studied her at great length. She'd been pale when she returned from wherever she'd been, but not nearly so pale as she was now. He picked up the cup and took another swallow of the dark, rich coffee. "I would like to know where you were just now and who you went to see. I do not like secrets."

She opened her mouth to say something, then halted. Her gaze hardened, but not before he noticed a hint of fear in her eyes.

"In time you'll learn to trust me, Abby. Stephen and I may be bound by the same blood, but that is the only similarity between us."

She stared at him, and for a moment he saw the determined look in her eyes weaken. For a moment he thought he saw a glimmer of softness. Then it was gone.

She breathed a heavy sigh that nearly cried out in pain, then lifted her fork again and shoved the food around on her plate with no more interest in eating than she'd shown before.

The air hung heavily between them as they ate in silence. He was thankful when Palmsworth entered the room. "George said the carriage is loaded and ready to depart."

"Good." Ethan shoved his plate away and sat forward in his chair. "Have Bundy and George leave as soon as possible. I want everything ready at your mistress's town house when we arrive later. Tell them we should be there before dark. You may go with us, Palmsworth."

Abigail dropped her fork with a loud clatter, then cast the butler an open look of panic.

"No. Palmsworth needs to stay here. Bundy may take us, and Freddie may go with George."

The determined look on her face gave him cause for thought. Whatever the reason, it was very important to her.

"You are sure you do not want Palmsworth in London with you?"

"No. He is needed here. Please, I will have Stella. And there is a staff in London."

He focused for a long time on her desperate look. "Very well. Palmsworth will stay here." He turned to Palmsworth. "Bundy may drive us. Have George and Freddie leave with the first carriage as soon as possible."

"Yes, sir." Palmsworth gave him a respectful bow and left the room.

"Another secret, Abby?"

She dropped her chin, the guilty look on her face plain for him to see.

"Hopefully, you can rest on our way to London." He looked at the dark circles forming beneath her eyes and the pale complexion of her face. "I would like to leave before long."

"I'll be ready, sir." She rose. "I would like a moment to visit my father's grave before we go."

"Of course. And your mother's, too," he said, knowing it had not been that long since she'd lost her mother.

What little color she had left on her cheeks drained, but there remained an empty look in her eyes. Without a word, she left the room.

Ethan watched her take the stairs slowly, her grip on the polished oak banister clasped with white-knuckled desperation.

What could have happened to cause someone so young and with so much of her life ahead of her to have so many secrets?

He would not rest until he had an answer.

. . .

Abigail shifted her shoulder to another spot inside the carriage and struggled to find a comfortable position in which to sit. She was so tired her mind had ceased thinking long ago. Every muscle in her body ached from the millions of ruts Bundy unintentionally managed to hit. And the journey was worse now. Ethan had tied his mount to the back of the carriage and was sitting on the seat opposite her and Stella.

She knew it was not so, but even with her eyes closed, he seemed to take up every empty inch of the carriage. His broad shoulders seemed to span at least half the width inside, and his long, muscular legs angled perilously close to hers. Every time he shifted against the squabs, she felt his touch—the heat of his knees or ankles or soft leather boots—which left a river of fire that blazed through every layer of her petticoats until it reached her skin.

She refused to look at him, not wanting to see if he watched her. Not wanting to remember how safe and secure she'd felt when he'd comforted her in the night. She did not want to get used to him being there. Marriage to him was an impossibility, and if she let herself care for him, she would be even more alone when she walked away. Stephen had taught her a very painful lesson, but it was one she would never forget. She would never give her heart away only to have it shattered and broken.

She shifted again in the corner, inching as far away from him as she could.

"Here." He exchanged places with Stella and sat down beside her. "Lean your head against my shoulder and try to get some sleep."

Abigail sat up with a start. Her eyes popped open to find him but a few inches from her.

"Don't worry, Abigail. Stella is here to guard you."

"I'm fine where I am." She slid closer to the carriage door.

"No, you're not. You're as restless as a dog with an itch, and you haven't slept a minute since we left Fallen Oaks."

She lifted her brows and tried to keep from laughing at him. *A dog with an itch. How ridiculous.* "I'm not tired." She locked her hands in her lap with as much an air of propriety as she could muster.

He laughed. Not a shallow, empty laugh, but a full, rich sound that sent fiery shivers racing along her limbs.

"You're so tired, you look like the walking dead. Doesn't she, Stella?"

Stella clamped her hand over her mouth to stifle a giggle. "You do look a might weary, miss," she answered, then took out some embroidery to keep herself occupied. The maid gave her a sympathetic look before she concentrated on her handiwork.

"How descriptive," Abigail said, pulling the edge of her skirt from beneath his leg. He helped her shift the volumes of fabric that was the fashion, then slid closer, as if she'd moved her skirt to make more room for him.

"Have you missed town life?" he asked, shifting on the seat, which only served to make his nearness more confining.

She turned to look out the window, but his arm pressed against her side. A river of fire burned a path to the tips of her toes.

"Not necessarily." She turned to look straight ahead. That position held the least threat. "I've never enjoyed the rounds of parties and teas. I fear I have too much of my father in me. He wasn't fond of the social life either."

"What about your mother?"

"She thrived on it. She hated the isolation at Fallen Oaks and was her happiest in London during the height of the Season."

"My mother feels the same."

"And you?"

"I'm afraid I'm just like you. I hate the feigned camaraderie, the fake adherence to social rules that gives free rein to all manner of indiscretions. That's why I spend so little time in London. I'm used to a life much different."

She leaned back in the seat, relaxing against him just a little. Surely that would not hurt. "What is your plantation like?"

She heard a deep sigh and knew without looking that he'd smiled. "It's a paradise, lush and green and beautiful, with a peacefulness I can't describe. The sunsets are more gorgeous than anywhere on earth, and the sunrises so beautiful you swear God created special colors that He only uses there each morning. It's hard to describe a life so perfect: tropical breezes that warm you year-round, and flowers so alive with color you'd swear they could talk to you."

Abigail was enthralled by his vivid descriptions. She fought the urge to travel there to see such wonders. Even Stella held her needle still to listen, a faraway look of fascination in her eyes.

"We grow spices on my plantation and fruits unlike anything you have ever seen or tasted. It's a place different from anywhere else on earth. I truly miss it when I'm gone."

"Do you ship spices, then?"

"Partly. I've spent the last few years selling anything to the colonies I can get my hands on. Primarily to the Southern states."

She sat straight. "You are a blockade runner?"

He smiled at her. "I guess that is what you could call me. Does that disturb you?"

"No, but isn't it dangerous?"

"Not if you're careful." He flashed her a smile that caused her heart to stutter. "And I'm always careful."

"Why do you do it?"

"For the money. There's a great deal of profit to be made by blockade running right now. One of the North's strategies is to starve out the South. The Southerners are desperate and willing to pay a decent high price for anything that can be smuggled in to them."

"And your cargo allows people to eat."

"I would not be honest if I didn't admit it bothers me to know people have nothing to eat when food is so plentiful."

Abigail could imagine him daring Northern warships to stop him, just as she could imagine him captaining his own ship, slicing through the storms and the waves, with the wind whipping through his hair and the sun beating against his skin.

She closed her eyes to stop such thoughts, then stifled another yawn. Stella already leaned against the corner with her head dropped to her chest and her eyes closed. The carriage was warm with him sitting beside her. Abigail yawned again. She'd had to get up so early to visit Mary Rose one last time before they left. Her lack of sleep was finally catching up with her.

"I cannot imagine such a war," she said on a sigh. "It must be terrible there. They are all Americans, some of them even related."

He shifted to make a more comfortable spot for her to lean against. The temptation was too great for her to resist taking modest advantage of it.

"I know. It's not easy on either side. The North sees cutting off the South as the answer to ending a war that is killing their young men by the thousands. The South sees the war as an end to a way of life they've cherished for generations."

"The elimination of slavery?"

"Yes."

"Have you seen the slaves in the South?"

There was a noticeable pause before he answered. "Yes."

"What is slavery like?"

"I'm not sure I can answer that. I don't think anyone can who has not lived surrounded by slavery."

She let herself sink more heavily against him and gave up her fight to stay awake. "I've heard there are antislavery sympathizers who sneak into Southern harbors in the dark of night and smuggle whole families of slaves out of the South and take them to Canada so they can be free."

His only answer was an indiscernible sigh barely

loud enough to be heard. If he said anything more, it was lost on her.

Sometime just before she fell into a deep sleep, she felt his arm wrap around her. He brought her toward him.

His muscled chest became a pillow for her head.

His powerful strength became something far more dangerous.

She leaned against him and slept better in the small, cramped, bouncy carriage than she had ever before.

Chapter 9

"Abby, wake up. We're here."

Ethan spoke in a hushed whisper. He was afraid he might startle her. She slept so peacefully he was tempted to have Bundy drive around London a while longer so she could get the rest she needed. But that wasn't a possibility.

"Abby, wake up." He ran his fingertips down her silky smooth cheek.

"Is it morning?" she asked, burrowing her face deeper against his chest.

He smiled, then nestled her closer to him and brushed back the coppery tendrils that had fallen onto her face while she lay against him. Stroking her hair was like touching burnished brass, cool and vibrant, startlingly alive. Touching her face made his flesh sing with life. "No, Abby. It's not morning. We're in London."

"Oh," she sighed, her tone filled with disappointment.

Her body stiffened in his arms as she realized what it meant to be here. It did not take her long to push herself away from him and sit up straight. "I'm sorry. How rude of me to sleep all the way."

Ethan looked at her, and a warm molten heat swirled deep in his belly. Her cheeks burned rose-red, glowing with the bright innocence of a woman newly awakened. A heaviness settled in his loins, an uncomfortable weight that ached to be soothed.

He opened the carriage door and stepped to the ground. He was eager to put some distance between them before he revealed more of himself than he wished to. He helped Stella disembark first, then turned to Abigail. He took her hand and led her up the short walk to the town house that, according to her father's will, now belonged to her. George held the door for them, then took their cloaks.

"Thank you, George," Abigail said, handing George her bonnet. She stepped to the middle of the room, then stopped. She turned around slowly, as if she either couldn't quite remember what the house should look like or was not certain she wanted to. Watching her, Ethan wondered whether memories of living here were happy. He wasn't certain they were.

A maid introduced as Genevieve led the way to a set of doors to their right. "You warm yourself by the fire, mistress," she said, bustling through the entrance. "I'll bring you each a nice hot cup of tea right off. Cook says she will have dinner ready whenever you like."

"Thank you, Genevieve," Ethan answered. "Tell Cook she may serve as soon as we've settled in."

"Very good, sir," Genevieve said, then rushed from the room.

Ethan walked over to the windows and pulled the draperies closed. He wasn't sure why, but he suddenly felt the need to isolate Abigail from the outside world. He wasn't certain he wanted her in London any more than she wanted to be here. Bringing her here could put her in danger.

He turned to find her studying this room as intently as she'd studied the foyer. "Is something wrong?"

She shook her head, but the frown on her face said something different.

"It's just been so long since I've been here."

"It's a beautiful property." Ethan took note of the rich oak paneling on the walls, the thick Persian carpet covering the floor, and the exquisite furnishings arranged to perfection throughout the room.

"This was my mother's. It was her home, her showpiece."

"Does it bother you to be surrounded by what was your mother's? Or does every memory of your mother bother you?"

She shot him a closed look, a look that told him he'd stumbled into an area of which she didn't wish to speak. "I don't wish to discuss my mother."

"I took the liberty of instructing one of the lads at Fallen Oaks to care for her grave. It looked as if it had been left unattended since her death."

She turned. Whatever the hurt, the wounds were still too tender and exposed.

She stood on the other side of the room, holding in her grasp an exquisite china figurine of a mother holding a child. "Did you know my mother?"

"No. She was ill the day I came to tell you Stephen had left. I only met with you, then later your father."

She turned the figurine over in her hands. "She was a very beautiful woman."

"No doubt, if her daughter resembles her in the slightest."

She lifted her gaze to his and smiled, but her smile was bittersweet. None of its beauty or warmth reached her eyes.

"I was always a disappointment to her. Mother was

the belle of Society, the center of attention. She was thirty-eight when she died, and she still attracted men like bees to honey. I was never fashionable enough, or popular enough, or courted by enough dashing, eligible young bachelors to gain her approval."

"Stephen desired you."

"Stephen desired my dowry."

Ethan stared at her pale face, a face void of all expression. He wondered if he would ever find out all that had happened to make her feel this way.

"I was not cut out to lead the life my mother led. I was more content to stay at home with Father, or go with him to the shipyards to watch one of his ships dock or set sail. Mother couldn't tolerate such common trivialities. She couldn't believe she'd produced a daughter who did."

"What about your father? What was he like?"

She smiled, the first genuine smile he'd seen on her face. "He was fifteen years my mother's senior, far too absorbed in his ships to keep up with Mother's social life. They were worlds different from one another."

She placed the figurine back on the shelf. "It was impossible for Mother to pretend interest in Father's ships, so he left her to her rounds of parties and social obligations, and concentrated on spoiling me. There was nothing I lacked. Nothing I wanted that he didn't get for me."

"And you wanted Stephen?"

She studied her empty hands.

"After Stephen left, why didn't you return to London?"

"I do not want to discuss this."

"I do."

She lifted her chin. Her huge green eyes stared at him with hard resolve. "Because I did not want to. Stephen's leaving caused a large enough scandal. Even though our engagement hadn't been announced, everyone assumed we would marry. Then Mother became ill." She stepped around him. "I did not want to marry after that. I still don't."

"So you've said."

"Yes, so I've said," she repeated on a sigh. "For what it's worth. We women really have very little control over our lives. No matter what our worth, we are still at the mercy of someone else."

"You mean a man?"

"Yes."

"You are not without power, Abigail. More than even you realize yet."

She stared at him, the vibrant green of her eyes filled with thoughtful questioning. "Do you still intend to use my ships to get Stephen out of debt?"

"Yes. That has been my intent from the start. Once Stephen is out of debt, it will be his responsibility to stay that way. What he does after that is his concern."

"Why do you care what happens to him?"

"Because the estates are not just his. They were my father's, and his father's before him. I can't just sit by and let Stephen lose it all."

"Even though you will never have any of it."

"I have never wanted it. Stephen may have it with my blessing."

"Do you care for him that much?"

He paused. "Yes. He is my brother."

"What if he doesn't come back?"

"He will." Ethan walked to the fire and placed another log in the flames. "This is not the first time you've hinted that Stephen may not return. Why do you think he may not?"

Ethan stared at her. She was visibly uncomfortable.

"It's been eighteen months," she continued. "Even

you have to admit that is far too long to stay away. Perhaps he does not want to come back to face..."

"Face, what?"

She shrugged her slender shoulders. "His debts. The loss of his estate. Whatever else he cannot address."

"You are indeed a lady of mystery, Abigail. You know far more than you are willing to say, and yet..." He reached out and placed his hands atop her shoulders. Her eyes opened wide.

A blistering heat warmed his fingers. "What will you do when I discover your secrets?"

"No, sir," she taunted. "The real question is, what will *you* do when you discover my secrets."

He reached up and stroked her cheek with his fingertips. "You're wrong, Abby. I have nothing to lose. I'm a second son. I left here five years ago with nothing except the clothes on my back and a determination to succeed. All I have amassed I have done so by my own labor and sweat. If I were to lose it all today, I still have the clothes on my back and that same determination to succeed."

"Except now you would have me."

He touched her lips with the callused pads of his thumb. She was so soft, so yielding. So ready to be kissed. "You think you are that much of a burden?"

"In time, perhaps you will think so, too."

He lowered his head and leaned his forehead against hers. He closed his eyes to drink in the feel and smell of her. "Perhaps," he whispered.

"Please, don't," she whispered.

He stood straight. "Don't what?"

"Touch me like that."

"It's hard not to."

He lowered his head and pressed his mouth to hers. He expected her lips to be soft and yielding beneath his own, but instead he received none of the fiery passion he'd hoped for. None of the burning thirst or the mind-jarring hunger that would jolt every nerve and set it to singing.

He lifted his lips from hers and looked down. Her face was ashen white. Her fingers clutched the sleeves of his jacket until the cloth bunched in crinkled wads in her fists. Her chest heaved with her labored breathing.

"What's wrong?"

She opened her mouth to speak, then shook her head when no words would come.

"Why are you so frightened?"

A thousand thoughts ran through his mind at the same time. Of all the secrets she harbored, this one confused him the most.

Ethan wrapped his arms around her and held her closer. Her slight body trembled against him.

For a long time neither of them moved. He knew if he opened his arms, she would run from him. He refused to let her go. He kept his hold loose, his touch gentle, never tight enough to be confining. Just secure enough for her to feel no threat.

She let him hold her. In time, her trembling ceased. The grip she had on his clothing relaxed. Finally, she moved her hands and placed them on his chest atop his pounding heart. But she did not wrap her arms around him.

"Are you that afraid of me?" he whispered.

"It's not what you think," she said.

But it was. She was fighting for breath like a frightened animal.

"Then what is it?"

Her gaze lifted to meet his, the emerald in her eyes the deepest green imaginable. "I—I just was not...expecting you to..."

He held her, his pride not allowing him to let her go. This was the woman he would marry, the woman he would take as his wife, the woman who would be the mother of his children.

She trembled in his arms. "I'm sorry," she whispered. "It's just that..."

Ethan tipped his head back on his shoulders and closed his eyes. Perhaps he had startled her. She was, after all, still an inexperienced young woman. Although he could not imagine it, perhaps Stephen had never made such advances. Perhaps she had never been kissed.

He could not bring himself to release her. She belonged here, nestled in his arms. When she pulled back to look up at him, he lowered his head and kissed her on the forehead.

A deep sigh echoed in the silence as if she welcomed this new experience, then she leaned against him again.

They stood locked in each other's arms while the clock in the foyer ticked away the minutes. Only when George cleared his voice to tell them that dinner would be served in an hour did he release her.

He accompanied her up the stairs to her room to rest until dinner. It would take time for her to accustom herself to him.

But he had time.

Chapter 10

Ethan Cambridge had gone to the Burnhaven town house to change for dinner. Abigail used the time that he was gone to rest and to try to calm her nerves. But all she could think about when she closed her eyes was how her body had reacted to him when he held her. When he kissed her.

She didn't want to feel anything when she was near him, but she did. There was something about his strength that caused her to want to remain in his arms. And she wasn't referring to his physical strength. She was more drawn to an inner strength that made her feel safe. That caused her to want to rely on him to take care of her. And to take care of Mary Rose.

But she couldn't allow herself to give in to those feelings. She could never forget what had happened. She could never forget what she'd done.

The blood ran cold through her veins. Instead of wanting to step into his arms, she should run as far away from him as she could. Instead of considering marriage to him, she should be planning a way to escape him. And she told herself she would. As soon as she was alone for more than just a few moments. As soon as she could clear thoughts of Ethan Cambridge from her mind.

She rose and dressed for dinner, then left her room. He was waiting for her when she entered the study. He greeted her politely, and together they went in to dinner.

They ate in silence. He didn't comment on how little she ate or prod her to eat more. It was as if he'd vowed not to make her feel self-conscious or uncomfortable about anything. As if he'd decided to give her time to become accustomed to their situation.

She appreciated what he was doing. She was not the one, after all, who was forcing their marriage. He was. The least he could do was grant her time to come to terms with the magnitude of what he expected from her—even if she had no intention of going through with a marriage to him.

"Did you manage to rest at all while I was gone?" he asked, placing another helping of roast beef on his plate and nodding his thanks to the footman who served them.

"A little, yes."

"I'm glad. I know the past several weeks have been difficult."

Abigail looked away. It wasn't only the past several weeks, but the past several months. Eighteen, to be exact, since the night her world changed forever.

"I've upset you," he said. "Forgive me."

She tried to wave off the guilt he felt. "No, you haven't upset me. My father was ill for several months. I'd prepared myself for his death for many weeks."

A tear filled her eye and spilled down her cheek. Abigail wiped it away with her damask napkin.

"Except when he passed away, you discovered you weren't as prepared as you thought you were."

She lifted her head and locked eyes with him. It was almost as if he understood.

"It was the same with my father." Ethan set down his wine glass and seemed to speak to it rather than to her. "He'd been ill for quite some time, but no matter how much I'd prepared myself for his death, it affected me more than I thought it would."

"Were you close to your father?"

"Yes. Closer than Stephen was, actually. Father considered it his duty to make demands of Stephen so he was prepared to take over the earldom when the time came. Those demands weren't required of me." A smile lifted the corners of his mouth as he looked up at her. "He wasn't as harsh with me as he was with Stephen. In time, I believe we almost became friends."

"That's the way I felt about Father. He was a friend more than a parent."

Their conversation continued, and Abigail was aware of a different side of Ethan Cambridge than she'd seen before. A softer side. A more human side.

The footmen filled their water glasses, then served tea with their dessert. There wasn't an overabundance of discussion. They didn't know—or trust—each other enough to reveal too much, but neither was there complete silence. It was during one of those times of silence that Abigail heard voices from the entryway. Angry voices. And one was particularly shrill.

"Bloody hell!" Ethan said, obviously recognizing the intruder's voice.

Abigail turned as a woman stormed through the open doorway. Her heart plummeted to the pit of her stomach when she recognized Ethan's mother.

"How dare you!" the Countess of Burnhaven cried out, clasping one hand to her throat, while fanning her scarlet cheeks with a lace handkerchief clutched in the other. "I could scarcely believe it when I heard you were here. And that my son was with you." The countess took another step into the room. "How dare you show your face, you vile creature."

Abigail pushed back from the table. She evaluated how difficult it would be to escape, and realized it was impossible.

Suddenly, strong hands reached for her, and Ethan stepped partially in front of her as if to protect her.

"Mother! Quiet!"

The Countess blinked, shock written on her face. It was obvious that no one had ever spoken to her in that tone before. Her courage faltered, but only for the briefest moment. With renewed bravery, she braced her shoulders and counterattacked. "I will not keep silent. This woman is a schemer and a fraud. A common harlot. No wonder Stephen refuses to come home. One can hardly expect him to return, still believing he will have to take her for his wife!"

"That is enough!" Ethan bellowed. This time the Countess staggered back and clamped her hand over her mouth.

"Well, I never," she gasped, clutching the back of a delicately carved Louis XIV chair and lifting a bejeweled hand to point an accusing finger in Abigail's direction.

Abigail focused on the icy hatred in the countess's eyes, and was reminded of eyes that same color. Eyes that belonged to Stephen.

The Countess of Burnhaven was still a handsome woman, tall and thin, striking in appearance, with a regal air of authority. She was one of the few women who could have caused, and probably did cause, Abigail's mother a degree of competition when she was alive.

A magnificent diamond necklace sparkled around

her neck, the breathtaking opulence of the jewels unhindered by the open collar of her black velvet cloak.

Glimpses of her gown could also be seen, a creation styled after the latest London fashion, the full skirt tiered with layers of the darkest rose.

Large ruby gemstones fastened together by a delicate filament of woven sliver strands were entwined amidst her golden curls, the same golden blonde as Stephen's.

Abigail risked a sideways gland at Ethan and found herself lost in the azure blue of his eyes. His deep mahogany hair was the antithesis of Stephen's. The antithesis of his mother's. He was as dark as she was pale.

"Why are you here?" Ethan demanded.

The Countess narrowed her icy glare. "I heard you had arrived with her. I refused to believe it, so I delayed my arrival at a small dinner party nearby to see for myself. From the look of the two of you together, I came none too soon."

Ethan stood taller, a stalwart protector.

The Countess of Burnhaven took a menacing step closer. "I see she has used her seductive wiles to sink her claws into you, too. Just like she trapped Stephen—"

"You have said enough, Lady Burnhaven." Abigail faced the vile, vindictive woman on her own. "I think it's time you left. George..." She tried to keep her voice as steady as her anger would allow. "Please show the Countess to the door."

Ethan's mother's jaw dropped. "You have no right—"

Abigail cut off the Countess's retort. "On the contrary, my lady. I have every right. You are in my home. While you are under my roof, you will cease your vicious accusations. You have overstepped your bounds, and I will not tolerate such an outburst."

The Countess clutched her hand to her throat. "And

to think Stephen thought to take you as his wife."

"Mother," Ethan interrupted, his voice cold and hard. "I think it would be best if you left now."

"You are standing up for her? You are siding with this...this...harlot, against your own mother?"

"Stop!" Ethan leveled his mother a look filled with disgust. "I will not have you make one more accusation against Miss Langdon."

Ethan Cambridge wrapped his arm around Abigail's waist and brought her to him.

"I have asked, and Miss Langdon has agreed, to be my wife."

Abigail thought the countess would suffer from an attack of apoplexy.

"You cannot mean it," she said, clutching her hand to her throat.

"Oh, but I do. I am most grateful such a wonderful and gracious woman has consented to marry me. As should you be."

The countess's mouth opened.

"Without Miss Langdon's most generous dowry," he continued, "you would be destitute within a few months. And Stephen would end up in debtor's prison the moment he returns."

Lady Burnhaven struggled from the shock, then puffed her shoulders and glared at him in haughty disdain. "I don't believe you. You have been jealous of your brother since the day you were born. And now you want this creature because she was to have been Stephen's. You have always wanted what was rightfully Stephen's."

The grip holding her tightened until it almost hurt. Abigail peered from beneath her lowered lids and saw the knot that was formed at his clenched jaw.

"That is enough," he warned. The icy tone of his quiet

voice was enough to send even the bravest man fleeing. It affected Ethan's mother only the slightest.

"No. You will hear me out," she bit back. "You cannot abide that Stephen was born first and is heir to the great Burnhaven dynasty. You have always hated him because of all he has. You've always coveted his title and the place he's made for himself in Society. And now you covet the woman he was to marry. Well, take her with my blessing. She was never good enough for Stephen anyway."

"Enough!" Ethan roared.

The Countess of Burnhaven gave Abigail a look so malicious and filled with hatred and blame it sent shivers up and down her spine. "It is your fault Stephen is gone. You drove him away. I will never forgive you for what you have done."

Ethan broke the explosive situation by grasping his mother by the elbow and ushering her from the room. "Leave, Mother. Before I say something I will regret, no matter how much you deserve to hear it."

"Very well, but you have not heard the last from me."

She pulled out of Ethan's grasp and walked to the door with the same fury as she'd entered. Before she reached the entryway, she turned around and hurled her final insult with all the venom she had left. "You are no different than your mother. The whole of Society knows what she was. And you are the same. The same! No wonder Stephen cannot bring himself to come back to you."

Ethan took a step toward his mother and escorted her out the front door.

Abigail stood alone for several moments, then sank to the nearest chair.

The countess's accusations caused more pain that she imagined words could cause.

I am not like my mother. I am not!

. . .

"Abby?"

Abigail pushed herself to her feet and slowly turned until her gaze locked with Ethan's.

"I'm so sorry." His soft voice wrapped around her like a warm shawl. The regret in his eyes added a layer of comfort that was like a soothing balm.

He took one step toward her, then another.

Each remained fixed upon the other.

Abigail didn't know if the rawness in her emotions was that obvious. Or her desperation to be comforted that apparent. But he understood what she needed most and opened his arms.

Without hesitation, she stepped into his embrace.

Slowly, as if not to frighten her—or perhaps to give her time to avoid what she knew was about to happen—he lowered his head and pressed his lips to hers.

His kiss was slow, almost hesitant, as if asking permission to continue. Abigail accepted the sweetness of his kiss, and returned his kiss with an eagerness that expressed her acceptance.

He deepened his kiss and caressed her lips with an aching need that should have surprised her, but didn't. Her desire to give in to him matched what he was asking.

His tongue traced her lips, and Abigail opened to him as if she understood what he wanted. What he needed.

He entered, explored, then found what he sought. A blast of emotion unlike anything she'd ever experienced surged through her. The rush of emotion caused by the mating of their tongues nearly took her to her knees. She eagerly and completely surrendered to the passion of his kisses.

He kissed her again, showing her a depth of emotion she didn't know existed. And she welcomed what he offered.

He kissed her one last time, then turned his head, breaking the kiss.

Abigail gasped for air. She wasn't sure she could breathe on her own. Wasn't sure she could stand on her own.

As if he realized how weak his kisses had left her, he wrapped his arms around her and pulled her to him.

She pressed her cheek against his chest. The rapid pounding of his heart beneath her ear matched the thundering of her heart in her breast.

She remained in his arms for several long moments. A part of her never wanted to leave the warmth and strength he offered.

Another part of her was frightened to death because of those same virtues. What was wrong with her? How could she give in to him as she had? How could she have forgotten that she could rely on no one?

No one.

Especially the brother of the man she'd killed.

Chapter 11

Abigail paced the room once more, then sat on the sofa to try to forget how Ethan had held her and kissed her. It had been three days, and she could still feel his lips pressed against hers. Could still feel the blood thunder in her head when he held her. Could still feel her flesh tingle where he touched her.

She clenched her hands in her lap and tried to forget the wondrous sensations that warmed every part of her body. Stephen had never kissed her like that. His touch had never set her on fire. His nearness had never caused such a violent turbulence to swirl deep within her.

Only Ethan could disarm her like that. Only he was able to make her forget the danger he posed to her or to Mary Rose. He exuded a magnificence she could not understand. A strength in which she could find refuge.

How could she allow herself to yield to his power? Didn't she know how dangerous it was to give in to the riotous emotions that pulled her toward him? Hadn't she been fooled once already by a man's handsome face and vows of love?

Hadn't that experience turned into a nightmare?

She could never let him close to her again, and yet, a part of her wanted to go to him, to talk to him, to try to take away the sting of his mother's cruel words. Even though he pretended that scene with her had never taken place, she knew her accusations still ate away at him.

He pulled deeper within himself as he settled into the role of the determined protector out to save her, and to save what Stephen was in jeopardy of losing.

He spent hours with Sydney Craddock, working out the details that would give her complete and immediate rights to Fallen Oaks just as she'd demanded. Papers that would give him immediate possession of her father's ships, including the *Abigail Rose*.

Once the papers were finished, they would sign them and it would be finished. Fallen Oaks would be hers. Mary Rose would be safe.

She should be happy, and she was, but a part of her ached, knowing that she'd given up the ships. Given up the *Abigail Rose*.

She chided herself for feeling such emotions. All she wanted was to have Fallen Oaks in her grasp. Fallen Oaks would be her haven, her sanctuary where she could protect Mary Rose from the outside world. She would do whatever she needed to provide for herself. Whatever she must so she did not need him or the ships to take care of her.

She clutched her hands together in her lap and watched the growing rays of sunlight filter through the open draperies he'd warned her to keep closed. She wasn't comfortable deceiving him into believing that they would marry. But marriage wasn't something she could consider. Not with all her secrets.

"Are your thoughts so terribly distressing?"

Abigail lifted her head and focused on his tall,

muscular frame as he leaned against the oak door jamb.

By the saints, he was a handsome man. Thick, dark brows stretched in a hard line above eyes the same color as a bright blue sky on a clear spring day. The noble cut of his high cheekbones arched with the strength of a fearless warrior, while the uncompromising line of his jaw angled in well-defined firmness.

She tried to smile. "I was just thinking."

He pushed away from the door frame and walked toward her, his gait slow and easy. "Upon what troublesome concern were you concentrating, Abby?"

She locked eyes with him. "You, sir." She took a deep breath. She had to say the words, offer him an escape one last time. Offer herself an escape.

"It's not too late to change your mind, Ethan. We don't have to go through with this."

His brows arched high, his answer to her statement a questioning frown. "Are you having second thoughts? Is my name too high a price to pay even for your precious Fallen Oaks?"

How dare he. "It isn't necessary for you to marry me to get my ships. I've offered them openly in exchange for my estate."

"Which the creditors will take away from you before you can begin to enjoy your secluded life in the country."

She smiled an insincere smile. "How noble of you. Your freedom for mine." She turned her face from him, loath to lower her eyelids and show her defeat, yet unable to match the power of his gaze.

"What brought this on, Abby? Why doubt your decision now?"

"The truth?" she asked.

He nodded.

"Your mother, sir. All the accusations she made the other day, the accusations you refuse to face. The guilt I see in your eyes, guilt that's been eating away at you like a cancer, growing and festering until I fear you will burst from the need to strike out at something— someone. You don't have to fulfill all of Stephen's responsibilities, Ethan. You don't always have to be his substitute. No one expects it."

"Is that what you think I am doing?"

"Why else would you demand I marry you? I've offered to give you what you want without taking me as your wife."

"Perhaps it's not enough." He took a step closer to her. "Perhaps I *want* to marry you."

She shook her head. He couldn't mean that. "Surely you realize Society will think you married me only to take me away from Stephen."

"Bloody hell, woman! Do you think I care one whit what my mother or Society believes?"

"Yes. I think you have always cared but have refused to let anyone know."

He froze, every muscle in his body clenched. "Well, I don't. I learned long ago it does no good to care what anyone thinks, especially my mother."

"She must have hurt you terribly," she said, studying the hard look on his face.

"She didn't hurt me at all. She hardly ever noticed I was around."

"Which in itself is painful."

He shrugged, as if whatever he'd felt then no longer mattered.

"It's not too late to change your mind," she repeated

"Yes, it is. Our intentions have already been announced. I have just returned from my mother's. Although I doubt you will receive the apology you deserve, she now understands that marriage to you is the only way to save Stephen's inheritance. Which is the only way she will be able to live in the style to which she is accustomed." He walked to the sidebar and splashed some brandy into a snifter. "Even though it galls her to know she is indebted to you, she is astute enough to realize when she has been bested."

"She's agreed to our marriage?"

"She knows she has no choice but to pretend our decision meets with her approval." He turned to her, giving her his full attention. "Our marriage will take place in three weeks, after the reading of the banns. By then I will own the ships, and you will have the deed to Fallen Oaks."

"And then what?"

He walked to the windows and pulled the draperies closed. "I don't know what you mean."

"Yes, you do."

Abigail rose. She was unwilling to finish this discussion having to look up. "You have been like a trapped animal, pacing back and forth in a small, confining cage, closing draperies so no one can see inside, refusing to allow me to leave the house. What has you so concerned?"

"It's nothing."

"I think not," she countered. "And I think I know what it is."

The look of shock on his face took her aback. She suddenly realized that the secret he was keeping from her had nothing to do with his mother, or her accusations, or what Society thought of him. And she was frightened—for him.

He took several steps toward her, not stopping until he could reach out and touch her. "What secret do you think you know?"

She shook her head and turned away from him.

"What? Or are you afraid that if I divulge my secret, I'll expect you to reveal one of yours?"

"I told you, I have no secrets."

"Oh, yes," he said on a laugh. "You are enveloped by them. You are a woman shrouded in mystery. I still have your father's message, don't forget. His warning was clear. You have something to hide, and it's only a matter of time until I discover what it is."

She felt as if she'd been struck.

"I have a number of questions to ask you." He stepped up behind her and turned her in his arms. "Will you answer just one of them? Allow me to solve just one of your mysteries?"

She forced herself to focus on his disconcerting eyes. She would not be able to answer even if she wanted. Her mouth was too dry to try.

"I think you were the last to see Stephen before he left. I think you know what happened that made him leave so suddenly. Will you tell me what it was?"

A tremor of fear rushed through her. A heavy weight pressed painfully against her chest.

"You've repeatedly said you didn't think Stephen would come back. You must have a reason for believing that. What is it?"

He paused for several uncomfortable seconds.

"What did your father mean when he wrote that you have something of the greatest importance that belongs to Stephen? What do you have, Abby? What is it you won't give to me?"

"Nothing," she whispered. "I don't have anything that belongs to Stephen."

"Why are you so desperate to keep Fallen Oaks? What is there that you are hiding?"

He towered over her. The muscles at the juncture of

his jaw knotted in frustration.

She struggled to pull out of his grasp.

"Who did you go see at the crack of dawn that morning before we left?"

"Stop!"

"Can you give me just one truthful answer?"

She held his gaze, outwardly facing him with all the bravery she could muster, while deep inside she cowered in fear.

"I thought not," he said, the corners of his lips curving upward. "But someone besides yourself knows. I wager it's Palmsworth." He studied her. "Is he the one who can answer all my questions? Is that why he stayed behind at Fallen Oaks? Would he tell your secrets if forced, Abby, or is he such a loyal servant he would take them with him to his grave?"

Her heart leaped to her throat. She couldn't breathe. "You are only grasping at straws."

He continued to hold her. "You are terrified I might find out what you are hiding. What do you stand to lose, Abby? Just tell me that."

She steeled herself, then lifted her chin to face him squarely. "Everything," she said, wishing the word would not have come out so pathetically weak.

For a long time he did not move. "The day will come when I will find out each of your secrets. A day for which you had best prepare."

He said no more, but dropped his hands from her and walked over to the bell pull to ring for George.

"Yes, sir," George said almost immediately.

"Have Bundy bring round the carriage, then have Stella bring her mistress's cloak and muff."

"Yes, sir," he nodded, backing from the room.

"Where are we going?" Abigail asked.

"To the docks. I have arranged a meeting with your

father's old friend Captain Parker. I thought you might like to be present to hear the arrangements that have been made as per your father's will."

"Yes. Thank you."

They stood in uncomfortable silence, neither of them brave enough—or foolish enough—to say more. When she couldn't stand another minute of the torture, she attempted to break the silence. "Ethan—"

He held out his hand to stop her. "Unless you are offering an answer to one of my questions, I think we have talked enough for today. Here," he said when Stella came into the room. "Put this on. There's a chill in the air despite the bright sunshine."

He wrapped the cloak around her shoulders, his touch lingering a moment longer than necessary.

The gesture seemed tender and considerate. Abigail wanted to turn in his arms and have him hold her like he'd done before.

She wondered what would happen if he found out what she'd done. What they had all done.

She reminded herself that she couldn't let herself care for him. She couldn't trust him. Or rely on him to protect her.

Mary Rose would not be all she lost if she did.

. . .

Ethan sat on the seat opposite Abigail as the Langdon carriage rumbled down cobblestone streets that led to the wharf.

What the bloody hell does she have to hide?

He breathed in the heavy air. His lungs took in the smell of the docks like a fish breathes in water. How he missed the sea, the freedom. The power and the vastness. How he missed knifing through turbulent water with a thousand ton of iron and wood beneath his feet.

It wouldn't be long now. The moment Stephen's creditors heard he had a clipper ship at his disposal to deliver a shipment of precious China tea, they would extend his credit, and Ethan would be free to leave. By late spring he would be married and could take Abigail and go home. Go far away from here, leaving behind him any reminder of his mother and the Burnhaven legacy.

And Stephen be hanged.

He had saved his brother's sorry backside twice while he'd been gone, and it was twice too often. Let Stephen squander his inheritance. Ethan didn't give a damn. Stephen could drown in his expensive brandy while his mother choked on her vicious tongue, and it wouldn't make any difference to him. Not any longer.

Ethan turned his face away from the window and found Abigail watching him. For all her secrets, there was still something natural that passed between them.

He willed her to keep looking at him, and he smiled when she did just that. She smiled in return—not a wide smile, but a warm smile. It was remarkable how comfortable he was with her once he put her secrets behind him.

"Would you like me to move beside you to keep you warm?" he said.

"No. You're fine where you are."

"Very well. Tell me, Abby," he said, turning to a more serious matter. "How much faith do you have in this longtime friend of your father's?"

Her eyes opened in astonishment. "Fenny?"

Ethan rolled his eyes. He could just picture a bandy-legged old sea captain. "Yes. Fenny." He leaned forward to rest his elbows on his knees. "I know he's been with your father for quite some time, and given your father's age, well...do you think Captain Parker is young enough to command any ship, especially the *Abigail Rose*?"

She leaned back in her seat. Surprise was evident on her face. "Are you worried Fenny might be too old to handle such responsibility?"

"Well, yes. I know what your father's will stipulates, but before I meet with...Fenny...I'd like to know your opinion."

"That's quite revolutionary of you, sir. To ask a simple woman her humble opinion."

"Does that mean you don't have an opinion?"

"No, sir. I always have an opinion. It's just that you are one of the few males I have ever met, other than my father, who has had the courage to ask it."

"Your father seemed to have great regard for what you thought, and I hope your opinion will make it easy for me to come to a decision."

"Well, if you're wondering if poor old Fenny is ready to be put out to pasture, or dry-docked, or lagoon-logged, or wherever it is they put rheumy-eyed, ancient mariners who no longer have their sea legs, the answer is no. I'm sure the doddering old sea dog has a few more voyages left in him."

"You would even trust him with the *Abigail Rose*?"

Her composure did not waver the smallest bit. "I would trust him with my life."

Ethan's brows arched. With a slight tilt to his head, he leaned back in his seat and crossed his arms over his chest. "I cannot wait to meet this ancient paragon of noble virtue and most able-bodied sea captain."

"And I cannot wait for you to meet him." The smile on her face broadened and seemed to light the whole carriage.

When the carriage pulled up at the end of the street near the docks, Ethan helped her descend. Her steps were light as she made her way across the wooden planks that served as a walkway connecting the long row of shipping offices bearing a variety of renowned titles. They stopped before the painted sign that read *Langdon Shipping*, and Ethan threw open the door. Abigail entered first.

Ethan quickly scanned the room. "Fenny" was obviously late, because the only man to occupy the clean, well-organized shipping office was a muscular sea captain who looked about the same age as himself. The man lifted his head. His dark eyes glowed with recognition when he spotted Abigail. He pushed his chair back and rose to his feet.

There were very few men Ethan had ever been forced to look up to in order to look in a man's eyes. The man facing him was one such man. He was a good two inches taller than Ethan, with shoulders as broad as his own, and muscled arms that showed years of hard, physical labor. The man's size and stature were indeed impressive.

The bronzed tan of his skin showed hours spent in the sun. Ethan recognized someone who would do backbreaking work alongside his fellow crew members to get a job done, and Ethan's respect for him soared.

Whoever this man was, Ethan would make sure he was assigned a place alongside old Captain Fenny. The doddering old sea dog could probably use all the able-bodied help and assistance he could get.

The sailor stepped around the desk and came toward them. "Miss Langdon." The captain reached out to take Abigail's hands and held them. "Are you all right?"

"Yes, I'm fine."

He did not drop her gaze. Or her hands. "We'll miss him."

She nodded as if words would not come. Moisture gleamed in her eyes, and Ethan felt a special connection pass between the two.

"He'd be proud of her, the *Abigail Rose*. She's a beauty."

"I know. I'd hoped he'd live long enough to see her. Owning a clipper was his lifelong dream."

The broad-shouldered man nodded, and Ethan swore he saw a glimmer in his eyes, too.

"We'll sail her just like he intended, Abby. Just like he would have himself."

Abigail nodded.

Ethan stepped forward. His blood surged hot. A warning. *The captain just called her Abby.*

"Mr. Cambridge," she said, clearing her voice. "I'm pleased to introduce Captain James Fenimore Parker. Fenny, Mr. Ethan Cambridge."

Ethan looked up at the tall, overpowering sea captain. He tried to disguise his shock, but knew he'd failed. The broad grin on Abigail's face told him as much. He gave her his most ferocious frown.

She put a gloved hand over her mouth to stifle a giggle. "The look on your face, Mr. Cambridge, was worth the wait."

Ethan took the man's hand and shook it, then dropped his head back on his shoulders and laughed.

Meeting doddering old Fenny was indeed a hilarious surprise. He should be angry with her for teasing him, but he wasn't. Instead, he wanted to pull her into his arms and hold her. And claim her as his own. And he knew the reason why.

Doddering old Fenny, who'd called her Abby in a most familiar way, was still holding her hand.

Chapter 12

"She's the only person to ever call me that and live to tell about it," Captain James Parker said with a warning frown that made her laugh. "My mother had a fondness for anything written by the novelist James Fenimore Cooper and named me after him. Abby discovered my middle name when we were young and has used it to blackmail me ever since."

"The two of you knew each other when you were young?"

Abigail heard a twinge of something akin to envy in Ethan's voice. "We grew up together," she said.

"Not exactly together," Parker corrected. "My father captained one of Lord Langdon's ships. His ship went down around the Cape during a monsoon. When my mother died of typhoid a year later, Lord Langdon found me a home with one of his captains. I spent my youth with the sailors here on the docks. The pest," he said, casting a glance in Abigail's direction, "came 'round with her father nearly every day. She was like a shadow no one could escape. She nearly drove us all mad."

Abigail gave him a good-natured shove he accepted with a grin, which brightened his tanned face, a face Abigail had always considered handsome. The look in Ethan's eyes hardened.

"Would you like to take a tour of the *Abigail Rose*," James asked, taking note of where Ethan had placed his hand. "Or should we get down to the reason you're here?"

"We'll tour the ship first," Ethan said, more as a command. "Miss Langdon has been dying to see her namesake."

"And you haven't?" she asked, giving him a smiling glance beneath lifted brows.

He relaxed. "I admit it. I have, too."

"Then we'll tour the *Abigail Rose* first," Captain Parker said, then led the way to the door.

Abigail took Ethan's proffered arm with a relaxed ease she found reassuring. They had this in common at least: the ships, and their love of the sea.

Ethan asked Fenny about every aspect of Langdon Shipping, while Abigail listened. He wanted to know about the goods they shipped, the ports where they were loaded, and the routes the ships took to get to and from London. He absorbed every detail with relentless tenacity, firing one question at Fenny after another, until the beautiful clipper ship with its three towering masts came into view before them.

He stopped to stare at the sight in awestruck wonder. So did she. "Your father would have been proud," Fenny said.

"Yes, he would have," she sighed.

"Has she been tested for speed?" Ethan asked. His look of admiration was plain.

"Not with a full load," Fenny answered, "but she'll average fifteen knots easy."

Ethan stayed focused on the *Abigail Rose* as he put pressure on Abigail's elbow to usher her toward the clipper. The moment they stepped aboard, a change came over her, a change more startling than she'd experienced any time before when she stepped aboard one of her father's ships. She could barely contain the excitement that engulfed her.

Ethan's eyes mirrored that same excitement, the vibrant exhilaration and powerful anticipation of what it would be like to feel such a magnificent vessel flying through the wind with the waves smashing beneath you.

She and Ethan walked in reverent admiration as Fenny gave them a detailed tour, covering every inch of the clipper from the captain's stateroom, to the officers' quarters, to the carpenter's shop. From the galley to the lower deck and the hold where the chests of tea would be stored. There was even a pigpen and a chicken coop, for fresh meat and eggs, and a forward hatch, a booby hatch, and a main hatch that led below.

Abigail took in everything, rubbing her hand along the polished wood railings and the shiny brass trim. Her father would have been so proud.

She breathed a painful sigh and was thankful when Ethan stopped to examine the deck winch and Fenny was called aside by his first mate. She needed time to herself.

She leaned against the starboard railing and looked out to the open water. She didn't know how long she'd been there before Ethan came up beside her.

"You love the sea, don't you," he said, catching her staring out at the endless strand of blue-gray water that would carry her ships to the open sea.

"Yes," she whispered on a sigh. "My father's legacy to me. It's such a humbling yet powerful force. One moment the clouds roll by in such carefree abandon you feel you can reach out and touch them. The next, they gather like a rebellious crowd and stir the waves and whip the wind with vicious ferocity, striking out to destroy everything in their path. The sea's power is frightening, yet awesome."

"And yet you love it?" he asked, smiling up at the clouds floating by, as if he understood exactly what she meant.

"I could be content to spend my life living where the sea met me at my back door."

"The plantation I own is like that. It's a paradise, surrounded by water and untouched by crowds. A place where the days are magnificent, the nights enchanting. It promises a life as perfect as anywhere on earth."

"How could you leave it to come here?"

He tightened his grip around the polished wood railing. "I had little choice. I received a letter from Sydney Craddock I couldn't ignore. It seems a number of Stephen's creditors had been holding off foreclosure because of his promised marriage to you. When he absconded without your dowry, they panicked. Stephen was about to lose everything."

Ethan turned to look at her. "I received a report this morning from one of the runners I have looking for Stephen, a Mr. Walker. He is on his way home with news concerning Stephen. News too confidential to put in writing."

He had to reach out to steady her. Her knees buckled beneath her while the blood rushed from her head, spinning the world around her.

"Abby?" He kept his arm fastened around her waist. "Take a deep breath."

She took in several, but it didn't help. It would only be a matter of weeks before Ethan would know the truth.

Terror consumed her. A fear she struggled to control. Someone knew. Someone knew Stephen was dead. Perhaps they even knew she had killed him.

She braced her shoulders and took a step away from him. "Did this Mr. Walker say any more?"

"No. Only that he would inform me of everything when he returned to England. He evidently found Stephen and knows his whereabouts. Perhaps he will bring him home with him."

There is nothing to bring home, she thought, fighting the wave of panic that made her gasp for air.

"Once Stephen returns, everything will be back to normal. In a few weeks, you and I will be married and can go to my island. I would like for you to see my plantation before I must set sail for Australia."

A cold dread fell over her. "No. You cannot expect me to go with you. The purpose for marrying you is to keep Fallen Oaks. Not to leave it."

"You will keep Fallen Oaks. That is why we are marrying, so I can use the profits from the shipments of tea and wool to keep your estate."

She shook her head. "I have no intention of leaving."

"It won't be forever. Only for a while. Then we'll return."

The more he said, the less in control she felt. She needed the deed to Fallen Oaks in her hands. She needed to go home where she would be safe, and hold little Mary Rose in her arms. She needed to get ready for when Mr. Walker returned and Ethan found out what she'd done.

Abigail's legs trembled beneath her. She'd never been so frightened in her life. Not since...

"I am going home, back to Fallen Oaks," she said, struggling to keep her composure.

"We will soon."

"No. You may stay in London if you like, but I'm going home."

"We will speak of this later."

"Abby?" Captain Parker's voice echoed from behind them.

Abby turned her head and found herself staring into the murderous look of a friend bent on protecting her from a man he wasn't sure he should trust. Ethan stiffened when he saw the look on Fenny's face.

"Are you all right?" His lips pursed into a tight line, his jaw clenched in angry concern.

She tried to smile. "Yes, Fenny. I'm fine. I was just a little overwrought for a moment. It is not as easy as I supposed to come aboard the ship Father dreamed for so long of sailing and realize he never will."

Fenny relaxed, and he released a deep breath. "Ah, Abby. I'm sorry. I should have known how hard this would be for you."

"As should I," Ethan said. "Perhaps we should finish our business and go."

"Yes, please," she agreed.

Ethan led her toward the gangplank, and they made their way back to the office.

"Why don't you wait for me in the carriage," Ethan suggested, motioning for Bundy to come for her. "I have some details to discuss with Captain Parker. It won't take us but a moment."

Abigail nodded, then walked with Bundy to the waiting carriage. Every muscle in her body trembled with indecision and fear. She'd been such a fool, such a thickheaded idiot. How could she have thought what she had done would not catch up with her? She should have known agreeing to marry Ethan would not protect Mary Rose, but would increase the risk of losing her.

Her breath caught in her throat. Once he discovered

all she'd done, the list of reasons for him to hate her would be too numerous to count. Even the ships would not be reason enough to want her.

Her steps faltered, and Bundy held out his hand to steady her. She should have done what she'd planned from the start. She should have demanded he accept her offer of the ships in exchange for Fallen Oaks. But he'd given her no choice. He'd threatened to take her away from Fallen Oaks that very day. How could she have left without taking Mary Rose with her?

Abigail leaned back against the soft leather seat of the carriage and cursed her father for writing the letter that had brought Ethan to her.

And she cursed her traitorous body for wanting something she could never have.

. . .

Ethan closed the door to the Langdon Shipping office and turned to face Captain Parker. The dark look in the captain's eyes hinted at a temper that smoldered beneath the surface. His hard countenance established him as a formidable opponent.

"I intend to speak openly and frankly, Captain Parker. I expect you to do the same."

James Parker walked to a heavily marred wooden cabinet in the corner of the room and opened a small door at the side to pull out a half-full bottle of whisky. "Very well," he said, pouring a generous amount into two glasses and handing one to Ethan. "Then perhaps you would begin by explaining your intentions toward Miss Langdon." He sat down behind his desk and leveled Ethan with a glare as hard as the tone of his voice.

"I'm going to marry her."

Parker's glass halted midway to his mouth. "Does Miss Langdon know this?"

"Yes."

"And she agreed?"

"Reluctantly, but yes."

"Why?"

"Because I possess the deed to Fallen Oaks."

"You bastard."

"Perhaps. The marriage was not originally what I intended. Her father left her Langdon Shipping, as you are well aware, and a cousin she had never met inherited Fallen Oaks. I acquired it. The easiest solution would have been an exchange of properties, which is what Abigail wanted. But Fallen Oaks can never support itself. In a year—two at the most—Abigail would be forced to sell off small portions of the property to keep out of debt. In time, she would become destitute without a home in which to live. Marriage is a solution which benefits us both."

"So now, upon your marriage, you will not only have Langdon Shipping and Fallen Oaks, but a beautiful bride in the bargain."

"Yes. I will have it all."

"And what will Abigail have?"

"She will have a husband who will always care for her, a life where she will want for nothing, plus the assurance that Fallen Oaks will always remain hers." Ethan leaned back in his chair and took a long swallow of the excellent whiskey. "And now, Captain Parker, I would like to ask you a question. Just what is your relationship with Miss Langdon? Unless I'm mistaken, your feelings for her are stronger than those of mere friendship."

"I love Abby. I always have. But she doesn't love me.

We've been friends too long for her to consider me as anything more."

Ethan looked at the honesty in Captain Parker's eyes. And the loss. To love, knowing that affection would only be returned as a deep friendship, was a torture all its own.

The captain took a swallow of his whiskey, then set the glass down before him on the desk. "I won't let you hurt her, Cambridge. Your brother did enough of that to last a lifetime."

Ethan's grip tightened around the glass in his hand. "What do you know of the night Stephen left?"

Captain Parker didn't flinch, but kept his hardened eyes riveted on Ethan's face. "Only Abigail knows the answer to that question."

Ethan studied his adversary. "I want you to know," he said, "I will never let anything hurt her."

"Neither will I," Captain Parker countered.

Ethan waited to give them time to let their tempers cool. Then he continued their discussion. "How do you intend to run Langdon Shipping?"

"Exactly as I have been since the day Baron Langdon put me in charge."

Ethan nodded. "How many ships are out?"

"All of them. The *Wind Sprite* and the *Night Journey* are both on their way to the Orient for cargoes of silk and spices. The *Pegasus* should return from Australia with shipments of wool within the week."

Ethan sat forward. "How soon can you have the *Abigail Rose* ready to sail?"

A certain excitement shone in Parker's eyes. "By the end of the month. Earlier, if we don't have trouble getting enough supplies."

"The May tea harvest in China should be ready to ship by the first of June. Can you get there in time?"

"Yes."

Ethan nodded. "The clipper is yours, Captain. Make good use of her."

Any remark James Parker intended to make was cut off by a sharp rap on the door, followed by the entrance of a burly sailor with fiery-red hair and a beard to match.

"Beggin' the Cap'n's pardon. Them same men as was here the other day inquirin' after Mr. Cambridge is back."

Ethan's blood ran cold.

Parker sat forward. "Thank you, Cooley. Keep them busy for a while, would you?"

"Sure thing, Cap'n. We'll take them to the docks, away from the carriage."

Ethan waited until the door closed, then walked to the window to catch a glimpse of the two men he knew Stafford had sent to find him. When he turned around, he faced as lethal a glare as he'd ever received in his life.

"The men are from the colonies. They're looking for you."

"They've been here before?"

"Two days ago. They came with a bag full of questions."

"What did you tell them?"

"The truth. I'd not laid eyes on you. Evidently, whoever they're working for knew you would come around eventually." Parker walked to the window. "That means they've connected you to Langdon Shipping and to Abigail." Parker took one step closer. "I won't let you put her in danger."

"She isn't. She's perfectly safe." Ethan prayed his statement was true.

"And what about you?"

"I can take care of myself. You worry about getting my clipper ready to sail, and I'll worry about keeping Abigail safe."

Ethan walked out the door, knowing he had more to worry about than the men Stafford had sent to find him. He could still see the look of panic on Abigail's face when he told her he'd had news of Stephen. He could still see her look of defiance when he told her he wanted her to leave England.

Whatever was keeping her here, it was hidden at Fallen Oaks.

He'd bloody well have to find out what it was before too long. He wasn't safe in England any longer.

Chapter 13

Abigail paced her room, her nerves stretched to the point of snapping. When Mr. Walker returned, Ethan would know what happened. What if he pressed charges? What if they put her in prison? Or worse. What would happen to Mary Rose?

Her heart raced until she feared it would leap from her chest. She had to tell Ethan she could no longer marry him. She had to do what she should have done from the very start—trade him the ships he wanted for the deed to Fallen Oaks.

She had to get the papers from Sydney Craddock and leave London. She would take Mary Rose and run. Perhaps to France. Or the colonies. Someplace where he would never find her.

Abigail lifted a pillow from the bed and threw it down in frustration. What had she been thinking? What had made her think agreeing to marry him was the answer? What made her think no one would ever discover what she'd done?

She wiped her sweating palms against her nightgown, then threw on a heavy robe. Sleep eluded her.

Worry consumed her. She knew Ethan Cambridge still sat in her father's study downstairs on the pretense that he needed to go over some of her father's papers. Now was the time. She needed to tell him she could never marry him. She needed to convince him she could manage Fallen Oaks by herself. She needed to sever all ties with him.

She pulled her wrapper tighter around her shoulders and crept down the stairs. She didn't care what she had to give up to get Fallen Oaks. Nothing was too great a sacrifice.

Abigail stepped across the foyer, skirting the round table in the center of the entryway, then walked past the chair outside the study door. How often had she followed the same path when she'd come down to sit with her father while he worked late at night? A heaviness weighed against her heart. So much had happened since those times. So much tragedy.

Abigail took a deep breath, then raised her hand to knock on the study door. Her arm halted in midair at the sound of angry voices beyond the door.

"What the bloody hell did you think, Ethan? I told you weeks ago Stafford's men were here."

"What did you expect me to do, Mac? Hide away in some corner until they tired of looking for me and went home?"

"No. But I didn't expect you to go around London without a care in the world."

"I didn't. I had to meet with Langdon's solicitor, then talk to the captain of Langdon's ships. I wanted to make sure he was qualified to sail the clipper to China."

"And is he?"

"Yes. He's good. Captain James Parker is as good as the reports you gave me. He's more than capable. He'll have the *Abigail Rose* ready to sail by the first of next month."

"Then get the hell out of England."

"I can't."

"Why the blazes not? You know what will happen if Stafford's men find you."

There was a long, deafening silence. Abigail sank down into the chair beside the door and clasped her hands over her mouth.

"Maybe it's time I quit running, Mac. Maybe it's time I faced Stafford and got this whole mess behind me."

"Have you taken leave of your senses? The man's insane. You made a fool of him in front of everyone. You took his slaves out from under his nose and gave them safe passage to Canada."

"What did you expect me to do? He would have killed them. He whipped the one called Henry nearly to death before I stopped him."

"That doesn't matter. Beating them was within his rights, Ethan. They belonged to him."

Abigail started at the loud sound of a fist slamming against something solid. "Listen to yourself, Mac! How can you say such a thing when you know you would have done the same?"

"That's not what's important. What you did was a crime in the colonies, and will be as long as slavery is legal. Stafford's never going to let you go. Do you think he's sent runners all the way to England to thank you for humiliating him like you did?"

Abigail twisted her hands in her lap while the interminable silence knifed through her.

"Bloody hell, Ethan," the man called Mac said, his voice almost a whispered plea. "Get out before Stafford finds you. If they catch up with you, they'll kill you."

"Do you think I don't know that?"

"Then why are you still here?"

"It's time this was over. I can't run any longer."

"Why the hell not?"

"It's not just me anymore. There's the girl. I've got to make sure—"

Abigail's hand trembled as she reached for the latch. When she pushed open the paneled oak door, Ethan's face lifted to stare at her. The words he intended to say died on his lips.

"Ah, hell," he said, impaling her with a harsh glare that soon softened.

Ethan's white lawn shirt hung open halfway down his chest, the dark bronze of his skin glowing beneath it from the fire that danced in the grate. His hair was mussed, as if he'd raked his long, sturdy fingers through it in frustration more than once tonight. The muscles across his shoulders bunched, his lips tightening to two thin lines, and his heavy brows knitted together across steely-blue eyes.

The other man in the room stood. She gave him a brief nod, then concentrated on Ethan.

Ethan stepped around the desk, taking one step then another, until he stood mere inches from her. He raised his hand and brushed the backs of his fingertips down her cheeks. The soft toughness of his skin sent riots of shocking currents through her body.

"You shouldn't be here."

"I wanted to speak with you."

He placed his arm around her shoulder and led her further into the room. "I want you to meet someone." He stopped in front of the man she had only heard through the door.

The dark-haired man stood at his chair. He towered above her, his height nearly as great as Ethan's. The width of his shoulders was nearly as broad as Ethan's, the muscled expanse of his chest and arms an equal match. His eyes were dark and warm, even though the frown on his handsome face indicated an undercurrent of doubt and concern.

"Abigail, I'd like you to meet my friend, and the captain of one of my ships, Malcolm MacDonnell. Mac, may I present Miss Abigail Langdon."

"Miss Langdon," Malcolm acknowledged, saying her name with a light Scottish lilt. The tone of his voice as well as the look in his eyes emitted a warmth and a friendship she knew were genuine. "'Tis a pleasure to meet you, miss. It truly is. I've heard much about you."

"Thank you, Captain MacDonnell. I regret I cannot say the same." Abigail turned to Ethan and gave him the full force of her next comment. "I can see I'm not the only one with a secret or two."

The frown on Ethan's forehead deepened, and he nodded his head in acquiescence. "Why don't you come and sit over here by the fire," he said, leading her to the sofa and covering her with a blanket that had been thrown over the back of a chair. "You'll freeze to death down here dressed as you are."

For the first time, Abigail realized her lack of appropriate attire and felt a twinge of embarrassment. "I'm sorry," she said, wrapping the blanket around her shoulders. "I didn't realize you had a guest."

"I was about to leave, Miss Langdon," Captain MacDonnell said, taking a step toward the door.

"Please, don't leave on my account."

A broad smile brightened his features, showing her an amazingly handsome face.

"Believe me, if the choice were mine to make, I'd gladly stay as long as you graced us with your presence. Unfortunately, I have a number of details to take care of yet."

The captain walked to the door. "'Twas a pleasure to meet you," he said, then left.

Ethan followed him out into the foyer and Abigail held her breath, waiting to hear what they said.

"Have a care, Ethan," Captain MacDonnell warned in a voice just loud enough for Abigail to hear. "Barney is waiting in a carriage around the corner and will keep watch through the night. If anyone comes round, he'll let you know."

The rest of his words were lost to her when they reached the front door. She waited for Ethan to come back.

Her path was set. Captain MacDonnell's warnings were plain. Ethan had to leave. Marriage would only tie him down, keep him in England where the man named Stafford would find him.

She pulled her legs up against her chest and rested her chin on her knees. She was more determined than ever to break their betrothal. Surely he would agree now, too.

The soft click of the latch at the front door told her Captain MacDonnell was gone. She lifted her head and watched Ethan walk into the room. Without a glance in her direction, he went over to the fireplace.

"Are you warm enough?" He placed another log onto the fire.

"We have to talk, Ethan." She kept her voice soft, yet firm.

"No." He stood tall, then braced both arms against the mantel. "I don't want to hear it, Abby."

"You must." She waited for him to turn to her, to give her some sign that he acknowledged what she was going to tell him. When he didn't, she continued in the most confident voice she could find. "I've always known how foolish it was for us to marry. Now you do, too. Between the two of us, there is too much to overcome."

"Too many secrets?"

"Yes."

"They wouldn't be between us if you'd share them with me," he said in a soft whisper.

"They will always be between us. More so after you discover what they are." She clenched her hands tighter around her knees and breathed a deep sigh. "We can't marry, Ethan. I've known it from the start and only agreed to your proposal because I was desperate to do everything possible to save Fallen Oaks."

"Then you must realize why we still have no choice but to marry."

"You may have the ships, Ethan. Just leave me the deed to Fallen Oaks."

He shook his head, his refusal as determined as before.

"I heard what Captain MacDonnell said. You have to leave. Staying only puts you in danger."

"I will apply for a special license first thing in the morning. It shouldn't take long. We'll be married immediately. I'll make all the arrangements."

"No! Didn't you hear me? I'm not going to marry you!"

"You will or you'll never set foot back on Fallen Oaks. I own it now."

"You wouldn't dare."

A sardonic smile crossed his lips. "Wouldn't I? Refuse my offer and you'll be left without your precious Fallen Oaks, and I'll be left without the ships to save Stephen's inheritance. We'll both end up the loser."

"Don't you understand? I don't need the ships. I can survive on Fallen Oaks without your help. With a few improvements to the farming practices, I am sure I can make the estate self-supporting in a few years' time."

He swiped his hand through the air. "What do you know about farming practices, about crop rotation or terrace farming or irrigation or cultivation or—"

"Nothing right now," she interrupted. "But I can learn."

"You're no more a farmer than your father was. His first love was his ships, as is yours. Fallen Oaks was only a haven to escape the hectic social life he couldn't abide. It was never a working estate. He didn't know how to make it one, and neither do you."

"And you do?" she said, dropping her feet to the floor and sitting forward on the sofa.

"No. But with the money I make from your ships, I'll find someone who does. At least I'll be able to keep you out of debt."

"You aren't responsible for me."

"I can't abandon you and hope you survive."

"Yes, you can."

He shot her a look filled with disbelief. "What happened between you and Stephen that made him leave without a word? What happened that night to cause this whole tragedy? What are you so desperate to hide that you can't see how essential it is for us to marry?"

She felt the color drain from her face, but refused to look away. She lifted her chin and stared at him until he turned away to stare at the flames licking upward in the fireplace.

"You can't stay here, Ethan," she said. Her anger was gone, replaced only by a deep-seated fear that he wouldn't be safe if he stayed. "I heard what Captain MacDonnell said. You have to leave before it's too late."

"It's already too late."

The hollow tone of his voice brought her to her feet. She watched him walk to the window and pull back the soft satin drapery.

"Come here." He held out his arm for her to join him.

Abigail stepped in front of him, and he wrapped his

arm around her while he still held the curtain.

A thousand tiny shivers raced through her body when he touched her. Heaven help her, she didn't want his nearness to affect her so.

"Watch down this street. In a little while you'll see a carriage approach."

Abigail did not have to concentrate on the shadows very long before a carriage rumbled closer. A gaslight burned in front of her house, lighting the street enough to make out the strange vehicle.

"Is that him?"

"Yes," he said. "It drove by the first time when we arrived earlier and has been making its rounds every thirty minutes to check if I'm still here.

"Leave, Ethan. Get out of England before it's too late."

"I'm not running again, Abby. You heard Malcolm. You know why Stafford will never let me go. It's time I faced him. You and I will say our vows as soon as possible, then I'll take care of what is between Stafford and me."

Abigail started to scream her objection, then stopped. Something did not make sense. Why did he insist on marrying her first?

An icy chill raced through her body. "If something were to happen to you today, who would get what belongs to you?"

"Stephen."

"But if we marry?"

"Everything would go to you. I'll make sure of it."

She backed one step away from him then another. Her eyes burned dry as they opened to stare at him in disbelief. Her heart pounded inside her breast as if a door had opened to reveal her most frightening nightmare.

"You don't think you will survive, do you?" she whispered.

He turned away from her and stared into the flames. "There's always that possibility."

"Leave. Do as Malcolm suggested earlier and leave England."

"And run for the rest of my life?"

"Yes! I'll not have you marry me just to make me your widow!"

He shook his head. "I'm tired of running, Abby. And too big a coward to live with the guilt of what he might do to anyone he considers important to me."

He turned to face her, their gazes locked in an understanding that terrified her.

"This is madness," she said, fighting the panic growing inside her. "I'm not worth the sacrifice. Don't you understand? I'm not worth it!"

What was she to do? How could she stop this tragedy from happening? How could she convince him to get out of England and leave her behind?

She clutched her arms around her middle and held tight. The look on his face didn't change. His eyes were like blank pages, the knowledge he harbored a hidden glimpse into a future she could not see.

"Go to bed, little one," he said, lifting his arm and brushing the backs of his fingers down the side of her face. He stopped and cupped her cheek in the palm of his hand. "Tomorrow will be a long day."

"I can't marry you, Ethan. Even if I wanted, I couldn't."

"Tell me why."

She lifted her shoulders and faced him squarely. "There are things you don't know. Things about me you could never understand. I won't marry you, then live with your hatred for the rest of my life."

"I could never hate you, Abby. I care for you too much to ever hate you."

She couldn't believe what she'd heard.

He cared for her.

She ached with a need she could not explain, a need so intense she couldn't suppress the shiver that shuddered through her body. She cared for him, too. More than cared for him.

He opened his arms in invitation. She knew it wasn't possible to have a future with him, yet she desperately wanted one.

She hesitated, then stepped into his embrace. His arms wrapped around her like a warm, protective cocoon, sheltering her, shielding her from the worries that had plagued her since the night Stephen had shattered her nearly perfect world.

The soft ticking of the clock on the mantel, the hushed whisper of the flames whisking in the fireplace, the muffled snapping of the charred logs. These were the only sounds that intruded into the quiet of the room. The only sounds that seeped into the silence. He held her close for endless minutes. Without saying the words, she told him goodbye. Leaving him was the only choice she had.

She pressed her cheek against his chest and inhaled the clean male smell of him, a smell so wondrous, so masculine. One she never wanted to forget.

His lips brushed against the top of her head, his kiss a tender gift, then his hands moved higher, clasping her on either side of her neck, his fingers raking softly through her loose hair. "You have no choice, Abby. You must marry me."

Ever so slowly, he tilted her head back and looked with warm earnest into her eyes. With the kindest of intent, he lowered his head and kissed her on the forehead.

His breath whispered across her cheek as his thumb slowly outlined her lips, causing them to tingle in anticipation. He lowered his head until he was a hair's breadth from her. Abigail closed her eyes and breathed a shuddering sigh as his lips claimed her own.

The kiss was slow and sweet, filled with the most innocent sharing of emotions. He kissed her once, then kissed her again, lingering only long enough to tease and torment, without fulfilling the greater promise, then pulled away.

"Go to bed, Abby." He walked away from her and filled a glass with brandy.

"Ethan—"

"Go to bed," he repeated, then took a great swallow of the amber liquid.

Abigail waited, but she knew the moment was gone. He'd distanced himself from her as if her absence was just as necessary for his protection as his absence was essential for her.

Abigail left the room. Her mind and heart clashed in greater turmoil than when she'd come downstairs. Before, she'd been determined to leave him because it was the only way she could protect herself and Mary Rose. Now, it was the only way to protect Ethan.

. . .

Abigail made her way through the dark side-street leading away from her town house, with Stella close on her heels. Bundy had taken the carriage over an hour ago to wait for them in an alley five blocks away. When Abigail was certain everyone was asleep, she and Stella followed on foot.

Abigail rounded the corner, keeping in the shadows until she spotted Bundy sitting behind the two horses with the reins in his hands.

"Did anyone notice you?" she asked, coming up on him from the side furthest from the street.

"Bundy jumped down to open the carriage door. "No, Miss Langdon. Mr. Cambridge didn't see me leave from the back and neither did that other man he had watching the front."

"Good." She motioned for Stella to get inside. "We have to get home as quickly as possible, Bundy."

"We will, miss," he said, helping her inside.

Abigail leaned back against the soft leather squabs and closed her eyes as the carriage jerked into motion. They should reach Fallen Oaks before Ethan discovered they were gone.

She prayed he would realize her leaving was for the best and know he was free to leave England without feeling responsible for her.

Chapter 14

The sun was just peeking above the horizon, the sky turning muted shades of pinks and purples and blues. Abigail thought they'd reached the halfway mark a little over an hour ago. They should be at Fallen Oaks by noon.

"There's an inn ahead, mistress," Bundy called down from above. "Did you want to stop, or should we travel on?"

Abigail wasn't sure she wanted to lose such precious time, but one look at Stella's exhausted form huddled in the corner and she knew she had no choice. "We'll stop, Bundy. Perhaps they will have a loaf of warm bread or a muffin to take with us and something hot to drink. We will stay just long enough to get warm, then be on our way."

"Very well, mistress." Bundy pulled off the road and followed the short half-circle drive that curved past the Arm and Anvil Inn. He stopped in front of the door and jumped down to help them from the carriage. "I'll take care of the horses, miss, while you and Stella get yourselves something to eat."

"Thank you, Bundy. Come in when you're finished."

"Very well, miss."

Abigail led the way through the door to the inn. The potent smell of strong ale and stale tobacco smoke left over from the night before assaulted her nose, but the inside of the room looked clean, and the warmth from a big fire blazing in the hearth beckoned her. She hadn't realized how cold and hungry she was until the aroma of freshly baked bread hit her.

"Find a table over by the fire, Stella, while I arrange for some food. I'll ask the proprietor where we might freshen ourselves."

"Yes, miss." Stella clutched her shawl tighter around her shoulders and headed for a table by the fire.

By the time she'd ordered something to eat and drink and accompanied Stella to the small 'necessary' shed behind the inn, Bundy was sitting at the table with a pitcher of hot tea and a platter of warm bread. Abigail poured the tea while Stella cut the bread and put a slice in front of each of them.

"Do you suppose the master has discovered you've left?" Stella asked, casting a worried glance in Abigail's direction.

"Most likely. I imagine he's just now coming in from the watch he's kept all night. No doubt he'll want me to break my fast with him. I told Genevieve not to volunteer any information, but not to lie to him, either."

"He's going to be mighty angry with you, miss," Stella said, shaking her head.

"No doubt. But I'm sure when he calms down and thinks about it, he'll realize my leaving is for the best."

Abigail raised her eyes just in time to see Bundy roll his own heavenward.

A wave of trepidation bolted through her. Something deep inside her echoed Bundy's doubts. Even though she knew Ethan would be furious with her for leaving, she prayed he would understand why she'd gone. Why she had to return to Fallen Oaks, so he could get himself and his ship out of London on the first tide.

"Pack up the leftovers, Stella. We've spent enough time here. I want to be at Fallen Oaks before lunch is served. If Mr. Cambridge does happen to follow us, I don't want to meet up with him on the open ro—"

The front door flew open and slammed against the wall. The loud crash of the wood echoed through the room like a gunshot. Abigail's gaze darted to the entryway.

Ethan's massive shoulders dominated the opening as completely as his anger consumed the rest of the room.

He slowly scanned the interior. His focus halted when he came to the table where she sat. He didn't pay attention to Stella and Bundy but only stared at *her*. His black look turned furious with rage.

A man and his wife and two small children sat at a table nearby. When the man saw the scowl that covered Ethan's face, he moved his family to a table on the far side of the room.

Two men at the table on the other side of the hearth leaned back in their chairs anticipating the fireworks to come, their faces brimming with looks of expectant enjoyment.

Not a sound could be heard in the long, narrow room except the hollow pounding of Ethan's boot heels as he made his way to where she sat. He stopped in front of the table.

"Bundy, ready the carriage to leave," he ordered. His lethal glare didn't leave her.

"Yes, sir," Bundy said, pushing away from the table.

"Go with him, Stella," he ordered again.

With a quick nod, Stella jumped up from the table and followed Bundy across the floor.

Ethan towered over her, his feet braced wide, his hands knotted in tight fists anchored at his waist. Dark circles rimmed his eyes, evidence of his lack of sleep. The muscles on either side of his jaw knotted in rage.

The hems of his doeskin breeches beneath his great-coat were spattered with mud. There was not one inch of him that seemed soft or yielding, one inch of him that did not exude fury.

Abigail kept her head high, a look of confident determination firmly planted on her face. "I did not intend for you to come after me."

He leaned forward and braced the palms of his hands flat on the top of the table. "What the bloody hell do you think you are doing?" he hissed, his voice soft and slow and dripping with anger.

"I am going home, sir. Back where I belong."

"You belong with me," he answered. A vein stood out on the side of his neck, evidence that his temper threatened to explode. "Where I can watch you. Where I can protect you."

"I don't need you to watch me. I can take care of myself."

He jerked out the chair opposite her and sat down, crossing his arms on the tabletop and leaning close to her. "I do not have time for this, Abigail. I don't have time to chase you all over England."

"No, you don't. You don't have time to do anything but get aboard one of *your* ships and sail as far from England as you can get. I intend to return to *my* home, where I will be content to live peacefully without obligation to anyone."

He leaned a little closer and glared at her with eyes brimming with fire. "Fallen Oaks is not yours, Miss

Langdon, until you marry me to get it. As your ships are not mine until I marry you to get them."

She shook her head. "Oh, Ethan. Don't make this any more difficult than it already is. The papers have been drawn up. All it will take is our signatures, and we will both have what is best for us."

"You have no idea what is best for me, Abigail, or you wouldn't have left London."

His words caused her to pause. "Yes, I do. We can't marry. I heard what Captain MacDonnell told you. You have to leave before this Stafford fellow finds you."

Ethan sat back in his chair and stared at her, the look in his eyes filled with concern. He took a deep breath, but not before she glimpsed a hint of fear.

"Gather your things," he said, his rigid composure back in place. "We have to leave."

"Where are we going?"

"I'm afraid we have no choice but to go to Fallen Oaks. It's too far to go back to London, and the horses are too tired to make the trip back."

"You don't have to go with me. I'm perfectly safe traveling by myself."

"You think so?"

"Of course," she retorted. "I have Stella and Bundy with me."

He stared at her a moment, then shook his head. "You don't even know what you've done," he whispered so softly she wasn't certain she heard him correctly.

He rose from his chair and offered her his hand. When she took it, he wrapped his strong, sturdy fingers around hers and held tight. A feeling of safety engulfed her, and she wondered what she could possibly have feared before.

He didn't look at her, but led her out of the inn and across the cobbled yard. The midday air still had a chilly nip to it as they made their way to the waiting carriage. Bundy sat atop, ready to set the horses in motion. Stella sat bundled inside, her shoulders huddled in the corner, sending a look that said *I told you he'd be angry*. Ethan waited until she was inside, then closed the door and walked away without a word.

Abigail settled herself, then peeked out the window to see him give last-minute instructions to Bundy. She couldn't hear his words, but saw from the excited bobbing of Bundy's head and the deep frown that covered his face that Ethan's orders were important.

When he finished, he mounted his steed with the practiced moves of an expert horseman and sat ready to ride. He leaned forward to pick up the reins and at the same time jabbed his hand into the side pocket of his greatcoat and pulled out a pistol, which he moved to the right-hand pocket of his dark velvet jacket.

Abigail's heart skipped a beat. Why would he possibly think he needed a weapon so close to Fallen Oaks? No one had been attacked or robbed anywhere near here for years. No one had even seen a highway robber since she was a little girl.

Ethan urged his horse forward, and the carriage followed with a jerk that shifted Abigail back against the seat. They traveled at a fast clip—Ethan riding even with the carriage, his head swiveling to the left then to the right as he kept watch.

Abigail studied him from her window, praying the nervous fear roiling through her was a result of her imagination and not a premonition of something yet to happen. Surely the man called Stafford wouldn't have followed Ethan here. Surely she hadn't put him in danger by leaving London.

She knew the answer to her questions even before Bundy's gut-wrenching warning cry cut through the air. Before the first shot rang out.

"It's a trap!" she heard Ethan bellow. "Get her away from here, Bundy!"

His order was followed by the loud slap of the reins hitting the horses' backsides. The carriage lurched forward, tossing her against the back of the seat.

Stella screamed, then crumpled in a heap on the floor.

Abigail righted herself just in time to see Ethan pull the weapon from his jacket and turn his horse around. Just in time to see the end of a whip snap out and wrap around his chest. The force of the long leather cord pinned Ethan's arms to his body and pulled him to the ground. The gun he held in his hand flew forward, leaving him with no way to protect himself.

"No, Ethan!" she cried. "Bundy, stop!"

The carriage didn't slow, no doubt because Ethan had given orders to get her to safety. Then, without warning, the carriage jerked to a halt.

Before she had time to collect herself, the door flew open and a big, burly man pulled her from the coach.

Her first sight was that of Bundy's still body lying on the ground, a thin stream of blood running down the side of his face. "Bundy!" she screamed, struggling to go to him, but the man held her back.

"Abigail, run!" Ethan cried, a look of frantic fear in his eyes as he fought against the whip that circled his body. "Get away!"

She struggled against the arms holding her, biting and kicking and scratching in her attempt to get away. She needed to go to Bundy. She needed to make sure he was still alive. She needed to get the weapon Ethan had dropped on the ground. She needed to free him from the man she knew wanted to kill him. From Stafford.

Dear God, she silently pleaded, looking at Ethan.

Help him. Please, help him.

This was all her fault. If only she hadn't left London. If only she'd have stayed where they would have been safe.

Somehow, Ethan managed to free his arms. With lightning speed, he landed a strong punch to Stafford's face, then another, and another. Stafford fell to his knees. But before Ethan could attack again, two of the men with Stafford rushed forward and grabbed Ethan from behind. Each held one of Ethan's arms behind his back while Stafford bounded to his feet. His swelling face darkened with rage. He doubled his fist and hit Ethan in the jaw, then in the stomach, while the other men held him.

"You aren't so high and mighty when the tables are turned, are you, Captain Cambridge?" Stafford said, swaggering over to Ethan. "You're not so cocksure, now that you're outnumbered, are you?"

"Go to hell, Stafford," Ethan slurred, the cut on his lip poorly shaping his words. "You wouldn't be standing if you had the courage to face me by yourself instead of relying on these bullies to do your fighting for you."

"Oh, the fighting is fair, Captain. My men are going to handicap you, just like your men handicapped me. Like your sailors held their guns on me while you loaded my property onto your ship and sailed away with it."

"Those were people. Not property. You were going to kill them."

A slow, sardonic smile lifted the corners of Stafford's lips. "I was punishing them. Just like I'm going to punish you, Captain."

"No!" Abigail screamed. She struggled harder, but it was no use. The man holding her was too strong.

"How touching," Stafford said, walking over to Abigail

and lifting her chin with his finger. "I'd almost forgotten about the lovely lady."

"Leave her alone!" Ethan pulled against the two men. One of the men lost his grip and Ethan lunged forward, only to be stopped by Stafford's whip handle coming down across the side of his head.

Ethan staggered, giving the second man time to grab his arm and fasten his hold. A cut opened above Ethan's eye, a small river of blood flowing down the side of his face.

"You touch her and you're dead, Stafford."

"My, my. The Captain is certainly protective, isn't he? Just like I tried to be the night he humiliated me in front of my wife and my friends."

Stafford turned to Ethan. "My wife still reminds me how weak and inept I was against you. How I failed to stand up to a handful of incompetent British sailors to save what was mine. How I let you sail away with every slave I owned."

He lifted his hand as if he wanted to strike Ethan, then stopped. "Do you know how it feels to be laughed at by your wife? By your friends? I am ruined. As a Southern gentleman, I am disgraced. And it is your fault. You humiliated me and took away all I own. I think it is only fair I do the same to you."

The look in Stafford's eyes burned with hatred, a vile and vindictive glare that bordered on insanity.

Abigail looked for a way to help Ethan. She scanned the ground to find the pistol he'd dropped.

Ethan cast her a frantic look. The helplessness she saw on his face mirrored her own ineptitude. This was all her fault.

"Strip him and tie him to the carriage." Stafford snapped his whip in the air. "I owed Henry twenty lashes for his insubordination. Since it's your fault he's not here to receive them, you will take them in his place."

"No!" Abigail screamed again, but she knew her pleas would go for naught.

"And you, my dear," Stafford said, walking over to her, "can watch and listen while the brave and courageous Captain Cambridge receives his punishment. We will see how long it takes for him to beg me to stop. And then," he said, "I will take you away with me, just like the good captain took all my slaves. It's only fair, don't you think?"

A painful knot tightened in the pit of her stomach.

"Let her go," Ethan bellowed. "Do what you want with me, Stafford, but let her go."

"Oh, no. I want you to know how it feels to have what you cherish taken away. I want this lovely lady to see how weak you really are."

Stafford laughed—a harsh, shrill laugh that shot chills down Abigail's spine.

"My wife was privileged to watch you hold me at gunpoint while you stole everything that was important to me. I will afford you the same courtesy. Strip him!"

Ethan fought, but it was no use. There were too many of them.

First they pulled his jacket from his shoulders, then ripped his white lawn shirt from his back, stripping him bare to the waist. Next, they stretched his arms out and tied him to the carriage, making sure he could not move.

Ethan turned his face toward her, impaling her with a look that exposed his vulnerability. Black fury raged across his face, the frantic helplessness spearing through the charged air, twisting in the pit of her stomach.

She couldn't breathe.

"I'm sorry," she whispered through hot, heavy tears that streamed down her cheeks. "I didn't know. I didn't know."

Stafford raised his arm, then brought the whip back. The long leather strap halted as if suspended, then sliced through the air. It snapped with a loud crack as it met its target—Ethan's flesh.

His back arched. His muscles bunched. His body jerked once before he clenched his hands around two metal strips on the carriage and held tight.

A part of her died.

The whip snapped again. And again. And again.

"No!" She struggled against the muscled arms that held her. The look in Ethan's eyes blazed hollow, vacant, as if he needed to detach his mind from the pain being inflicted on his body. The breath that left his lungs hissed through his teeth, as he quivered in obvious agony.

Each snap caused another bloody stripe to mar his smooth, bronzed skin. Lashes crisscrossed with one another until they meshed like an ugly patchwork with no particular design.

With each downward swing of Stafford's arm, another cut appeared. Ethan's blood flowed in small rivulets toward his waist.

His face paled, and twice his legs buckled beneath him. But he did not cry out.

Abigail felt as if her heart was being ripped from her breast. His head dropped to his chest as he fought to maintain consciousness.

She watched as long as she could, willing him her strength. When she couldn't stand to see Ethan's body recoil in pain another time, she pinched her eyes shut.

Another snap echoed in the stillness, followed by a muffled groan. It was worse not to see. She opened her eyes, focusing first on the ground, then on the carriage wheel, then on the dull metal object behind it. Ethan's pistol.

Her heart beat faster. Her breath quickened. She had to get it. It was the only way she could stop Stafford.

Without considering if her plan would work, she raised her foot and brought it down hard on the instep of the man holding her. At the same time, she lowered her head and bit his arm. With a loud yelp, he released her.

Before the man could stop her, she dove for the weapon beneath the carriage wheel and grabbed it in her hands. She heard Ethan's weak voice yell a warning, but nothing could have deterred her. It was her fault Stafford had found Ethan. Her fault that blood ran from his flesh. Her fault she may be too late already, and he may die.

She jumped to her feet and turned. She aimed the pistol to the middle of Stafford's stomach. "Put the whip down. Now."

He held the whip high, poised to strike once more. The look in his eyes questioned whether or not she knew how to fire a weapon, or had the courage to do it.

"Put the whip down, sir, or I will blow a hole in you as big as my fist. I'm sure you know that a wound to the stomach is almost a guaranteed death sentence. And a very painful way to die."

Stafford laughed. "You expect me to believe a delicate woman such as yourself would have the courage to kill a man?"

She stepped between Stafford and Ethan and smiled. "I pray you give me the smallest excuse to answer your doubts."

The condescending smirk left his face, replaced by an obvious hint of concern.

"I spent most of my youth on London's docks with my father. He considered it essential that I learn to protect myself. Although the pistols I used were usually much smaller, I assure you, they were just as deadly."

The frown on Stafford's face grew darker.

"Drop the whip, sir, and take your men and leave." She motioned to Stafford's men and they moved to stand beside him.

Stafford hesitated a moment, as if considering what she would do, then lifted the corners of his mouth in a wide grin. "As you command," he said, bowing in mock conciliation, then lowering his whip to his side. But not dropping it to the ground.

He turned to his men and nodded, but his look was not one of surrender. Instead, it seemed more a signal for alertness. Every nerve at the back of her neck prickled in fear.

The next few seconds happened in the blink of an eye. With a loud cry, Stafford put his hand in his jacket and pulled out a gun.

Before he could fire, Abigail pulled the trigger.

Stafford's gun fell to the ground and his eyes opened wide, the look on his face filled with disbelief. He stared at her, then down at the blood oozing through his fingers that clutched his side.

"You bitch!" he yelled, his voice raspy and harsh. "You filthy bitch!"

The men in Stafford's employ stopped. They gaped at her as if they could not believe she'd pulled the trigger. As if they feared she might pull it again.

"Kill her," Stafford bellowed. "Kill them both!"

Abigail turned toward the men. She knew she couldn't stop them all, but she would stop at least one. And that one would be Stafford.

She shifted the gun from the three men standing

beside Stafford to Stafford.

His eyes opened wide. "You would shoot an unarmed man?"

Abigail hesitated. Could she?

She kept the gun aimed at the center of Stafford's chest. Mary Rose's sweet face flashed before her. She would be lost to her forever. So would Ethan. But with Stafford dead, at least Ethan and Mary Rose would live.

She lifted the gun, ready to shoot.

"Riders coming!" one of the men with him shouted.

The men abandoned Stafford and raced to their horses, but Stafford didn't move.

"You'd better leave now, Stafford," one of his men said, holding Stafford's horse, "or you ain't going nowhere."

If she was going to kill him, she had to do it now.

Stafford glared at her with a look that held more hatred than she'd ever seen before. As if he realized she wouldn't kill an unarmed man, he bellowed to the men turning to leave. "Help me. I'm hurt bad."

Two men helped him mount his horse.

"We're not finished," he growled, before his men led him into the trees.

Abigail heard yelling, and from somewhere, a shot rang out. Men shouted, horses thundered, gunshots went off all around her, but she couldn't move. She clutched Ethan's pistol in her hand and kept it pointed to the spot where Stafford had been, as if she expected him to come back.

"Abby," Ethan whispered, his voice a small echo in her mind. "Abby."

"He's gone, Ethan," she said, still pointing the gun to the empty spot. "I—I shot him, but...he's—he's gone now."

"'Tis all over now, Miss Langdon," Malcolm MacDonnell said, placing his arm around her shoulder. "'Twas a fine job you did here, but 'tis all over, and you're safe."

Abigail looked at the pistol, then handed it to Mac.

She'd just shot a man. She would have killed him if she had to. Just like she'd killed Stephen.

Her stomach recoiled and she thought she might be ill. What kind of person did that make her? What kind of woman brought a rock down on another human being's head? What kind of woman would shoot another person, even if it were the only way to save the man she loved?

Abigail clutched her hand to her roiling stomach.

"Mac," Ethan said, his voice soft and ragged. "Help her. She's not…"

"Save your strength, Ethan. I can see the lass is having trouble. I'll take care of her."

Abigail felt Mac's arm tighten around her. "Come on, lass," he whispered in her ear. His voice was a soothing lilt that made things seem not quite so bad. "Ethan needs you, lass. He's hurt. He needs you to take care of him."

Abigail looked into Malcolm's dark eyes and saw the concern there. She blinked, and the fog cleared from around her. She turned to Ethan, then took a step toward him.

"That's a lass," he said, and followed her to Ethan.

"Abby," Ethan whispered, his voice barely loud enough to be heard. "Are you all right?"

"I'm sorry, Ethan. I didn't know—"

"Shh. It's over now." Ethan leaned his bruised cheek against the side of the carriage. "Everything's going to be all right."

"Galton! Barney!" Malcolm interrupted. "Come help me with the Captain. Each of you, take an arm."

The men each took one of Ethan's outstretched arms, while Malcolm took out a knife and cut the ropes that bound him. Ethan's low moan echoed when they lowered him to his knees.

"Ah, friend," Malcolm said, supporting him. "'Tis a fine mess you've gotten yourself into this time."

Abigail knelt down with Ethan and let him lean against her. "You're going to be all right, Ethan. We'll get you to Fallen Oaks and you'll be fine. Stella," she said to the maid, who'd finally crawled out of the carriage. "Tear some strips from your petticoat, then check on Bundy." She looked at the big Scot. "I need some water. There's a stream just over there." She nodded to the side of the road.

"Right away, miss."

They put Ethan in the carriage and Abigail sat with his head in her lap. She placed wet cloths on his back to help with the pain and to keep the wounds moist until they could be properly tended to.

A wave of guilt washed over her. What had happened to her today had changed her. She'd almost killed another man.

She looked down at the blood-encrusted stripes that had been torn deeply into Ethan's flesh and swiped away any guilt she felt. She would have killed a dozen men to protect Ethan.

She would have killed a hundred men to save the man she loved.

Chapter 15

Abigail sat in a cushioned chair next to Ethan's bed and watched his restless sleep. It had been three days since Stafford had flayed him raw. Three days when she didn't know if he'd survive the next day. Or even the next hour.

Stafford's intention had been to kill Ethan. And he'd almost succeeded. There were places on Ethan's back where the skin had not only been ripped to jagged shreds, but the flesh beneath lay open and exposed.

And every brutal stripe on his back was her fault. Every deep tear was because she'd fled London and he'd been forced to come after her. She clutched the quilt tighter to her, as if the soft warmth could assuage her guilt. Why hadn't she listened to him and stayed in London?

She swiped at a tear that spilled from her eye, then pushed the cover from her shoulders and rushed to his bedside when he released an anguished moan and tried to push himself from the bed.

"You're safe, Ethan. Nothing can hurt you anymore."

"No!" he groaned. His struggling intensified.

"I'm here, Ethan. You're all right."

"Run, Abby! Run!"

His attempts to free himself became more frantic. "I'm safe, Ethan. Lie still."

"No," he moaned again. "Run!"

Abby tried to hold him steady while whispering in his ear. She needed to calm him before he tore the stitches that had taken Mac over an hour to sew. Thankfully, strong hands reached in to help her hold him down.

"Lie still, Captain," Mac's commanding voice said. "That's an order."

Ethan's movements didn't calm completely, but at least enough to keep him from doing more damage.

Abigail knelt by his bedside and whispered comforting words in his ear. Eventually, he calmed, then slept.

"Has he rested at all since I left?" Mac asked when Ethan was still, and Abigail had returned to her chair.

"A little."

"When was the last time you gave him laudanum?"

She looked at the clock on the mantel. "About an hour ago."

Mac shook his head. "Dammit. It's too soon to give him more."

Ethan released a painful sigh, and Abigail rose to place a cool cloth on the back of his neck.

"Tell me what happened between Ethan and Stafford," she said when she returned to her chair.

Mac watched Ethan's restless sleep. "I guess you deserve to know," he said, then leaned back in his chair. "We were delivering a shipment of French wine to Stafford's plantation. The voyage hadn't gone well from the start. First, we hit bad weather and lost part of our rigging. Then we ran into a patrol searching for blockade runners and were nearly caught. It was time to go home. The crew looked forward to unloading the cargo and leaving hostile waters."

Mac rose from his chair and rinsed the cloth in cool water, then placed it back on Ethan's neck. "We arrived at Stafford's plantation in the middle of celebration. I'm not sure what Stafford was celebrating, but there must have been thirty to forty friends and neighbors gathered there. Ethan went ahead to tell Stafford we were there, and the crew loaded our cargo into smaller boats and rowed to shore.

"Stafford invited us to join the party, but Ethan told him we were in a hurry to leave to avoid any more run-ins with Northern patrols. He understood and ordered several of his slaves to help unload the cases of wine."

Mac pushed himself to his feet and walked to the window. "Ethan and I had seen evidence of Stafford's cruelty before, so we knew what he was capable of. But that day we got a firsthand look at how brutal he could be.

"There was a slave—Henry. He walked with hunched shoulders and a limp. His hair was white and his face wrinkled with age. He should have been sitting in a rocker on the porch of his hut, but Stafford still expected him to carry cases of wine as if he were a man of twenty."

Mac braced his fist against the window frame and looked out. "As Henry walked past Stafford, he tripped. The case of French wine hit the wooden dock and several of the bottles broke. Within seconds, Stafford snapped back the whip he always wore at his waist and brought it down on Henry's back.

"I held Ethan back the first three lashes Henry suffered, but he broke away from me on the fourth. When Stafford lowered his arm to whip Henry a fifth time, Ethan grabbed Stafford's wrist and stopped him."

"What did Stafford do?"

"He told Ethan that his slaves were his to do with as he saw fit, and that Ethan's interruption cost Henry ten more lashes."

Mac pushed himself from the window and returned to his chair. "I knew we were in trouble. The crew knew it, too. No one is more honorable than Ethan, and, to a man, they'd give their lives to protect him. When Ethan pulled out his gun, the crew followed suit.

"Of course, Stafford and his guests weren't armed, so what happened next went smoothly. Ethan ordered several slaves to pick Henry up and put him in one of the boats. I think Ethan's plan was only to take Henry, but a female, obviously Henry's wife, rushed forward. Then two little children, maybe grandchildren ran forward, crying that they wanted to go, too."

Mac swiped his hand over his face. "One look at Ethan's face and I knew what he was going to do. I know you heard me tell him how foolish he'd been, but I've never been more proud of another human being in my life. He looked at the group of slaves and told them he'd take anyone who wanted to go with him."

"And they all went," Abigail answered as tears streamed down her cheeks.

"To a last one. Even a frail old grandmother who had to be carried to the boats."

"Where did you take them?"

"To New York. Stafford's slaves weren't the first slaves we'd taken north. When we reached New York, Ethan contacted a group of sympathizers, and they took them where they'd be safe."

Mac stood again and rinsed the cloth in cool water, then replaced it on Ethan's neck. "I knew Stafford wouldn't stop until Ethan was dead. And it's not over. As soon as he recovers, Stafford will be back."

A wave of panic rushed over her. "What are you going to do?" she asked.

"That's not the question, Miss Langdon." Ethan's friend locked his gaze with hers. "What are *you* going to do?"

. . .

Abigail rinsed the cloth in the water again and with tender, fleeting touches, washed Ethan's back, then applied more of the strong-smelling ointment the doctor had given her to ward off infection. More than once in the first week, she was certain he would die. He hadn't. It had been eight days now, and today he'd stayed awake even longer before falling back to sleep.

Abigail poured some wine into a glass, then added a few drops of laudanum. When she replaced the glass on the table, she rolled her shoulders to ease her aching muscles.

"Why don't you lie down and get some rest?" he said from behind her. "You look tired."

Abigail started, then turned around to check on him. "I thought you'd gone back to sleep."

"I've slept enough the last week to last a lifetime."

She smiled, then placed her hand on his forehead to make sure there was no fever. She sighed in relief when his skin was cool to the touch.

She pulled her hand back and took a step away from the bed. It was more difficult each day to be near him. Her traitorous body reacted in a way she didn't understand. In a way she knew was dangerous. "You needed to sleep. Your body needs rest to heal."

He reached for her hand and held it. "What happened wasn't your fault, Abby."

She turned her face, unable to look him in the eye. She could still see the end of the whip tearing at his flesh, the rivulets of blood streaming down his back, the pain in his eyes.

"Do you need something to eat or drink?" she said, pulling her hand free. "Cook just took a beef pie out of the oven. It smells delicious."

"Ignoring what I'm saying won't make it go away."

"I know that," she answered, "but talking about it won't, either. I know what I did. I know the danger I put you in. I know what almost happened that day."

"If Stafford hadn't followed me there, he would have found me somewhere else. And you wouldn't have been there to save me."

"Oh, Ethan. If I hadn't left London—"

"Why did you? Why did you leave?"

"I had to. You know that."

"No, I don't. You didn't have to leave."

"Can't you understand? Nothing has changed."

He breathed a sigh. "You're right. Nothing has changed. I still need your ships, and you are still intent on having Fallen Oaks."

Abigail walked to the window and looked down to the cobbled drive leading to the front entrance. She would give the world if things could be different, if she could tell him about Mary Rose. If he wouldn't hate her when he found out the rest.

"You don't understand," she said, turning toward the bed, looking into his eyes.

"Another secret, Abby?" he said, his voice angry.

"Yes."

"Then share it with me. Whatever it is you're hiding, we'll find a solution."

"There is no solution. Some problems cannot be solved."

"They can, if a person wants to solve them badly enough." His voice was surprisingly determined for someone so weak.

She couldn't answer him. There was no answer.

"Am I interrupting something?"

Abigail turned to see Malcolm MacDonnell standing behind them in the doorway.

"No, Captain MacDonnell," she said, trying to appear relaxed. "Please, come in."

"Thank you," he said, walking across the room. "I think, Miss Langdon, it's past time you called me Mac, like the rest of the world does."

He offered her one of his heart-warming smiles, and she couldn't help but return it. "I would like that, Mac. And you will call me Abby, as only a few in the world do."

They both laughed. Even Ethan gave a quiet chortle. But when he looked at her, his expression told her their conversation wasn't finished.

Abby indicated a chair beside the bed. "Won't you sit? I'm sure you have things to discuss with Ethan in private, so I'll leave you two alone."

"Before you leave, I have a message for you from Captain Parker. He wants you to know he will be ready to set sail by the end of next week. He thought you would like to witness the maiden voyage of the *Abigail Rose*."

Abigail looked down at Ethan, but before she could make an excuse, he answered for her.

"Of course. We'll all be there."

"No," she argued. "You are not nearly ready to travel yet."

"I will be by the end of next week. I've spent enough time in this blasted bed. It's time I left it. And there's nothing I'd rather witness than the *Abigail Rose* setting sail."

She could hardly argue when there wasn't anything she'd rather see. "Please, tell Captain Parker that nothing could keep me from being there when he takes the *Abigail Rose* out for the first time."

"It will be my pleasure."

"Thank you. Now, if you gentlemen will excuse me, I have some work to take care of."

Abigail felt Ethan's eyes on her as she softly closed the door behind her.

Somehow, she still had to convince him she couldn't marry him. Somehow, she had to keep Mary Rose a secret from him. And somehow, she had to find a way to survive the rest of her life knowing he was lost to her forever.

Chapter 16

"What on earth do you think you're doing?" Abigail rushed into her father's study where Ethan sat behind the desk. "You should be resting." She couldn't believe it when Stella told her Ethan had not gone up to rest all day.

"Good afternoon to you, too," he said.

He lifted his head as she took off her bonnet and gloves and handed them to Palmsworth, along with her heavy woolen cloak. There was something different in the way he looked today, something predatory. Something that whispered a warning.

"Have you been out again?"

"I needed some fresh air."

He shoved the papers that littered the top of the desk forward and laid down his pen. "Your father's estate records are a disaster. It's a wonder Fallen Oaks has stayed afloat this long, even with the help of Langdon Shipping."

She ignored the truth of his warning and walked cautiously across the room. "You shouldn't be out of bed, Ethan. You're not strong enough yet."

"We leave for London in two days. I've got to be ready."

She looked at him, at the deep color of his cheeks. "You look flushed. Are you feverish?"

"I'm fine. You still haven't told me where you went."

"Just out." She reached over and felt his forehead.

"See?" He clasped his fingers around her wrist and held her. "I'm fine."

The feel of his flesh against hers sent waves of molten emotions gushing to every part of her body. Every day it was harder to fight the pull he had on her, the yearning she felt deep inside her when she got too near him. "You should be in bed."

"Not yet."

He studied her with more intensity than she wanted to have to battle. How could his mere gaze do this to her? How could his touch affect her even more?

He rose to his feet. "Is everything all right?"

"Of course. What could be wrong?"

He lifted his hand and touched her face. Fiery tendrils spiraled to the tips of her toes.

"Your cheeks are warm," he whispered, cupping her cheeks more intimately.

She turned her face away from him. "Don't, Ethan."

He placed his hand on her upper arms and pulled her back against him. The air caught in her throat. Every inch he touched heated as if she'd sat too close to the flames of a fire.

"Why are you trying so hard to ignore what is happening between us?"

"There is nothing happening between us," she said, turning out of his arms.

"You can't deny it, Abby. There is something between us."

She shook her head, wanting to deny his words even as her traitorous body proved her denial a lie. He stepped up behind her and wrapped his arms around her waist.

"Please, don't," she whispered, her breath coming in short, rapid gasps. "I can't."

Her chest heaved, whether from fear or anticipation she couldn't tell. Without warning, he lowered his head and nestled his face in the crook of her neck, touching her sensitive skin with his lips, sending her emotions soaring out of control.

"Abby." He pressed a kiss against her neck, just below her ear. "You smell of lilacs in the springtime."

His fingers spanned the black bombazine stretched across her small waist, splaying outward and upward, coming perilously close to brushing against her breasts.

She moaned, a cry for him to stop his torture turning to encouragement for him to touch more of her. With a confidence that told her he knew her need, he turned her to face him.

"See, Abby?" He touched his lips to her forehead, then kissed her cheeks and the tip of her nose. "See how perfectly we suit one another?"

He cupped her cheeks in the palms of his hands and tipped her chin upward. He took possession of her eyes with a look that granted no quarter.

With the gentlest of touches, he stroked her lips with his thumb, then lowered his head and pressed his lips against hers. He touched her softly at first, then with more intensity, then with a desperation that matched her own. He molded his lips to hers, sampling, then tasting, then taking what she couldn't help but offer.

His relentless thumb pressed downward on her chin, and she opened to him. The velvety warmth of his tongue skimmed her lips, her teeth, then broached the opening she created for him.

Her breath caught in her throat when their tongues

touched. Starbursts of light exploded behind her closed eyes, bright white and shimmering silver. Her knees crumpled beneath her. There was no explanation for what he did to her, for the havoc he caused in her body, the mind-numbing explosions shattering inside her head.

She wrapped her arms around his neck, as she rationalized her desperation with the excuse that her legs wouldn't support her if he let go.

That was only a half-truth. In reality, it was the only way she could gather more of him to her. She needed to feel him against her, around her, within her, touching her, taking her, making her a part of his strength, his warmth. He was all she wanted, needed, ached to have take possession of her heart—fill the void deep inside her even little Mary Rose couldn't fill.

Mary Rose. Mary Rose.

Every kiss made it harder for her to push him away, more impossible to keep him from stealing her heart, the heart she'd guarded with such care. How could she have forgotten what a threat he was to her? How could she have forgotten how much he could hurt her?

She turned her head to break their kiss.

A wave of cold emptiness slapped against her, painfully wrenching her heart from the welcoming place it had found.

A soft, agonizing sigh escaped from deep within her. She tried to stand on her own and couldn't. She could not separate herself from him just yet.

Thankfully, she didn't have to. He held her tight.

Abigail leaned her forehead against him. His chest heaved in and out in small waves of uncontrolled distress as he struggled to catch his breath. Her breathing came no easier. She clung to him in desperation because she didn't ever want to let go. She didn't ever want to lose him.

Through the soft fabric of his white lawn shirt, she could feel the unbridled pounding of his heart. It equaled her own, wild and frantic, a violent thudding in counterpoint to the rhythm beating within her breast.

"Do you think you can stop what there is between us?" he gasped, the words coming with effort.

"I have to. I have no choice."

"Can't you bring yourself to turn to me for help just once? Can't you trust that I will overlook what great transgression you think you have committed?"

"No," she sighed past the lump in her throat. "Not even you are that magnanimous."

She turned out of his arms and stepped across the room.

"Abigail."

She halted with her hand on the door latch.

"Turn around. Look at me."

She slowly turned. The deep blue of his eyes became almost black as they pierced her with his riveting glare.

"Would it be that impossible for you to be married to me?"

Her breath caught in her throat. "Yes," she whispered.

"Why? Is there someone else?"

She turned her face, afraid he might read the truth in her eyes.

He glared at her, his look filled with astonishment, as if he finally understood. "Bloody hell," he said, a look of disbelief on his face. "Is it Stephen? Are you still in love with him?"

She opened her mouth to deny what he implied, then stopped. What did the reason matter? All that was important was that he understand that she could never marry him.

For just an instant, her pent-up fear receded, and she

saw the hurt she'd caused him. He turned his back to her and walked to the window. For several long, agonizing minutes, he stared out into the late winter sunshine. The muscles across his shoulders bunched, and the hand at his side fisted. When he spoke, she heard the fury in his voice. "How badly do you want Fallen Oaks?"

"More than anything in the world."

"Then it's yours."

The air left her lungs. Relief and regret surged through her at the same time. Along with a pain she couldn't explain. "You will give me the deed to Fallen Oaks and take the ships?"

"Yes."

"With what conditions?"

"None. The deed is yours."

She couldn't believe she'd heard him right. She couldn't believe the battle was finally over.

She'd gotten what she'd demanded. She should feel like celebrating her victory, but she didn't. She hurt too much. More than she'd ever hurt in her life.

She stared at his back, rigid and straight, the tense muscles across his shoulders pulled taut against his white lawn shirt. "Why have you changed your mind?"

He laughed, but his laughter rang bitter and hollow. "It's simple. I can't fight you any longer. Fallen Oaks will be yours. The *Abigail Rose* will be mine. You can keep the other ships. They should earn enough profit to keep Fallen Oaks from going bankrupt, provided you manage well. We'll see Sydney to take care of the final details when we return to London."

He turned away from her and walked to the small table that held a decanter of her father's favorite brandy and a half-dozen cut crystal glasses. He picked one of them up and filled it with the amber liquid.

"You are not going to change your mind?" she asked, watching his tense movements as he brought the glass to his mouth.

He lowered the glass a few inches and smiled at her. "Why would I insist on marrying you, knowing it's Stephen you'll always want in your bed?" He threw a swallow of the brandy down his throat and looked at her again. "As you reminded me yourself, even I am not that magnanimous."

Abigail felt as if he'd stabbed a knife through her heart. His words hurt more than she thought possible. And there was nothing she could do to lessen the pain she had caused him.

Abigail left the room, knowing she should feel happiness and relief. But all she felt deep inside was a hurt that wouldn't ease. She had won, and yet, somehow, she feared she had lost.

Lost more than she would ever know.

. . .

Something woke him.

Ethan opened his eyes to nothing but murky darkness. He remained quiet and listened.

From the blackness that surrounded him, he calculated it was the middle of the night. He listened to the sounds of a house gone to sleep many hours ago. Then he heard it again.

Muffled voices. The soft thudding of doors quietly opening and closing. The padding of footsteps rushing down the hall past his room, then fading as they descended the long flight of stairs. His heart quickened in his chest, an uneasy warning of things not right.

Agitated tones and anxious words echoed from

below. He couldn't make out what was being said, but he knew Abigail's voice was among them. There was a rush of activity, then the front door closed. All was quiet.

Ethan threw the covers back and leaped from the bed, then gasped in pain. The cuts on his back were well on their way to healing, but still tender enough to let him know he'd not given them the care and consideration they demanded.

He stretched his shoulders, then rushed to the window. He pulled back the drapery in time to see a carriage drive away from the house and turn at the end of the lane.

A feel of unease washed over him. Every nerve in his body grew tense. Surely Abigail hadn't gone out in the middle of the night?

Fear followed by anger welled inside him, building with ferocious intensity.

He threw on his clothes as quickly as his back would allow and opened his bedroom door just as Stella walked past.

"Where is your mistress?"

Stella looked up at him, her eyes rimmed red from tears, her face pale and puffy. Without explanation, she lifted the corner of her apron and wiped at her eyes.

"Where did she go?"

"Out, sir."

"Where?"

"Oh, sir," she said, sobbing into her apron. "There's nothing you can do. Nothing anyone can do."

"What are you talking about?"

"I can't say. I swore I wouldn't."

"Tell me, Stella! Where has she gone?"

Stella fidgeted with her apron, wringing the corners together until the threads threatened to break. "Oh, merciful heaven. I swore I wouldn't."

"Tell me!"

"Oh, Captain Cambridge. It's Sister Constance. She's ill."

"The sisters can't tend their own? Your mistress had to go to them?"

"Oh, sir. You don't understand." Stella sobbed uncontrollably into her apron, her whole body shaking. "I told her not to go."

"What are you talking about, Stella?"

"I begged her," she ranted, the tears coming afresh. "I told her she couldn't help."

"Couldn't help what?"

"Oh, sir," she wailed. "What if she becomes ill, too? Oh—"

"Cease, woman!"

Ethan stared at the servant, waiting for her to calm. When he thought she was rational enough to talk, he asked his questions again. "Tell me what I don't understand. Explain why the sisters at the convent are not able to care for each other, and your mistress had to go."

Stella twisted the soaked cloth in her hand, then stopped and looked up at him. "It's the typhoid, sir. Sister Beatrice fears Sister Constance has the typhoid."

Ethan's heart skipped a beat, a cold chill raging through his body. "And Miss Langdon went to help? Why in blazes did they send for her?"

"Oh, sir," Stella sobbed again. "I couldn't stop her."

Ethan grabbed his cloak, then raced for the door.

"No! Don't go. It will do no good. You are too late to stop her." Stella raced after him with a look of panic on her face. "You will only put yourself in danger."

Ethan ignored her warning as he ran to the stables to saddle his mount. He could think of nothing except trying to reach Abigail before it was too late, before she reached the convent. But he knew his efforts would be futile. He had lost too much time already.

As he made his way over the unfamiliar ground, he realized her carriage had too much of a head start, and Bundy knew the way better, perhaps even a shorter way to get there.

He kept his eyes focused on the road ahead, praying he would see her carriage, but he didn't. It wasn't until he reached the convent that he saw it. But he was too late. She was already inside the walls.

"Don't go in," Bundy warned as Ethan dismounted. "She'll not want you there."

Ethan gave him a look filled with all the anger and frustration he'd given himself free rein to feel on the ride over. He marched past Bundy and pounded on the oak door as if he intended to break it down.

It didn't take long for a timid sister to open the heavy barrier a crack, but it was enough for him to push his way inside.

"Where is she?" he bellowed at the sister.

"We have a sickness—"

"I don't give a damn—" His fingers clenched as he struggled to hold his temper. "I don't care. Where is she?"

The sister looked at him, and he could see her debate what to do. "Take me to her, or I'll search every room in the convent until I find her."

With a quiet nod, she bowed her head and turned to lead him through the quiet hallways. They walked in aggravating slowness down one long dark corridor, then up a narrow flight of stairs, and another, then down a second long corridor, finally coming to a halt in front of a door at the end of the passageway. Without waiting to knock, Ethan threw open the door.

Every muscle in his body froze, his heart falling to the pit of his stomach.

Abigail sat in a rocker at the side of a small bed, cradling a babe in her arms. A babe with hair of spun copper, just like Abigail's, and deep brown eyes and dimpled cheeks.

Just like Stephen's.

Chapter 17

Abigail clutched Mary Rose close to her, but kept her gaze riveted on Ethan's towering fury as he stood in the doorway.

Neither of them spoke. There was nothing to say. From the look on his face, he'd already noticed the resemblance to her, and to Stephen. From his dark expression and the clenched fists at his sides, he was as disappointed as she knew he would be.

Mary Rose struggled in her arms, making tiny squealing noises to tell Abigail she was holding her too tight.

"Shh, sweetheart." She released her grip enough to stop Mary Rose's squirming, then brushed her coppery red hair from her face. "It's all right. Go back to sleep."

Ethan stepped inside the room and closed the door behind him. "This is what you couldn't tell me."

At the sound of his voice, Mary Rose leaned forward to peek around Abigail's arm. She was curious to investigate the stranger with the deep, rich voice more closely. The first male voice she'd ever heard. Her eyes widened in appreciation, an impressive look of approval on her face.

He stepped closer. Mary Rose's little face tilted upward in awestruck wonder. Abigail was sure that to someone as small as Mary Rose, Ethan must seem like a giant.

"This is where you went each day."

He said the words more as an accusation than a question that required an answer, so she gave none. What could she say? There were no excuses to make, no point in expecting him to understand, and from the scowl on his face, no hope that he could forgive.

"Does she have the illness?" He watched the babe with the same curiosity as Mary Rose showed him.

"No. She's just unsettled because she was awakened in the middle of the night."

"The sister at the door said—"

"The doctor is with Sister Constance now. Sister Beatrice is afraid it may be typhoid."

"If it is?"

Abigail brushed Mary Rose's forehead, absently checking for a fever. "Then we will wait. We will know within a fortnight if she contracts it, too."

He reached down and touched the baby's forehead, then walked to the window on the other side of the bed. He stood with his back to her.

"What is she called?" he said, lifting back the curtain and staring out into the darkness.

"Mary Rose."

"Did you name her?"

"Yes."

"Why that name?"

"Rose has been a family name since my great-great-grandmother, Agnes Rose. Mary just...just seemed right."

"When was she…" He stilled. "How old is she?"

She could see the anger building in him. "Just ten months."

He spun around to face her. When he spoke, his voice was harsh, filled with bitterness. "Did Stephen know before he left?"

She lowered her eyes and shook her head. "No."

"But he knew there was a possibility?"

"Stop it! It won't do any good to place blame on anyone."

He looked at little Mary Rose, who still studied him intently, then turned back toward the window. He braced his hands on either side of the only outside opening in the room and hung his head between his arms. "How long did you think you could keep her hidden before she was discovered?"

"Forever! If you would only have left us alone."

He turned back to the darkness. "You couldn't have. Someone would have found out eventually."

She shook her head, refusing to believe he might be right.

"This is what your father meant. This is what he wrote you had that was of the greatest importance belonging to Stephen."

"He did not know what he was saying. He was sick and didn't mean his words."

"Yes, he did."

She stared at his back, willing him to turn around and look at her, to at least make an effort to understand. But he didn't say any more. There was nothing more to say. The shock of finding out about Mary Rose was now a bitter, impossible reality.

The chasm of silence widened. She could feel the gulf of disappointment and painful betrayal separate them. What they had shared before, or might have shared in the future, was moot. The feelings developing between them took an almost fatal blow when she let Ethan believe she still loved Stephen. The finality was even more painful now that he saw Mary Rose as proof of the love he thought she and his brother shared.

"What will happen now?" he asked, his voice a hoarse whisper filled with emotion.

"What I said would happen all along. I will stay here where I can care for Mary Rose, and you will go back to your plantation. We will sign the papers that give you possession of the *Abigail Rose,* and I will get possession of Fallen Oaks. We will both have what we want."

"You expect me to just walk away, now that I know about the child?"

"I never expected you to do anything else."

"Didn't you? Well, I expected more from you."

She wanted to defend herself against his cutting remark with one of her own, but couldn't. A knock on the door saved her from trying.

Sister Beatrice entered the room. "I came as quickly as I could to tell you the news. The doctor says Sister Constance doesn't have the typhoid."

The air caught in Abigail's throat. The news must have affected Ethan in the same way, for she heard a soft sigh from behind her.

"Thank God," Abigail whispered, swiping at an errant tear that spilled from her eye. She wouldn't allow herself to become emotional. She couldn't afford to. One tear would lead to a flood she wouldn't be able to stop.

She looked down on Mary Rose, now sleeping soundly in her arms, and kissed her cheek.

"Will Sister Constance be all right?" Abigail asked.

"Yes," Sister Beatrice said with a smile on her face. "The doctor says she has a severe stomach ailment caused by eating too much warm plum pudding. When she recovers, for penance she will be restricted from entering the kitchen for a month, and will go without sweets for two."

"Don't be too hard on her, sister. I'm sure she didn't mean to frighten us."

"Perhaps not, but..." The sister looked a little guilty. "I'm sorry I disturbed you needlessly at such an hour, but considering how concerned you are over the babe, I thought you would want to know."

"Oh, yes. Any time, day or night. I want you to promise you will inform me of anything that affects Mary Rose."

"That will no longer be necessary, sister," Ethan said from where he stood by the window. "Mary Rose will come with us tonight."

Abigail flashed him a desperate look. "No. She has to stay here."

His stoic expression did not change. The dark look in his eyes did not soften.

The blood swirled in her head, making her dizzy. "You can't mean to take her away from here."

"I can't leave her," he answered, ever so softly.

The first wave of fear rushed through her body—even more frightening than her terror that Mary Rose could have the typhoid. "You have no right to her. She's mine."

Ethan stopped, giving Sister Beatrice a nod of dismissal, then waited for her to leave the room. "She's Stephen's," he said when they were alone.

"No! She's mine, and mine alone!"

"I won't leave her here."

"You have to. Do you know what it will mean if people find out about her? She'll be a marked child. An outcast."

She clutched Mary Rose to her and stared at the man

who threatened to take away all she had left in the world.

The expression on his face remained hard, unyielding. The muscles in his jaw bunched in harsh determination, his lips pressed together in resolve, his eyebrows drew together to give him a formidable look.

"She is all I have left, Ethan. Please, leave us be. Go back to your plantation and forget you ever saw her."

"It's too late for that, Abigail."

She shook her head. She was desperate to find a solution. "No. What do you want from me? What can I give to you? I'll do anything, give you anything, be anything you want, only please, don't take her away from me."

"You are offering me your body?"

She hesitated. "If that will make you forget you know of her existence."

He sucked in his breath, his look turning more hostile.

Abigail felt her cheeks burn hot as she fought the waves of panic that washed over her. How was she to fight him? What could she do to protect Mary Rose from being discovered?

"Please, just leave us."

He shook his head. "I'll hold her while you put on your cloak," he said, leaning down to take the babe from her arms.

"No, Ethan. Please," she pleaded, pulling Mary Rose closer to her. "What more do I have that you want. It is yours. Anything."

"There isn't anything you have that I want, Abigail. Nothing that Stephen hasn't already had. Now, put on your cloak. We have to go."

Abigail was unable to move. Her cheeks burned as if she'd been slapped. Ethan took Mary Rose and cradled her as tenderly as if she were his own. He held her as if she might break. "Put on your cloak so we can go."

Abigail rose on wooden legs to fetch it. She wrapped her cloak around her shoulders, but her hands shook too much to fasten it. She couldn't think to take care of such mundane details, not when Mary Rose's future hung by a very thin thread—a thread which Ethan threatened to sever.

"Lay another blanket out on the bed," he said, pointing to a heavy quilt at the bottom of Mary Rose's bed.

When Abigail had it spread out, Ethan laid the sleeping babe in the middle. "Here," he said, turning to fasten her cloak. "You'll catch your death of cold if you're not careful."

She wanted to laugh. Her lips curved upward, belying the sickness she felt at how such humor struck her. "That would solve a multitude of problems. Wouldn't it, sir?"

"Don't, Abby."

"Why? Do you think you are the only one allowed to hurl accusations and insults?"

She turned away from him and wrapped Mary Rose in the second blanket, making sure the babe would stay warm on the ride home.

"I'll carry her to the carriage," Ethan said.

"No," she said, stepping between him and where Mary Rose lay on the bed. "She's not yours. I'll carry her."

He turned on her with lightning speed. "Stop it! Such bitterness will do no one any good. Surely you realize I can't let Stephen's child, illegitimate though she may be, stay locked away in a convent."

"She has not been locked away. She lives where she is loved and cared for. She's cherished as she will never be in the world in which you intend to thrust her. Who do you think will accept such a child? Your mother?

Society? You?"

He blanched.

"Don't you see? No one wants her but me. Your mother will despise her the minute she knows of her existence. Society will do nothing but condemn her. And you, sir, will be at your island paradise and will have washed your hands of both her and me. Please, Ethan. Just leave her here. At least until we can talk this through."

He turned away from her and walked to the window. The first faint tinges of sunlight had colored the midnight darkness to a lighter shade of black. He didn't move. His broad shoulders braced, stiff and unbending, his head stoically high, his hands clasped tightly behind his back.

Abigail stared at such magnificence and realized with a painful jolt all she would be giving up. All she would never know in her lifetime. She would only be able to dream of his handsome face, his high cheekbones and sharply defined features, his powerful strength and uncompromising integrity. The feel of his arms around her and his lips upon hers would be nothing but a memory. A memory she would struggle to keep alive her whole life.

"Put her back in bed," he said, impaling her with a look as dangerous as craggy rocks battered by the ocean. "She will stay here until I decide what is best for her."

Abigail clasped her hand over her mouth to hold back a cry of relief. The tears she'd been successful in withholding until now silently streamed down her cheeks.

"I will speak to Sister Beatrice and tell her our intentions. Say your goodbyes and be ready to leave when I return. We must still go to London in the morning."

With that, he left the room, leaving behind a small

remainder of his anger and fury, and enormous compassion.

Abigail picked up Mary Rose and sat on the edge of the bed with the sleeping babe cradled her in her arms. Back and forth she rocked, crying more tears than she thought she had in her, sobbing until her head pounded and her chest ached. Finally, she could find no more tears to shed and no more sobs to release. With nightmarish trepidation, she laid the sleeping babe in the small trundle bed and covered her up. She sat beside her and brushed back the coppery curls that framed her face. Dear God, how she loved her.

As if she were her own.

. . .

Ethan lifted his head from his arms flopped across the top of the desk and opened one eye. In the murky darkness, he saw two bottles standing on the edge of the desk, or perhaps there were four. Brave soldiers all of them, giving up their fine liquor for a good cause. To help him forget.

He couldn't be positive, but surely he hadn't drained all of them dry. He picked them up one by one. Surely one of them had some small amount in it.

He smiled when one seemed heavier than the rest. "The last brave soldier," he slurred, cradling the bottle to his chest as he searched for the glass he'd filled more times than he could count. He filled it again.

Damn, he was drunk. He hadn't been this drunk since...he didn't remember ever being this drunk.

This called for a toast. A toast to the most drunken state he'd ever survived—except he wasn't at all sure he would survive. And it was her fault. Hers and Stephen's.

He pushed his chair back, confident he needed to stand to offer such an important toast. The big winged chair toppled sideways, falling to the floor with a loud crash. With the bottle in one hand and the glass in the other, he saluted the fallen chair. All fallen soldiers deserved recognition. He lifted his glass, then threw the warm liquor to the back of his throat.

The room shifted beneath his feet. The big oak desk slammed into his hip, and the floor came up to meet his face. The leg of the fallen chair hit him squarely above his eye.

The sound was deafening: furniture breaking, decanters shattering, bottles crashing. The whole earth seemed to move in spiraling circles, never stopping.

He thought of saving himself, but protecting the only surviving half-full bottle of brandy seemed infinitely more important.

He lay amidst the shards of broken glass with the only unbroken bottle of brandy cradled in his arms.

· · ·

Abigail threw open the door to the study and stopped. There was broken glass and upset furniture everywhere. And Ethan lay in the middle of it.

"Don't move, Ethan. Lie still. You're hurt."

"Get out!"

She looked at Palmsworth, who followed her in. "Can you get to him, Palmsworth? There's glass everywhere."

Palmsworth nodded, then walked around the far side of the room. He made a path free of broken glass. "Here, my lady."

Abigail followed him and knelt beside Ethan on the floor. She reached to push back his hair from the gash above his eye.

"Get away, I said." He swung his hand through the air. His fist glanced off her chin, causing white stars to twinkle behind her eyes.

"That's enough, sir," Palmsworth said. He took the bottle from Ethan's hands and held his arms to his sides.

"Damn you, Palmsworth! Get the hell out of here and leave me alone."

"In a moment, sir. As soon as we have you back to your room."

"No!"

"Ethan, you're hurt."

"You ought to know," he slurred. "You did a damn good job of it. Not even Stafford knew how to do what you did."

The blood in her veins turned to ice. Abigail tried to dismiss his hateful words. She told herself it was the liquor talking. But with each step she and Palmsworth took to get him up the stairs and to his room, she knew the liquor alone couldn't be blamed for the painful words he shot at her. She was also to blame. As was Stephen.

When they got him to his room, she cleaned his cuts as best he would allow, then pulled up the covers and stepped away from him.

He slept soundly. The hooded frowns and angry creases had disappeared from his face. This was how she would remember him.

Tomorrow he'd wake feeling as if he'd been run over by a carriage.

A part of her was glad he'd hurt as much as she did.

Chapter 18

Ethan felt like hell. As if he'd been run over by a horse and wagon and no one had stopped to pick him up. The trip to London was brutal. He would have preferred to ride in the carriage to rest his throbbing head, but couldn't endure more torture. That's what sitting beside Abigail for the hours it took to reach London would be. Torture.

Plus, he needed to distance himself from her so he could think. He had to decide what to do.

He hadn't spoken to her during the journey. He'd stayed with the horses the two times Bundy had stopped for Abigail and her maid to eat and see to their needs. Food was the last thing his stomach could tolerate. Sitting near Abigail was the last thing his emotions could handle.

He was never more glad than when they finally reached the outskirts of London. He escorted her to her town house and instructed her on what time to be ready to go to the docks the next day to watch the *Abigail Rose* set sail, then left her.

He breathed a sigh of relief when he slid from his

horse in front of Stephen's town house. He'd thought of nothing else during the journey, but now—finally—he knew what he had to do. Even if she hated him for the rest of her life. He had to do what was best for her and the child.

And for him.

"Rub him down well, Georgie," he said, handing the reins to the stableboy.

"That I'll do, Mr. Cambridge," the lad said, then led the horse around back to the mews.

The front door opened before Ethan reached the top step, and Hargrove stood there with his usual air of dignified aplomb. "It's good to see you, sir," he said, bowing formally.

"Thank you, Hargrove. Are there any messages?"

"Yes, sir. This message marked 'urgent' arrived from a Mr. Harper," he said, holding out an envelope.

"When did this come?"

"Just this afternoon, sir."

Ethan snatched the letter from Hargrove's hand and walked into Stephen's study, closing the door behind him. His pulse raced as he ripped the missive open and scanned the words.

Mr. Cambridge,

I have important news concerning your brother. A man resembling his description was spotted on a packet a week out of London. I cannot swear this same man is your brother, the Earl of Burnhaven, but will verify his identity when the packet docks. You should know with certainty within the week.

Your humble servant,
Elvin T. Harper

Ethan clutched the corner of Stephen's mammoth oak desk as he reread the letter, then sat down in the plush maroon leather chair and buried his head in his hands. He had a week. A week. He wadded the letter in his fist and threw it into the fire.

"Hargrove!" he bellowed, throwing open the study door. "Send Georgie to me. I've messages to deliver."

"Yes, sir," Hargrove said, rushing to do Ethan's bidding.

With an anxious slap against his thigh, Ethan sat back down behind Stephen's desk and penned two messages. The first was a message that would summon Malcolm MacDonnell. The second, a message that would change his life forever, turning it to either a bliss-filled adventure he would never want to end or unfathomable days of hellish living from which there would be no escape.

. . .

The bells of the church tower clock chimed the noon hour as their carriage drove down the last narrow street to the place where the *Abigail Rose* was docked. Conversation had been practically nonexistent between them on the way, neither of them speaking unless absolutely necessary.

Abigail had expected it to be no different. She kept her gaze focused on the passing houses. She didn't want to concentrate on his hard indifference, the blank determination she could do nothing to change.

The dark circles beneath his eyes were still as prevalent as they'd been the day before, the deep furrows on his forehead just as menacing, and the serious countenance that masked his emotions equally as frightening. Nothing had changed since he'd discovered Mary Rose. He was as closed to her as if a door had been slammed in her face, his stiff aloofness an example of his cold resignation.

She wished she knew what he intended to do.

The carriage slowed to a stop as close to the docks as the driver could take them. Ethan dismounted, then turned to help her down the step.

"Captain Parker knows you are coming and has asked to speak to you before he departs."

"I would like that," she said, taking his proffered arm and walking with him toward the clipper. Fenny stood against the railing, looking down on them as if he'd been waiting. He looked so handsome in his uniform, his broad shoulders and towering height an impressive picture. He was the best friend she'd ever had, and for some reason, she desperately needed a friend right now. He walked toward them, then waited at the top of the gangway.

"Captain Parker," Ethan greeted, first with a salute, then a handshake. "Is everything in order?"

"Yes, Mr. Cambridge. We're ready to sail. We've been waiting for Abigail. I know how much this voyage means to her."

"Thank you, Fenny. I wish you the best of luck." She stood on her tiptoes to kiss him on the cheek.

"Captain Parker," Ethan said, his voice as lacking in emotion as the look in his eyes. "I have some important business I must see to before you leave. I wonder if I might impose upon your hospitality to see to Miss Langdon for a short while?"

"Of course," Fenny said, extending his arm. "I would be delighted."

Abigail cast Ethan a quick glance, but turned away when she couldn't read the meaning in his expression.

"I shouldn't be long," he said. "Then perhaps we can go over the bills of lading, loading dockets, and shipping manifests before you set sail."

"Of course. You'll find them all in order."

Abigail watched as Ethan strode down the walkway. She would be glad when this day was over. There was something wary in the way he kept himself so closed to her, so distant and far removed. Something that made her distrust what he might do. She didn't want to remember him this way.

"Is something wrong, Abigail?" Fenny asked, turning her toward the clipper.

"No, Fenny," she said, fixing a smile on her face she hoped he would think was sincere. "It's just a very emotional day. The maiden voyage of Father's clipper. Your leaving for such a long time."

"And your upcoming marriage to Ethan Cambridge."

Every muscle in her body stiffened. "Did Ethan tell you he intended for us to marry?"

"Yes. The last time you were here."

"I see."

"Are you sure that is what you want to do? You don't have to marry if you don't want. He cannot force you—"

She held up her hand to stop him. She couldn't tell him how much things had changed. "Oh, James," she sighed, touching his arm as if she needed the contact with him. "Things rarely end up the way any of us think they will."

He placed his hand beneath her elbow and led her to the railing where they wouldn't be overheard. "What's wrong, Abby? You haven't called me James since you were twelve and I knotted the ties of your pinafore to the mainmast rigging."

She smiled at him, remembering how carefree they both had been in their youth. She missed such freedom more than she thought possible. "I don't know. I suddenly feel terribly old, and terribly tired."

She hooked her arm through Fenny's, leaning against him as she'd done so many times in the past year.

He put his arm around her shoulders to hold her next to him. It would be eight months before he would return. So much could happen in that length of time.

"Ethan knows about Mary Rose."

He held her more securely. "What do you think he'll do?"

"I don't know. I'm afraid he'll fight me for her. She's Stephen's. Even if she is illegitimate, she's the only child they will ever have from him."

"You don't know for sure he's dead," he whispered. "Stephen could still be alive."

She shook her head. "If he were still alive, he would have come back before now."

He turned her to face him. "Leave with me, Abby."

She looked at him in surprise. "I can't leave. There is Mary Rose."

"We'll take her with us."

"We can't."

"Then I'll stay here with you."

She twisted out of his arms. "No. You have to go. We're all counting on you."

"But what about you?"

"I'll be fine. The moment I think I am in danger, I'll get word to you."

"I don't like leaving you, Abby. I don't trust him."

"Ethan?"

"Yes. He's used to getting his way. He's not above using force to get what he wants."

"Don't worry. He'd never harm me," she said, praying it wasn't a lie.

"Do you love him, Abby?"

Abigail didn't answer for a long time. "Sometimes," she said, finally. "When I forget I can't. When I forget he's Stephen's brother and will hate me when he finds out what I've done. When I forget the ships are the only reason he offered to marry me. When I forget I can never let him discover the truth about Mary Rose. Only then. Very stupid of me, isn't it?"

Fenny wrapped his arm around her shoulder again and held her. "Don't do anything until I return. If you are the least hesitant, hold off until I come back."

"Oh, Fenny," she cried, throwing her arms around him and holding tight. "What would I do without you?"

"I only want you to be happy," he said, keeping her close. "You deserve it. You've gone through enough."

"I'm just being maudlin," she said, not wanting to let him go. "Don't pay me any mind. I'm perfectly fine."

"Are you sure?"

"Yes. Don't worry about me. You just concentrate on having a good voyage and coming back to us safe and sound."

"Am I interrupting something?" Ethan's soft, dangerous voice asked from behind them.

Abigail pulled out of Fenny's arms. "I was just wishing Fenny a safe journey."

Ethan's black look shifted to lock with Fenny's. There was a warning in his glare that was obvious.

"I expect you to bring me one of those beautiful hand-painted fans from China that are all the rage," she said, trying to break the tense situation.

"It would be my pleasure," Fenny promised, all the while keeping his gaze locked with Ethan's and his arm wrapped protectively around her shoulders.

With slow deliberateness, he dropped his arms from around her and faced a man he considered his enemy.

"Are you ready to see the records now, Cambridge?"

Ethan didn't answer, but only nodded. "Would you care to join us?" he asked turning to look at her.

Abigail shook her head. "I think I'd like to stay here."

"As you wish," Ethan said. "It shouldn't take us long."

She nodded, then walked to the ship's bow and looked over the edge. The air crackled with an uncomfortable tension as Fenny led the way to the captain's cabin.

The feeling of apprehension and dread became even stronger. She'd let herself care for Ethan far more than she ever should have. That put her at a disadvantage. She felt more vulnerable now than when she only considered him a threat. How naïve she'd been.

How foolish.

Chapter 19

Abigail watched the *Abigail Rose* until it was no longer even a small dot on the horizon. The day was perfect. The sun shone brightly in the sky as a light southeasterly breeze carried the clipper on her maiden voyage out to the Channel that would carry her to the open sea.

She was a magnificent sight riding low in the water with a full cargo, her four towering masts pointed skyward, her sails tucked away, except for the mainsail on the mizzenmast. Fenny wouldn't fly a full set of sail until they reached the open waters.

"The *Abigail Rose* is a beautiful ship," Ethan said, when the royal flag high atop the mainmast slid beneath the horizon. "Your father would have been proud. He showed a great deal of foresight in commissioning her to be built."

She nodded, unable to speak past the lump in her throat.

He raised his arm as if he wanted to touch her, perhaps show her he understood, then paused. His arm dropped back to his side and she stood alone.

"I've seen enough," she managed, feeling a loss from which she knew it would take a great deal of time to recover. "I'm ready to go home now."

"I've some papers I need to go over before we leave. Would you mind coming aboard the *Emerald Gold* while I finish them?"

"Is that your ship?"

"Yes."

At the distant tone in his voice she turned her head to watch him, barely able to ignore the controlled resolve she saw in his eyes. His look was blank, unreadable. What had she expected? He'd discovered one of her secrets—a secret he couldn't live with. And he knew there were more.

She pushed aside any regret and told herself to be content with the way things had worked out. As soon as they were done here, Fallen Oaks would be hers. Mary Rose would be safe.

"I don't mind," she said, putting on a light front. "I'd like to see your ship."

She turned where he led. Everything would be better soon. By this time tomorrow, she'd have Mary Rose in her arms and could concentrate on forgetting everything she'd given up. Mary Rose would be safe. Nothing could ever threaten either of them again.

"Do you mind walking? The *Emerald Gold* is anchored a little ways from here."

"No. I'd enjoy the walk."

They strolled together down the waterfront, the bustle of activity fascinating her as it always did. Small armies of men loaded and unloaded both large and small crates of goods onto every ship they passed. Tall pulleys soared high in the sky, lifting and lowering cargoes too heavy to be loaded by hand.

She felt the touch of his hand against the small of her

back as he steered her through the maze of workers, carefully guiding her out of the path of any danger. Her flesh burned where he brushed against her, tingled with excitement, reminded her she must put a sharper rein on her body's traitorous response.

But resolve be damned, his nearness, plus the cacophony of sound and activity, continued to stir her blood, the commotion going on all around her bringing her to a fever pitch of excitement. She loved being here. She loved everything about the sea.

"Isn't this thrilling?" she said in awe. "Which ship is yours?"

"There she is," he said, pointing ahead.

Abigail's breath caught. "She's beautiful," she whispered, unable to hide her admiration. "You must be very proud of her."

"I am. She's served me well. She's not as fast as a clipper, but she can make the trip from the island to England in respectable time."

He pressed his hand against her back as they walked up the gangplank. The heat of his flesh against her caused a riot of emotions to rage within her. She didn't want his nearness to be so disturbing, but it was. She tried to walk further ahead as they stepped onto a clean, polished deck, but had to stop to stare at his magnificent ship. It was glorious. As perfect and powerful as its owner.

Mac stood at the top, waiting, as if he'd been expecting them.

"Good day, miss," he said, greeting her with that same warm smile that made her feel comfortable each time she saw him. "I watched the *Abigail Rose* set sail. She's a beauty."

"Thank you, Captain. This is quite a day. One I'm sure I'll never forget."

"Right you are, lass," he said.

Ethan stepped forward. "Abigail and I are going below. I've some papers to finish. Is everything in order?"

"Aye, Ethan."

He nodded, then took her arm and ushered her to a double stairway. He indicated they should take the stairs to the left.

"Where do those stairs lead?" she asked, pointing to the stairway to the right.

"To the crews' quarters," he answered. "Mac sleeps there, and any passengers we might carry."

He turned back to the stairs on her left, and she went down the six steps. At the bottom was a short walkway. She saw only one door at the end and knew it was the captain's quarters.

"Is the *Emerald Gold* preparing to set sail soon?" she asked when he opened the door and stepped aside for her to enter.

"Yes. We're loaded with a cargo of grain bound for Lisbon."

"Will you be going with her?"

"Yes."

Abigail felt a sense of regret, but she instantly pushed it aside. She should be relieved that he was leaving. It was torture having him so near. So why did the emptiness that gnawed at the hollow place in her heart ache so much?

She stepped inside the cabin and turned in a slow circle to take in her surroundings. The cabin was Ethan's domain. Every item was his—from the small telescope on the desk to the round globe on a shelf, to the chart-making instruments in a wooden cabinet with wire mesh doors affixed to the wall. This was where Ethan called home.

The room was not overly large. The most prominent piece of furniture was a huge oak desk, cluttered with maps and charts, placed near a large, round opening that let light into the room. Just steps away, his bed was secured to the wall, a bed much larger than most shipboard beds she'd seen before. She could see him lying here at night, the waves gently rocking him while he slept, the warm ocean breeze lulling away his cares, and the stars up above watching over him.

She ran her hand over the quilted spread, then touched the small square shelf that hung beside the bed.

An upright wooden chest stood in the corner. It no doubt contained his clothes. A second chest sat on the floor beside it. The room seemed crowded, yet neat and clean. And inviting.

Abigail envisioned him working late at night on his charts by light of the lamp that hung from chains bolted into the ceiling, and felt a strange tugging deep inside her. She pushed the thought aside. It would do no good to let her imagination run away like this.

She pulled herself back and concentrated on the sounds aboard the ship.

There was a rush of activity above her and the muffled sound of voices issuing orders. The sounds were familiar and brought back vivid memories from the times she sailed with her father. She hadn't realized how much she missed such excitement.

She watched Ethan work, his head bent over some papers, his rapt attention focused on what he was writing. He'd taken off his dark green jacket when she hadn't noticed and hung it over the back of the chair, along with his snow-white cravat. He looked at home, relaxed. Handsome beyond belief. That place low in her stomach gnawed uncomfortably.

She turned her face away from him to study the books on the long shelf in the corner. *The New American Practical Navigator* by Nathaniel Bowditch. Matthew Maury's *Wind and Current Charts*, and his *Sailing Directions*. These were some of the same books her father had cherished, books he said no captain worth his salt would be without.

From there she stepped over to the space on the wall next to the door, which was pinned with at least a half-dozen maps from all over the world. She went from one map to the next, taking note of the many routes Ethan had traced from one destination to the other, the current flows in every part of the ocean, and every port where a ship could dock. They were fascinating in their detail.

"How long will it take the *Emerald Gold* to reach Lisbon?" she asked, trying to locate the city in Portugal.

"Two, three days," he said, working on the papers in front of him.

"I see."

There was a loud thud from up above and a slight shift in the rocking of the ship. She looked up, startled. "Is it always this busy while she's docked?"

"Sometimes," he answered.

She didn't remember any of her father's ships being such a hive of activity until they were just about to set sail.

A shiver raced through her.

"When did you say the *Emerald Gold* was scheduled to set sail?" she asked, listening closer to the noises above her.

"I didn't."

The first wave of apprehension washed over her. Her skin prickled at the back of her neck, while tiny goose bumps rose on her arms.

She paced the room, trying to understand why she suddenly felt nervous. Why she was suddenly afraid. "Are you almost finished, Ethan?"

He didn't look up from his papers. She felt a stronger surge of panic.

She took her first step toward the door. "I believe I'll wait for you up top."

The springs of his swiveling chair creaked as he fairly leaped from it. "No. Please stay here."

He reached the door in two determined strides and inserted a key he'd taken from a nail beside the door. The loud click echoed in the room as the realization of what he'd just done exploded inside her chest.

He moved to the side of the door, his feet braced wide, his arms crossed over his chest. He didn't say anything, but he didn't have to. The look in his eyes told her what she didn't want to know.

Her heart fell to the pit of her stomach. "No," she cried, her voice a piteous moan.

He took a step nearer, towering over her, the serious expression on his face rigid and inflexible. "Sit down, Abby," he said, pointing to the bed.

His resolve was impenetrable, the set of his face harsh and unyielding.

Another wave of panic raced through her, just as the ship moved beneath her feet a second time.

"Ethan?" She shook her head in disbelieving horror. "No!"

She raced to the door, tugging on the handle, desperate to escape. His hands clamped around her shoulders to stop her.

"It's no use, Abigail. You can't leave."

She heard the scream that rose from her throat, just as the ship rocked again, rolling with the gentle sway of the waves as it moved through the water.

She twisted out of his arms and ran to the round porthole. She stood on her tiptoes to see out. The *Emerald Gold* was slowly, cautiously making her way through the maze of docked ships in the harbor and would soon be far away from London.

She felt the air leave her body. Her worst nightmare had suddenly become a reality. He was taking her away from England.

Away from Mary Rose.

Chapter 20

Abigail fought him with all her might, kicking and pummeling him in her attempt to escape. If she could escape from his cabin, she had a chance to get off the ship. They weren't that far from shore yet.

"Stop it, Abigail." He hauled her up against him and held her tight. "Fighting me will do no good."

Tears streamed down her cheeks. Her sobs nearly choked her as she struggled to get away from him. She was frantic to leave, frantic to get back to Fallen Oaks.

"Please," she sobbed. "You can't do this, Ethan. Who will take care of Mary Rose? She's used to me. She'll think she's been abandoned."

"Stop it, Abigail, and listen to me."

"No! It's not too late. Please. Put me in a small boat and let me go. I can make it back by myself. No one needs to go with me."

She struggled harder, her desperation driving her to fight him. Turning quickly, she twisted out of his arms. He grabbed for her, but missed. She looked around, frantic to find a means to escape, then raced over to the desk and grabbed the first object she saw to protect herself from him. A letter opener.

"Stay away from me," she threatened, holding the ivory-handled opener in her hand like a knife. "Open the door, Ethan."

"Or what?"

"Or I'll do whatever I have to do to get out of here."

"Put it down," he warned.

"Stay back! I won't hesitate to use it." Her hand trembled. She'd never been so frightened in all her life. "I won't let you do this. You can't take her away from me!"

A softness flashed in his gaze, the first hint that her pleas had touched him.

"Very well." He reached in the pocket of his breeches and removed the key. "Sit down on the bed."

"No."

"Sit down," he repeated. The tone of his voice issued an uncompromising demand.

With the opener still clutched in her fist, she sat on the edge of the bed.

Ethan walked to the door and put the key in the lock.

She watched with rapt attention as he turned the key and unlocked the door. He opened it just far enough to say something through the opening and turned back to her.

"Ethan, please. You mustn't take me away from Mary Rose. She's just a baby. She'd never understand. Please. Hate me if you must, but please, don't take it out on her. None of this is her fault."

He stared at her without speaking. His masked expression gave her no indication of what he was thinking. The unyielding expression on his face provided no hope.

A soft knock shattered the ominous stillness. He opened the door and stepped aside. Stella stood in the doorway with Mary Rose in her arms. Palmsworth stood behind them.

The air left Abigail's body in a rush and she ran across the room. With a squeal of delight, Mary Rose leaned forward and flung herself into Abigail's out-stretched arms.

Abigail held the babe to her, burying her face against her, smelling the clean baby smell she'd come to love. Her heart pounded in her chest, thudding in frantic rhythm as she struggled to understand why they were here.

"Take the babe back to your cabin," he said to Stella.

Abigail pulled her back. "No. I'll keep her with me."

He flashed her a look that broached no argument. "Her cabin is in the next corridor. You may see her whenever you like, but not now. You'll stay here so we can talk."

Abigail gave the babe over to Stella and watched the door close behind them.

She was alone with Ethan.

"You might as well make yourself comfortable." The tone of his voice was void of emotion. "You can put your cloak and bonnet in the upright chest."

Abigail hesitated, then untied the long satin ribbons of her bonnet and lifted it from her head. Her fingers trembled as she pulled the braided loops over each woven knot that fastened her cape, then dropped it from her shoulders.

On legs that were weak and unsteady, she walked to the wardrobe and opened the doors. Her breath caught in her throat. The dresses hanging there were hers.

She spun around to challenge him. He'd planned this down to the last detail, down to the clothes she would wear. How could she not have guessed he might do this? How could she not have seen it coming?

She opened her mouth to fire her accusations at

him, but he turned away from her. With stoic dignity, he walked across the cabin to the round porthole. He stood with both hands braced on either side of the glassed opening. The bulging muscles across his shoulders and back stretched taut the fabric of his white lawn shirt. For a long time, he did not move.

Her mind spun in dizzying circles. How could she have been so foolish as to trust him? Why was she so blind to his faults?

He was no different from Stephen. Even though he'd claimed they were not cut from the same cloth, now she knew otherwise.

He lifted his head. With a heavy sigh, he dropped his arms and turned to face her. "Have you calmed?"

"Where are you taking us?"

"Nowhere in particular. The *Emerald Gold* is scheduled to deliver cargo to Lisbon, then return with a full cargo. We're simply passengers."

"Why?"

His lips curled upward in a grin she couldn't even pretend resembled a smile. "You gave me little choice."

She took a step toward him. "I didn't ask you to kidnap us," she said, not bothering to keep the anger from her voice. "The only choice I expect you to make is to turn this ship around and take us back. You promised you would give me the deed to Fallen Oaks in exchange for the *Abigail Rose*."

"It's yours. There's a copy of the agreement on the desk."

"Then take me home."

He shook his head. "I'm afraid that's no longer a possibility."

"Why?"

When he spoke, she heard just the slightest tinge of regret mixed with his blatant resolve. "Because I didn't know about Mary Rose when I made that promise. I refuse to condemn Stephen's child to a life in a convent."

"You are not condemning her. She's loved and cared for and cherished there."

"You've shut her away."

"To protect her."

"To keep her there as if she does not exist."

"What would you have me do? Take her to London and expose her? Ride with her through Hyde Park as part of the five o'clock procession to show the *ton* what Stephen left behind?"

Her words stopped him. For several seconds he said nothing. When he did, his voice seemed more concilia- tory. It didn't last long.

"How long did you think you could keep her locked away? How long do you think she would have been content cloistered behind those stone walls with the sisters? Five years? Ten? Thirty? What kind of future would she have to look forward to after that?"

"Stop it. You have nothing to say in this. You're not responsible for us."

"That's not so."

His words struck her like a blow, taking the wind from her lungs. "Don't you dare think you have a right to Mary Rose. You have no claim on either of us. She's not yours."

"I know. She's Stephen's. But Stephen is not here to care for her."

"So you're going to take his place?" She stared at him in disbelief.

"I won't turn my back on her. Cambridge blood flows through her." He slashed his hand through the air, then walked to the desk. "I won't let you imprison Stephen's daughter in a convent until she's so timid and mousy she's left with no choice but to take her vows and stay hidden behind the convent walls."

"Ethan, listen to me. It won't be like that. She'll never lack for anything. I'll give her everything she needs."

"How?" Fury raged in his eyes. The muscles at the sides of his jaw clenched in anger. "By locking yourself away at Fallen Oaks? By condemning yourself to a future as empty as the life you'll give your daughter?"

"If that's what it takes! What chance does she have if Society finds out about her?"

"So you prefer to have everyone think you are so distraught over Stephen's absence that you can't bear to enter Society again."

She blanched.

"Or are you?"

She didn't like the look on his face. "Stephen has nothing to do with this."

His laugh indicated he was incredulous at her statement. "I wish Stephen would be the innocent one in all of this. But he's not." He looked at her for a long moment. "Don't you realize your plan to give up your father's ships in exchange for Fallen Oaks would have left you destitute?"

"I'd have survived. I'd have done whatever it took to provide for Mary Rose."

"Including prostituting yourself to do it."

She felt as if she'd been slapped. She remembered her offer and wanted to turn her face away from him in shame. Instead, she lifted her chin and glared at him. "Yes. Even that."

"Perhaps in the end that is what it will take."

She paused. She was afraid where this was taking her. "What do you mean by that? What are you going to do?"

"Exactly what I planned to do all along. I'm going to

make you my wife."

The air left her lungs. Surely he wasn't serious? She shook her head. "No."

"Captain MacDonnell will perform the ceremony. Don't worry. He has the authority. Our marriage will be legal and binding. I've brought the papers to prove it."

"I can't marry you."

"You have little choice in the matter, Abigail. I've Mary Rose now. If you want to be a part of her life, you'll become my wife."

She reached for the corner of the wardrobe. How could she marry a man who would hate her when he found out what she'd done? Marrying him would only be the start of her problems. At least now she had a claim to Mary Rose. Once they married, he'd find out her claim to Stephen's child was no more binding than his.

"Why are you doing this?"

"Don't you think I care enough for you to want to marry you?"

She wanted to laugh. Of course he didn't care for her. Just like Stephen had not cared for her, but had only wanted her for her dowry.

"No. I don't think you care for me. You care for the precious Burnhaven dynasty Stephen nearly lost, and will do anything to protect it from scandal and ruin. You care for Stephen and will do the same as you have done your whole life. The only action your conscience allows you to do."

"And what is that?" He lifted his dark brows as if daring her to come up with a believable answer.

"Protect Stephen from himself. Protect him with a blind loyalty that allows him to continue his careless, irresponsible behavior. Allow him to become more dependent on you. Protect him from losing everything your father and his father before him worked to pass down to him. You can't abide watching him answer for the mistakes he made, or be accountable for his own errors in judgment, or take responsibility for the reprehensible lifestyle he lived.

"You're not even close."

"Then, pray tell, why would you consider marrying me?"

"Because I want Mary Rose. I want to give her all the things you can't. I want her to have a real family and not the dismal existence you would force on her. And I want your ships. Marriage is still the only way to be assured I'll keep them. And—"

He stopped, the midnight blue of his eyes nearly black with intent, warning her how dangerous he could be. "And I want you."

She stared at him, unable to believe she'd heard him right. He couldn't want her. He did not know what she'd done.

"No, you don't."

His lips curved upward in a painful smile. "Why, Abby? Why do you think I can't want you? What is it you think you've done that is so heinous it can't be forgiven? Mary Rose?" He held out his hands, his palms upward. "That makes no difference."

"You don't understand."

"What? Another secret you're keeping from me?"

"Yes."

"Then tell me. Let me help you. Share your secrets so they can no longer come between us."

She shook her head. "This can't be fixed."

He turned to the door, as if her concerns were inconsequential. "Then we'll marry and fix it later."

She fought past the painful vice tightening inside her

breast. "And if I refuse?"

"You will lose Mary Rose."

She couldn't believe he'd threaten her like this.

"You may leave the ship at any time. I'll drop you at the nearest port the moment you say you want to leave. You may go with my blessing, and Mary Rose and I will sail on without you." He smiled. "But if you leave, I promise you'll never see her again."

"You can't mean that."

"Oh, but I do. The child stays with me."

Her blood ran cold. All she'd ever tried to do was protect Mary Rose. Now, she was in greater danger of losing her than ever.

She looked into Ethan's face and searched for a hint of the compassion and caring he'd shown her before. But his hardened look came back to her filled with resolve and resignation. He left her no choice. And he knew it. He knew she'd never leave Mary Rose. He knew she'd never go back without her. He knew in the end he'd get both the child and the ships.

She studied his face. If she saw a hint of gloating, she'd be able to hate him. Instead, she saw only sadness in his eyes. And regret.

She thought hard to find a way to protect herself. The thread connecting her to Mary Rose was so fragile. Marrying Ethan would weaken that thread even more. Then he would discover her deepest secret. The one she could never let him know.

She made one more attempt. "I'll give you—"

"Enough of your bargains, Abby. I have the child. If you want to be a part of her life from this day on, you'll consent to become my wife. The choice is yours."

"Damn you!"

He laughed—a harsh, bitter laugh that seemed inanely hollow. "Yes, Abby. I'm no doubt damned, and you haven't left me with even one way to save myself. From the moment we met, your secrets have been my undoing. Your stubborn independence and self-reliance my Achilles' heel."

"I told you from the start I couldn't marry you."

"You still don't have to." He lifted the corners of his mouth in a mocking grin. "You may leave any time you want."

She leveled every bit of her anger and disappointment against him. "You know you haven't given me a choice."

"But I have. You may leave. But if you stay," he continued, "there will be no more secrets. Do you hear me? None."

Gnarled fingers of dread clamped around her heart. How could she promise him that? Marriage to him would reveal an even bigger secret. The secret she'd guarded as carefully as she'd guarded Mary Rose.

"What have you decided? Shall we marry? Or should I issue orders for Mac to dock at the next port?"

Every nightmare she'd ever had flashed before her, suffocating her, stealing the breath from her body. What choice did she have? She could never give up Mary Rose. She could never go back to England alone.

Ignoring the lead weight that pressed painfully against her heart, she turned to him as if she were not alone and unsure and terrified, but as if she had a legion of soldiers at her back to validate her demand. "If it's my ships you want, they are yours. I'll marry you."

He had no reaction, as if he'd known all along that would be her answer.

"But I'll never be your wife."

A slow, sardonic smile lifted the corners of his mouth. "You refuse to offer me the body Stephen so freely enjoyed?"

Her cheeks burned with fiery heat. "If you choose to bed me, it will be by force."

"Then you have nothing to fear, Abigail. I've never had to force a woman to open her arms for me in the past, and I don't intend to begin the practice with my own wife."

Abigail turned her head, unable to battle the harshness she saw in his eyes. She wanted to scream out her renunciation, to tell him she hadn't meant her words, but it was too late. The damage was already done.

He lifted his shoulders and walked away from her. "We'll be married as soon as you change your gown," he said through clenched teeth.

She ignored his anger. She'd expected as much. She couldn't, however, ignore the hurt she'd caused. Never in her life had she intentionally set out to be cruel. She suddenly couldn't stand up beneath the guilt or the self-loathing. She reached for the corner of the bed to hold her steady.

"Your clothes are there," he said pointing to the two chests. "Choose something for your wedding that isn't black."

She searched for something to say that would make things better, but his outstretched hand stopped her.

"To you this may not be a joyous occasion, but you do not have to announce to the world how distasteful you find taking my name."

She stiffened beneath his latest assault. "I'll have Stella help me and will have all my clothes moved into the cabin with her and Mary Rose."

"You'll stay here. This is our room."

Her eyes opened wide as she glanced at the bed against the wall. "But there is only one bed. You said—"

"I said I'd not touch you, and I won't."

"You can't expect us to—"

"You've demanded enough for today." He threw open the door. "I'll send for you in an hour." The door slammed behind him.

She sat down on the bed, her head throbbing and her eyes burning with unshed tears. It was too late to feel anything now other than a hurt more painful than she ever thought she'd have to endure.

How dare he kidnap her and force her to marry him. How dare he take Mary Rose from the convent and spirit them both away. How dare he tell her he cared for her. Didn't he know what torture that would be for her? Couldn't he tell she cared for him, too, and that she would die a little each day when she had to bury her feelings?

Damn him for everything he'd done and for expecting her to dutifully obey his every command. She should have known to be wary of him when he'd first come to the house demanding she give him what belonged to Stephen. When he'd purchased the deed to Fallen Oaks. When he'd forced her to accept his offer of marriage. She should have known not to trust him.

But then he'd kissed her, and all reason had left her. And marrying him would only have made things worse.

She dropped her head to her hands and wept.

Chapter 21

Abigail stood at the railing on the deck of the *Emerald Gold*, waiting to begin the ceremony that would wed her to a man she was a fool to marry. It was the first time in over a year she'd worn anything but black, and even though the light-blue satin gown was slightly out of fashion, it was soft and feminine and made her feel special.

The fact that it had never been worn before somehow seemed important for her wedding.

The bodice was moderately low and square-cut, edged in gathered lace and trimmed with the daintiest clusters of blue embroidered flowers adorned with pearls. The full skirt had an inverted V-shaped inset of ivory satin that started at a narrow point at the waist and tented to a wide opening down the front of the gown. Yards and yards of ivory lace strips crowded atop each other in cascading tiers of ruffles. She smoothed her hands over the elegant fabric, the softness of the color almost succeeding in lightening her day.

"You make a beautiful bride," Ethan said from behind her. His soft voice sounded almost amicable, as if he wanted to reassure her what was happening was for the best.

Abigail turned her head to give him a look that showed him how much she disagreed. Her heart leaped to her throat. No one had a right to be so handsome, especially the man she'd ignore for the rest of her life.

She swallowed hard, then turned back to stare at the endless expanse of water in front of her. She tried to convince herself she could survive this. She told herself that as long as the marriage wasn't consummated, it could be annulled. She told herself that it wouldn't be that long before they returned to London. She tried to convince herself that she could avoid him for that long. If only he wouldn't hold her. If only he wouldn't kiss her.

He stood next to her and braced his hands against the railing. He looked out over the water with her. She imagined he couldn't concentrate on the gently rolling waves any more than she could.

"Stella has gone to bring Mary Rose up from below. I thought perhaps you'd want her to be with you. As soon as she arrives, we'll begin."

Abigail ignored her trepidation and took another deep breath. "If we didn't marry—"

"You would never see Mary Rose again."

She breathed a deep sigh and lowered her head. Was there nothing she could do to stop this from happening? His next words stopped her cold.

"Even if Stephen were to come back tomorrow, he wouldn't marry you, Abby."

She flashed him a look of disbelief. "You think that is why I don't want to marry you? Because I'm waiting for Stephen to come back?"

She couldn't stop an unnatural laughter from escaping. "I wouldn't marry Stephen if he came with the

Queen herself to plead his cause."

"Then why? Why is it so difficult to marry me?"

"That is not really the question, sir. The question is why do you want to marry me, knowing I'll never be a wife to you."

He smiled. "Because I've the patience to wait for you to change your mind. Never is a very long time. At sea, even the most novice seaman knows how drastically lives can change with the next passing storm cloud. We have all learned not to make threats or promises we aren't sure we can keep."

"But I'm sure."

"So you've said."

Every muscle in her body stiffened. "Will you make me one promise then?"

"If I can," he said, his voice containing a hint of wariness.

"Will you promise you will care for her as if she were your own and never threaten to take her away from me again?"

Ethan looked at her in wide-eyed astonishment. "Why are you afraid I'll want to take her away? You are her mother."

The air left her body.

He stepped closer to her, as if he could sense how concerned she was. "I'll make you this promise, Abby." He placed his hand over hers. "I promise there will always be a place for Mary Rose in the home you and I make together, and I promise to love her as my very own."

His words were meant to reassure her, but he didn't understand. He would never understand. The truth would only tear them apart.

She turned away from him, and her gaze locked with Captain MacDonnell's. He stood in the center of the deck with a small black leather book in his hands. Stella stood nearby with Mary Rose in her arms and Palmsworth at her side.

Several of the crewmen of the *Emerald Gold* stood in a semicircle, the smiling grins on their faces evidence enough that they thought this a perfect match for their captain. She wondered how they'd feel when they found out their captain had married a murderer.

Ethan held out his arm and led her forward. Abby looked at Mary Rose when they passed her. The babe, usually bashful and shy around anyone she didn't know, sat in Stella's arms as alert and interested in what was going on as everyone else. The tyke focused on Ethan, as if she would leap into his arms if he'd hold them out to her.

What she saw made her angry. She wouldn't let Mary Rose become attached to him. He offered them a life neither of them could have.

"I'll never forgive you for this," she whispered softly enough so no one heard her but him.

He turned and skimmed the back of his fingers down her cheek. "Yes, you will."

A riot of shivers raced through her. She struggled to hold on to her anger so she would never forget what he'd done to her.

Mac began the ceremony, saying the words every girl dreams of hearing from the moment she's old enough to suffer her first bout of lovesickness. They were words Abigail dreaded hearing.

"Do you take this man to be your lawfully wedded husband? To..."

She glanced over her shoulder to look at Mary Rose. The child's chubby arms reached forward for Abigail to hold her. Her laughing eyes were keen to everything happening around her. Her garbled sounds were the beginning of what would soon be words.

Mac had reached the part in the ceremony where she'd have to say her vows. The blood thundered in her head. Her heart pounded in her chest. She wanted to scream her refusal but couldn't take the chance Ethan would make good his threat to abandon her at the nearest port and take Mary Rose away with him.

In the end, she'd no choice but to take a deep breath and answer, "I do."

Mac repeated the words and Ethan answered with the same. "I do."

After an appropriate length of anticipation, she heard Mac say the words, "I now pronounce you man and wife."

It was too late. She was Mrs. Ethan Cambridge.

She looked down at the ring Ethan had placed on her finger, then up when Mac gave Ethan permission to kiss his bride.

She knew he intended to kiss her before he placed his finger beneath her chin and tilted her head upward. Before he smiled a satisfied grin and lowered his head. Before he covered her mouth with his.

She prayed for a chaste kiss, but knew he wouldn't oblige. She knew he would take this opportunity to show her what he intended for their marriage.

She wanted to break off the kiss, but he wouldn't let her. He wrapped his arms around her shoulders and held her tight.

The kiss was deep and possessive and hungry, his lips soft and warm and inviting. He kissed her like he had the other times. Until she could no longer think. Until she was powerless to do anything but lean into him and answer his demands with challenges of her own. Until she never wanted him to stop.

She couldn't do that now. Allowing him to kiss her

that way would be the biggest mistake she could make. She turned her head and broke the kiss amidst the raucous shouts and cheers of the sailors aboard the *Emerald Gold.*

Her cheeks burned fiery hot when he turned her around to face his still-cheering crewmen.

The noise startled Mary Rose. She wrinkled up her face with a look of fright, ready to cry, but before she could utter the first whimper, Ethan reached out and took her in his arms. Her fussing stopped.

He stood before the crew, holding Mary Rose in one arm and clasping the other around his wife's shoulder. The crew gave several more hearty cheers, then one by one went back to their duties. Mac held out his hand to offer his congratulations, as did Stella and Palmsworth. Then they, too, walked away: And she was left alone.

Alone with a baby who wasn't hers and a husband who never could be.

. . .

Ethan leaned back against his chair and watched her sleep. She was in bed now, where he'd put her. But that wasn't where he'd found her when he'd walked into his cabin long after he was certain she should be asleep. He'd found her curled in a tight ball atop a makeshift bed of blankets she'd placed on the floor beneath the porthole. It was almost as if she couldn't force herself to climb into his bed for fear he might find her there and think her presence was an invitation for him to join her.

The light from a full moon shone through the opening, casting her delicate features in opalescent splendor. He let his vivid imagination—and his eyes—roam.

Every detail of her face seemed even more perfect than before—the noble rise of her high cheekbones, the slight tilt of her nose, the lush fullness of her lips. He couldn't believe it was possible for one person to be so beautiful.

He remembered kissing her after Mac had pronounced them husband and wife. The look in her eyes had begged him not to, but he couldn't stop himself. He wanted to hold her in his arms and feel her lips beneath his. He wanted to unleash the passion she thought she could deny and prove she was not immune to his kisses. And he had. He'd felt her answer his kisses with a desire almost too powerful to restrain. She was a wealth of untapped emotions waiting to be released.

She breathed a deep sigh, then turned her head to the side. Even though she slept, her rest was not peaceful. He'd been afraid it wouldn't be. Much had happened to her today. If ever there was a time when her nightmares might return, he knew it would be tonight. He didn't want her to be alone.

He felt a twinge of guilt at what he'd done: deceiving her, then kidnapping her, then forcing her to marry him. But he'd had no choice. Stephen wouldn't come back to her. Harper's letter confirmed that. Stephen was as irresponsible today as he'd been nearly two years ago when he'd abandoned her. He couldn't let her live a secluded life waiting for Stephen to come back to her, without anyone to watch over her. Without anyone to love her. He cared for her too much to let that happen.

His heart shifted in his chest. He didn't know when it had happened, but he didn't want to spend the rest of his life without her. He was sure that in time she'd come to feel the same.

If she could bring herself to forget Stephen.

Her sleep became more restless. A frown deepened across her forehead. Deep worry lines stretched over the flat line of her brows. She tossed her head from side to side as she clutched handfuls of the quilted counterpane in her fists. He walked to the bed and sat beside her.

A soft moan echoed in the silence, then a whimper, and finally a cry.

"Abby, wake up." He brushed the coppery hair from her face. "You're dreaming. It's only a dream."

"Oh, no. Please. Don't. Please, don't."

"It's all right. Everything is all right."

"Papa, no! Oh, Stephen!"

She tossed her head from one side to the other. She slashed her fists through the air as if battling a legion of demons. Each breath was an agonizing gasp for air. A light sheen of perspiration skimmed her face as she fought to breathe.

Ethan clasped her shoulders and lifted her to him just as a heart-wrenching sob escaped her lips. "It's all right, Abby," he whispered, holding her close. "You're safe now. Nothing can harm you."

"I didn't mean to do it. I didn't."

He held her in his arms while she struggled with the invisible monsters that haunted her.

"Ethan?"

"Yes, Abby. I'm right here." He knew she was not awake. Not enough to realize he was holding her. She would have pulled away from him if she had.

"I'm sorry. I didn't mean to do it."

"I know you didn't, love."

"I'm so afraid."

"Of what, Abby?"

With a shuddering sigh, she nestled closer and fell back asleep.

He held her a little longer, until he was sure she wouldn't wake again, then laid her down and pulled the covers under her chin. There were still secrets that separated them. Secrets that acted as barriers to keep them apart. There was no hope for them until he knew what they were.

. . .

Abigail opened first one eye then the other as she tried to orient herself to her strange surroundings. It was morning. Bright sunlight shone through the window, indicating she'd slept much later than usual. She looked around the room to make sure she was alone. She was.

She wondered where he'd slept.

She stretched her arms over her head and looked at the makeshift bed on the floor. The blanket she'd wrapped around her shoulders lay in a crumpled heap.

She lifted her head off the downy pillow. She glanced about the room. His jacket hung on the back of the chair, his snow-white cravat lay on the desk, and the door to his side of the upright chest where he kept his clothes stood slightly ajar. He'd been here.

She squinted her eyes and held her hand to her forehead. Her head ached just like it did each time she'd had a nightmare. And he'd been here.

As if she was afraid he might return any moment, she thrust the covers back and jumped to her feet. She ran to the basin on the small table behind a screen and washed as quickly as she could, then dressed in her familiar black bombazine. A sudden, frantic need to see Mary Rose overwhelmed her. She didn't know why, but she needed to make sure the child was all right.

Abigail ran a brush through her hair, giving up trying to control the errant coppery tendrils that framed the sides of her face, then knotted the rest in a bun at the nape of her neck. She couldn't explain why she was worried. She'd checked on Mary Rose a final time just before she'd gone to bed and she was fine. Besides, Stella was with her.

Abigail grabbed her cloak as she left the cabin. She ran up the six steps to the lower deck, then around the railing that separated the two stairways, and quickly descended the other six stairs to an adjacent hallway. Three doorways exited off the corridor: the door to Mac's cabin, the door to Palmsworth's, and the door to the cabin Stella and Mary Rose shared.

She threw open the door and searched the room.

"Where is she?" she asked Stella, searching the room for the babe.

"Oh, the captain came to take her for a walk on deck."

"The captain...took her?"

"Yes, miss. He said the air would be good for her." Stella went back to straightening Mary Rose's empty bed. "You should have seen her. Happy as a little lark, she was. Went to the captain as if she'd known him her whole life."

Abigail pivoted out of the room and raced back up the stairs. She made her way across the deck, giving each crewman a quick greeting as she passed them, her gaze continuously searching for Ethan's tall figure. She saw him. He stood at the bow of the ship, holding Mary Rose in his arms.

A knot formed in the pit of her stomach. Mary Rose was wrapped in a warm, thick cover, with only her rosy cheeks exposed to the elements. A snug bonnet covered her head, its satin ribbons tied beneath her chin in such a way that only a few wayward coppery tendrils escaped to frame her face. He held her high, her little cherub face lifted to the sun, one arm reaching out to gather the wind, while the other wound possessively around Ethan's neck.

He wore no hat, his dark, mahogany hair mussed from the breeze. His face was clean-shaven, and he was as handsome as ever. He wore a long navy coat, the bright white of his buttoned shirt and cravat exploding in contrast against his bronzed skin. The unwelcome sensation swirled in the pit of her stomach, a feeling that came all too often when he was near.

She marched up to where he stood with Mary Rose and faced them. "What do you think you're doing?" she demanded, glaring at him with a ferocity that had been building in her since the day before.

"And good morning to you, Mrs. Cambridge. I hope you slept well."

She stared at him, wanting to say she had, when he knew she had not. "Do you want her to catch her death?"

"I doubt you have to worry about that. She's a healthy babe and has a natural love for the sea she must get from her mother."

A sudden strong breeze hit Mary Rose in the face, and she let out a squeal of delight.

"See?" he said as if her excitement proved his point.

Abigail was livid. She shouldn't let him become attached to Mary Rose. She shouldn't allow Mary Rose to become attached to *him*. "I'll take her back now," she said reaching for her.

"I promised her one more turn around the deck. I can hardly disappoint her."

"I don't have time to stroll the deck, Ethan."

"Then do what you have to do, and I'll bring Mary Rose to you when we're finished. Besides, Mary Rose and I need to get better acquainted."

"I don't want you to become better acquainted."

He shot her a hard look she couldn't hold for long.

Mary Rose pressed her tiny fingers against Ethan's cheek, obviously as fascinated by the smooth yet rugged texture of his face as Abigail had been. That cursed place deep in her belly warmed with the heat of molten lava, oozing slowly into every crevice as it pushed its way even lower.

She remembered touching his face, his cheeks, his mouth. She remembered him holding her, kissing her, wanting her. She shivered.

"Are you sure you don't wish to walk with us?" He turned down the collar of her cloak the wind had lifted. His fingers hesitated longer than necessary against her throat, burning her flesh where he touched her.

"I..." She wanted to brush his hand away but couldn't.

"Very well," he said, bouncing Mary Rose in his arms. "Come, Mary Rose. Let's see if we can find any more big fish in the water." He nodded politely, then turned away from his wife.

Abigail fought to stay behind but couldn't.

He walked slowly enough for her to catch up to him in just a few steps. "I'd like the key to my cabin," she said when she reached them.

"No."

"Excuse me?" She came to a halt, then continued when she realized he had no intention of stopping.

"You'll not lock me out of my own cabin, wife."

"But you said—"

"What I said, will be. But not because you have locked the door to keep me out. You'll learn to trust me to keep my word. Someday you'll even trust me with the rest of your secrets."

"Like I was foolish enough to trust you when you said

the deed to Fallen Oaks was mine, free and clear, then kidnapped me and forced me to marry you?"

"The deed is yours. As to the rest, I didn't know about Mary Rose when I made that promise. Your secrets are to blame for that."

He stopped and turned toward the sea. "Look, Mary Rose. See the fish?"

Mary Rose turned to where he pointed and made a loud squeal when she saw a school of large fish leaping out of the water as they swam alongside the *Emerald Gold*.

"Look at them, Abby." He shifted Mary Rose to the other arm, then wrapped his arm around her shoulders.

The warmth of his arm around her burned a path to her fingertips. Gooseflesh rose at the back of her neck. *Damn him!* She wouldn't let him do this to her. She stepped away from him.

He laughed, the sound of it deep and rich and filled with more understanding than she wanted to hear. "Do you know what, Mary Rose? Your mama is going to find sailing with us very uncomfortable for the next several weeks." He reached up and fingered a curl that fell against Abigail's face. "We will both have to be very patient with her until we return to London."

Abigail jerked her head out of his reach, then took Mary Rose from his arms and stepped back. "It's time for her nap. I'll not let you spoil her, Ethan."

"You can't run away, Abby. There's nowhere for you to hide aboard a ship. No place far enough to escape me."

She didn't dignify his statement with an answer, but held Mary Rose close to her and walked away.

He was right. The *Emerald Gold* was not large enough for her to hide from him.

The whole Atlantic Ocean was not large enough.

Chapter 22

Ethan had been right. There was no place she could hide from him.

No matter how early Abigail rose in the morning, Ethan already had Mary Rose up on deck to watch the sun rise. At midday, they strolled the length of the ship to "strengthen her sea legs" and watch the clouds roll by above them or the fish swim beside them. In the evening, he'd take her to the forecastle deck to watch the sun set. Ethan would stand with his long, muscular legs braced wide and Mary Rose in his arms. Her chubby arms would be wrapped securely around his neck, or her rosy cheeks pressed beneath his chin.

Abigail's chest tightened painfully each time she found them like that.

She tried to keep them apart, making excuses why Mary Rose needed to go below: she needed to take an early nap, she hadn't eaten enough at her last meal and needed to be fed again, she'd gotten dirty and needed clean clothes, one of the crewmen had made her a new toy and she wanted to play with it, she was getting too much fresh air, she wasn't getting enough rest, she was getting too much. The list was endless, and by the end of the week, the excuses were so lame even Abigail couldn't believe them.

"What is it today, Abby?" Ethan said when he saw her coming toward them. "It can't be too much sunlight. The day's more cloudy than not. It can't be too much fresh air. That was the excuse yesterday. Perhaps today the water is too wet?"

She glowered at him. A smile brightened his face, then a laugh. He was teasing her again. How could she stay angry with him if he constantly joked with her and never once got upset over anything she did or said?

"I must say, Captain Cambridge, that your *boat* seems to be taking its sweet time getting to Lisbon," she groused.

"Ah, you noticed," he grinned. "It seems our spate of fair weather has given our...*boat*...no reason to make haste." He played with Mary Rose's fingers as he spoke. "You don't mind that, do you, little one?"

Mary Rose gurgled and Abigail huffed.

"I thought you had a ship to captain, Captain Cambridge."

"I'm a passenger this trip," he answered, shifting Mary Rose to his other arm. "Mac is doing all the work. That leaves me endless time to get acquainted with Pud."

"Her name is not—"

He held Mary Rose out in front of him so she was eye level with him. "Have you noticed the black cloud that seems to follow your mama wherever she goes, Pud? If we can't get her to smile pretty soon, I'm afraid her face is going to freeze like that."

As if he'd held a baby his whole life, he lifted Mary Rose high above him, then brought her back down, causing her to giggle with glee.

"I don't have a black cloud following me, and don't call her Pud."

"Why not? That's what she is. A little pud of a thing, but she's quick. Listen, Abby."

Ethan sat the babe in the crook of his arm, then pointed a finger back at her. "Who's this?" he asked her.

"Pud," she answered, the word a garbled sound that could have passed for anything.

"See," he said with a grin that lit his face. "She knows her name. Now, who's this?" He pointed a finger at Abigail. "Who's this, Pud?"

"Bee!"

Abigail's heart swelled. "She's trying to say Abby," she said past the lump in her throat.

"No, Pud." Ethan pointed his finger at Abigail. "Mama. This is Mama."

Mary Rose repeated *Mama* so clearly no one could misunderstand her.

Abigail froze. "Sir, you will not presume to teach her that. She can never call me that."

Abigail lost the little composure she had. For nearly a week she'd avoided him as much as she could, staying out of his way during the day, then lying awake half the night, afraid he might come to her bed. Afraid she couldn't turn him away if he did.

She'd watched him steal Mary Rose's heart, then watched the bond that connected them grow stronger every day.

She had to stop him. The closer she let him get to either one of them, the harder it would be to forget him once they left. If he wanted a family, let him find another one. They could never be his family. Damn him for thinking they could.

"Do not dare to teach her that," she repeated.

"Mary Rose will know you are her mother. She will not grow up thinking we are ashamed of her."

"And what have you taught her to call you? Papa?"

The air bristled between them.

"No. I wish she could, but I'm not her father." He turned Mary Rose in his arms. "Who am I, Pud?" He pointed his finger at himself. "Who am I?"

"Cat," she answered with another grin on her face. "Cat."

"She's trying to say *captain*. She'll know Stephen is her father and you are her mother. And I am your husband. If she is satisfied calling me Captain, then I am, too."

Tears of anger and pain swelled in her eyes and threatened to spill down her cheeks. "You think you have everything figured out, don't you? Well, you don't."

"I've nothing figured out, Abby. You've kept too many secrets for me to know anything for sure. Tell me," he said, turning to step directly in front of her. "How old is Mary Rose?"

Inwardly, she pulled back. "A little under a year."

"How much under a year?"

"Three weeks."

"Then she was born the month your mother died," he said, the questioning frown on his face chilling the blood flowing through her.

She turned away from him.

"You lost your mother and had a baby. That must have been a very difficult time for you."

"Don't," she whispered.

"Is that what your father meant when he wrote he needed to atone for his greatest sin? Was he forcing you to give up Mary Rose?"

"Don't you dare judge him," she said, flashing him an angry glare she couldn't soften. "You have no idea what it was like for him. For any of us."

"No, I don't." He pulled the blanket up tighter around Mary Rose's shoulders. "How much of this tragedy do you lay at Stephen's door?"

Harsh fingers wrapped around her heart and squeezed. *All of it*, her mind wanted to scream. Instead, she turned her head and focused on the waves churning beyond them.

"We'll arrive in Lisbon tomorrow. We'll only spend the night in port, then return the following day, so we won't have time to see the sights."

"And then what?"

"Then we'll go to Fallen Oaks for a while, until I can make sure everything will run smoothly when we leave."

"And then?"

"Then you and I will take Mary Rose to Windswept Manor."

Fear rang in her ears. He intended to take her away. Away from where she'd be safe. Her mind reeled in confusion. Safe was with him, wherever he was, wasn't it? But that couldn't be. She couldn't face that.

She needed to escape. Needed to go where his dominance wouldn't consume her. "It's late. Mary Rose needs to go below now." She reached for Mary Rose, but he held the babe and didn't hand her over.

The look in his eyes turned dark and serious, and before she could stop him, he reached out and touched her cheek with the back of his fingers. "I'm not like Stephen, Abby. I'll never leave you like he did."

She wanted to tell him it wouldn't matter, because he wouldn't want her, either. Not after he found out the truth.

. . .

Ethan couldn't sleep. He couldn't forget what Abigail had said. He tried not to concentrate on how alone and frightened she must have been. How much she must have loved Stephen to give herself to him so young, then be betrayed by him and abandoned.

He rose from the bed in the storage compartment that had become his room. The bed was too short, the room too small, the light abysmal, but it was near Mary Rose's cabin. He could go to her anytime, night or day. Take her to see the sun rise the moment he heard her wake. Step in to watch her after she'd gone to sleep.

She never ceased to amaze him, never ceased to capture his heart with her ready smile, her happy giggles, her open arms that reached out to him. Everything about her was perfect.

He hadn't intended to become so attached to her, or let her become attached to him. He'd only paid attention to her at first as an excuse to be near Abby. But that changed the minute he held her. Now, he waited for her to wake up, or finish eating, or take her nap, so he could show her something new: the waves dancing on the ocean, the fish swimming beside the ship, the breeze pushing the *Emerald Gold* through the water.

For every wondrous experience he wanted to share with Mary Rose, Abigail invented a reason he couldn't. She also invented another reason she couldn't be around him.

A wave of frustration washed over him. He'd given her enough time, more than he thought it would take for her to accept their marriage. More than he thought it would take for her to come to him.

The whole ship knew something was not right between them. The tension was so electrifying that the night sky nearly lit up whenever they happened to be near each other. It took almost more self-control than he had left to keep from taking her in his arms and kissing her whenever she was near. Almost more self-restraint than he had left to keep from going to her at night and making her his wife.

He rubbed a palm along his stubbled jaw. Every minute away from her was torture. If he closed his eyes and concentrated, he could feel his lips covering hers, her arms wrapped around him, her firm breasts pressed against his naked skin. Just thinking of her caused a stirring deep inside him that wouldn't go away.

He threw the covers back in frustration. He had to walk beneath the moon and stars. Stand where the wind hit his face and whipped through his hair. Out in the wide-open, where he could think. And forget.

He took the stairs two at a time and filled his lungs with a deep breath when he reached the top of the stairway.

Everything was quiet, with two men at the helm and two more standing watch. He walked to the ship's bow, where no one would be at this time of night, and he could be alone without being observed.

The stars shone overhead, the moon full and bright. He took a half-dozen steps and stopped short.

Abigail's unmoving silhouette stood as a shadow against the railing at the bow of the ship.

His eyes drank in every delicate detail.

Her hair hung long and loose, glimmering in the moonlight like shiny strands of copper. She held her back rigid and straight, her slender shoulders curved slightly, as if they struggled beneath the heavy weight of the secrets she still carried. Moonlight outlined her features—the high arch of her cheekbones, the delicate slant of her jaw, the upturned tilt of her nose. She was pure perfection.

"Couldn't you sleep, either?" he asked, keeping his voice low and his tone easy.

He heard her gasp as she spun around. The moon reflected her startled expression.

"No." She clutched her cloak tighter around her shoulders. She wore only a white cotton night-rail beneath her cloak, its dainty lace collar peeking out around her neck. "I think it's the moon. It's too big and bright to ignore. I wanted to watch it for a while." She hesitated. "It's time I went back in."

"Don't go. Stay here with me."

She shook her head and stepped away from him.

He stepped closer, to block her way so she couldn't leave. "Please."

"Oh, Ethan."

He heard her sigh, but she didn't run away from him. Instead, she stepped back to the railing and looked up at the moon and the stars, then out at the water glimmering below them.

"I think we may have a serious romance budding between Stella and Cook," he said. It was the first thing that popped into his head. "Have you noticed?"

Her lips threatened to curve upward, but she stopped herself just before her expression could qualify as a smile. "Yes. Every afternoon when Mary Rose takes her nap, Stella disappears. I discovered she's spending her free time with Cook, but I didn't think too much about it until I noticed her rosy cheeks and the glimmer in her eyes when she returns."

Ethan laughed. "Cook has always had a turn of the tongue as sweet as the fruit tarts he bakes."

"It doesn't hurt that he's tall and handsome and has that smile."

"What smile?" Ethan asked, surprised at the twinge of jealousy that stabbed through him.

"You know. The one he gives Stella each time he sees her. And Mary Rose."

"And you?"

She sought his eyes. "Of course not. You've all but hung a sign around my neck that says the first crewman to acknowledge I'm even on board will get thrown into the sea."

"I have not."

"Yes, you have," she said on a sigh. "But it wouldn't matter. They all know how difficult it is between us and are giving us a wide berth to work things out."

"Is that what it will take?"

She pulled her cloak tighter around her, then gave him her back, as if she wanted to walk away. He reached for her and pulled her back against his chest. A tiny gasp escaped her lips, but she didn't pull away.

"You're not being fair," she whispered, unable to keep her voice from trembling.

"Why? Because you're afraid you might like it?"

She shook her head, but he didn't offer to let her go. He couldn't. He'd dreamed of holding her like this for too long. He'd envisioned having her in his arms, close to him, without Stephen or any more secrets to separate them.

She smelled of rose water and clean night air. He wrapped his arms around her middle, touching her just below her breast, and rested his chin lightly atop her head. She felt good here in his arms. Like she belonged.

"I noticed today how well Palmsworth has adjusted to sea life," he said, pushing her hair off her shoulder to expose her neck. "He had a needle in his hands and was sewing a rip in the canvas. He's still a sailor at heart."

"He's missed the sea," she said. "Every year, Father

gave him the chance to go back, but he always chose to stay with us. I think he knew neither Father nor I could get along without him."

Her voice sounded strange and unsettled, even to her own ear. She ran her fingertips against the shiny rail. They trembled. She looked up to study the moon in the sky, as if the answer to some great question were hidden there.

He couldn't stop himself. He had to touch her silky skin. He had to kiss her.

"You're beautiful, Abby. Beautiful." He lowered his head and kissed her at that special spot just beneath her ear. *Great heaven*, she smelled sweet, tasted so good, felt so wonderful. He couldn't make himself quit. He couldn't get enough of her.

He turned her in his arms and pulled her close, the feel of her breasts pressing against his chest a torture all its own.

The uncertain look in her eyes told him how afraid she was. The desperate look in her eyes told him how eager she was for him to kiss her.

He cupped her cheeks in his palms and tilted her face upward. His thumbs outlined her lips, the gentle lift of her upper lip and the soft fullness of her lower. They were perfect. Enticing. Kissable.

With a slowness he could barely force upon himself, he lowered his head and covered her mouth.

· · ·

Abigail felt his lips touch hers, and every nerve in her body exploded with want and desire. How could she let this happen? How could she give in to him when she knew the danger he posed? How could she want to kiss him when she knew it would lead to something she could never allow?

But she did.

She had wanted to from the time he'd put his arm around her the day of her father's funeral. From the time he'd held her against him and had become her rock and her fortress, her indomitable strength. From the time he'd held her in his arms and kissed her that first time, and showed her what it would be like not to be alone.

She wanted him like she'd never wanted anything in her life.

He tipped her head to the side and covered her mouth with even more desperation than before.

She lifted her hands and pressed her palms against the muscled ridges that spanned his chest. Her mind gave the warning to push him away. Her body ignored it. She'd avoided him for so long she couldn't do it any longer. She needed him to hold her, if only for tonight.

They stood in the open air, his towering presence blanketing her, sheltering her like a safe harbor in a raging storm. Yet, he was the storm, the turmoil she should run as far from as possible. And couldn't.

He ran his fingers through her hair, cupping her head in the palm of his hand, bringing her closer to him. She thought she would die from his touch. She'd dreamed of this for so long.

His lips moved over hers, tasting her, touching her, drinking from her with a fevered frenzy that set her on fire. She couldn't hold him close enough, couldn't give him enough of herself. She wanted him to kiss her and hold her until she forgot the night Stephen had changed her life forever.

For just this little while, she wanted what Ethan could give her. She'd endured so much. First, Stephen's betrayal. Then his death. Then Mary Rose's birth and Father's refusal to claim the child as his own. Then her mother's death. And finally her father's death.

Ethan was the balm to soothe her. The safe harbor to protect her.

His mouth opened slightly, and she parted her lips in anticipation. She wanted to feel him inside her mouth, their halting breaths mingling, then becoming one. His lips pressed hard against hers, his tongue mating with hers, then possessing.

She wrapped her arms around his neck and held him closer. For just this brief moment in time, she would pretend she could have the life she'd always dreamed of having. A life where someone would want her and love her. Where someone would choose her as his own. Not because of her mother's status, not for her legacy of ships nor her father's wealth, but for her and her alone.

"I need you, Abby," he whispered between his kisses. "I have since the moment I first saw you standing alone at your father's grave. I knew I needed you even more than you needed me."

He kissed her deeper, his tongue battling hers for dominance. Her heart raced in her chest and her legs buckled. Every bone in her body was as limp as a sail without a breeze. Her hips pivoted forward, needing to touch him, needing to feel him against her.

He ground his mouth against her once more, then kissed a line from her jaw to that special spot beneath her ear. "Ethan," she whispered, her lips finally free but her voice barely strong enough to be heard.

"Shh, Abby," he said, tilting her head to the side and kissing her neck. "Don't say anything if you're going to tell me to stop. I don't want to stop kissing you. I can't."

He brought his mouth back to hers, kissing her with

such desperation she barely felt her cloak slip from her shoulders. She sighed when his hands clamped around her waist, the thin cotton of her night-rail all that separated her from him.

"Let me make you mine," he whispered. His breathing was harsh and ragged, his chest heaving with the effort it took to take air into his lungs. "Let me make love to you like you deserve."

He brought his mouth down over hers again, pulling her close against him. She could feel the hardness of his body against the flat plane of her stomach. She knew if she didn't stop him now, it would be too late. She would never be able to stop him.

Let me make love to you.

His words washed over her like a splash of cold water. Her body ached for there to be more, but she could never allow it. Once she gave herself to him, it would be too late. He would know her secret.

She brushed her fingertips over the rippling muscles across his shoulders, not wanting to separate herself from him. Every part of her ached to feel his smooth skin beneath her touch, feel his naked flesh pressed against hers, but she couldn't give in to such weakness. If she did, she'd never be strong enough to walk away from him. She'd never survive the look on his face when he realized he'd loved a murderer.

Tonight was as much of herself as she could give him. More than she'd been wise to share with him. The heavy pain in her breast told her how careless she'd been.

She pushed him away from her. What a fool she'd been to think he would be satisfied with just kisses. What a fool she'd been to think her heart could escape unscathed. She hurt as if a knife had been thrust into her breast.

Large tears filled her eyes, threatening to spill down

her cheeks. She vowed he wouldn't see them.

"Ethan, stop."

"Abby, let me take you below. We can't—"

"No. Stop."

Every muscle in his body stiffened. He looked into her eyes, and with a loud moan, he dropped his head back on his shoulders and closed his eyes.

"Bloody hell, woman," he uttered through clenched teeth, his breaths coming in short, jagged gasps.

The black look in his eyes was filled with a vengeful anger she'd only glimpsed in him once before—the day she'd run away from him and Stafford had found them. "I'm sorry," she whispered, her voice sounding cold and heartless, even to her own ears.

"Bloody hell," he repeated, then pushed himself away from her and leaned against the railing. "A damn bullet to the head would have been kinder."

A tear wanted to spill from her eyes, but she busied herself with her gown to hide how much her heart ached. "Don't you dare blame me for what just happened," she said when she could speak. "I was not the one who started this."

"You didn't say no, either."

Her hands shook as she tried to fasten her buttons, the same ones he'd released with such ease. "You knew I'd never let you—" She couldn't say the words. "I warned you the day you forced me to marry you."

He pushed her hands away and fastened the buttons himself, then stooped to pick up her cloak. "You didn't say you would torture me every chance you got. That you wouldn't be satisfied until you nearly killed me, either."

"That's not fair."

"Don't you speak of fair. Nothing you did tonight was fair."

He turned his back to her and braced his arms against the railing of the ship. "Go back to your cabin," he ordered, keeping his focus on something far out at sea.

She searched for something to say that would give her the last word, that would make things better, but there was nothing.

"Go!"

She pulled her cloak tightly about her shoulders and walked away from him. She didn't regret what she'd done tonight. She'd wanted to have him hold her, and kiss her, and touch her. She remembered his mouth on hers, and her knees nearly gave out beneath her.

She knew what she'd allowed had been cruel. But she needed at least this one memory to sustain her after she left. At least this one night to fill her dreams.

Chapter 23

Storm clouds gathered overhead. Dark. Ominous. Threatening. As angry and violent as the storm that brewed inside Ethan since the night he'd kissed Abigail. It had been three days, and his frustration hadn't lessened. They'd docked at Lisbon long enough to unload their cargo and take on the cargo that would go to London, and not once during that time had she spoken to him.

Damn her and her secrets. How could he fight something when he didn't know what it was?

He walked the length of the *Emerald Gold*, feeling the dank uneasiness that always preceded a storm. The sailors busily prepared for what was coming, their gay laughter and rousing sea chanteys now as silent and eerie as a church after the door closes behind the last parishioner. Each man worked at his task, his hands busy preparing for the storm, while at least one watchful eye remained on the darkening horizon behind them.

Ethan climbed the five steps to the helm where Mac stood watching the line of building clouds. Out of habit,

Ethan picked up the compass and the latest page of charts and studied them. After making some calculations of his own, he set the instrument back in the little wooden box where it was stored.

A faint rumble echoed in the distance, a thunderous warning of the force and power bearing down on them. "This is going to be a rough one," Mac said in reverent awe, his voice an acknowledgment of the quiet calm that ushered in a raging storm. "I thought we could outrun it, but that black wall is gaining on us too fast." He clasped his hands behind his back and braced his shoulders and legs in readiness.

"The *Emerald Gold* is a sturdy ship," Ethan said, knowing even the sturdiest of ships were no match for the rampaging forces of nature. He opened the telescope and put the glass to his eye. A shudder raced through his body. The wall of angry black clouds was one the biggest, most threatening storms he'd ever seen.

"I have Abby below with Mary Rose. If something happens and I can't get to them," Ethan said, keeping his eye focused on the building clouds swirling above the horizon, "watch over them for me."

"Nothing is going to happen to you, or any of the rest of us, either."

"Of course not," Ethan agreed, giving Mac a smile he knew wasn't quite believable. "But if something were to go wrong, take her to Windswept Manor and keep her there until she can decide what to do. Maybe eventually she'll come to love it and realize Mary Rose will be better off there than in England."

"Let's just worry about this storm," Mac answered, his voice filled with emotions Ethan knew he couldn't bring himself to put into words.

The rumbling thunder echoed louder, the wind swirling around them in angry circles. Mac's next order brought the seriousness into perspective. "All hands!" he bellowed, cupping his hand around his mouth. "Furl the royals and topgallants, and double-reef the topsails."

A half-dozen sailors climbed the mainmast and made a line that spanned the yardarm, balancing on the narrow rope beneath their feet. Another group climbed the foremast and another the mizzenmast. One by one, they furled the sails as the wind blew even harder, its gusts becoming a steady gale.

Mac lifted his telescope and kept the glass focused on the building clouds racing toward them. A sharp bolt of lightning forked through the darkening sky, the thunder exploding with such ferocity that it seemed to rip the black wall into pieces. With the calm, steady hand of an experienced captain, he handed the instrument back to Ethan, then bellowed his next set of orders.

"Furl the topsails and close-reef the mainsails. Batten down!"

Men scattered to follow their captain's orders as the wind whipped around them and the rain slapped against their faces. The *Emerald Gold* pitched, then heaved with a great shudder as the first angry wave slammed against her. "Take the wheel, Ethan. Keep her course steady and straight. The sea is littered with tiny islands starboard side. We have to avoid the rocks."

They shared the confident look of two friends who had risked their lives before, but for Ethan, it had been easier then. He hadn't had Abby to worry about, or the responsibility of taking care of Mary Rose.

He took the steps to the wheelhouse and clasped his hands on the spokes of the wheel. Fighting an impending fear he refused to acknowledge, he braced his body to face the elements.

The wind increased to a howling gale. Huge, cold drops of rain pummeled the deck with a harsh splattering. Ethan knew the sea at its most violent was unstoppable. His heart raced as it always did when he had to bow to the elements. He thought of Abby and how he wanted to go to her, to hold her, and kiss her, and tell her everything would be all right.

With an angry roar, the wind slammed into them. Huge waves slapped against the side of the ship with a ferocity that caused the mighty *Emerald Gold* to buck sideways.

Ethan saw the wall of water bearing down on them and issued a prayer. "God help us," he whispered.

He lowered his head as the wind dashed the stinging rain against his face. He braced his legs wide, his physical stance in readiness for the ensuing battle. Insignificant man against a raging force so much more powerful. He knew the odds for survival. He thought of Abby again.

The muscles across his back and shoulders and down his arms screamed in pain. With unyielding tenacity, he held the ship steady as the next monstrous wave exploded over the deck.

· · ·

It had been hours. Hours that dragged by with such agonizing slowness she thought time had come to a halt, suspending them in this terrifying nightmare, refusing to let them escape.

Every muscle in her body ached from cradling Mary Rose close to her to keep her safe. With unrelenting fury, the angry storm tossed the *Emerald Gold* from side to side as if it were a toy, pitching her one way, then the other.

Even huddled in the corner, she felt no protection against the howling wind and violent waves. Each new assault slammed her against the wall, battering and bruising her arms and shoulders and hips.

She'd been through storms before with her father, but never anything of this magnitude. Never anything this violent. She thought of Ethan facing the elements, risking his life. She didn't want to think that something might happen to him.

Abigail brushed the coppery curls from Mary Rose's sleeping face and fought the fear that made her heart pound in her breast. The *Emerald Gold* shuddered and groaned, then threatened to break apart with each new wave that slammed against her. Yet Mary Rose slept on. She didn't know to fear the forces of nature. She trusted that the people around her would protect her and keep her safe.

A shadowy darkness enveloped the cabin, with only one small candle in an anchored bucket of gravel lit for fear any more might start a fire. The lack of light seemed suffocating. The only relief against its oppression was the frequent and blinding lightning that illuminated the room in brief flashes.

She thought of Ethan up above, fighting the raging winds, tired and losing strength. A painful ache clenched inside her breast. "Please, God. Please keep him safe," she prayed silently. "Please, don't make me live my life without him."

Before she'd uttered her silent amen, a deafening thud from up on deck shattered through the howling winds like an explosion. The ship trembled and groaned. Abigail's heart leaped to her throat. Mary Rose woke and stirred restlessly. "Shh, sweetling," she said, comforting Mary Rose in a voice much calmer than how she felt.

Another violent wave slammed into the *Emerald Gold*, then another in an explosive crash that rocked the shuddering ship. Abigail knew they'd lost one of their masts and said a quick prayer that the ship would hold together.

She'd heard of ships going down in storms. Heard of entire crews being lost. Heard of men being washed overboard. What if a wave crashed over the deck of the *Emerald Gold* and hurled Ethan into the churning sea? She swiped a tear from her eyes.

She wasn't sure she could survive if something happened to him. Every minute since she'd walked away from his kiss had been pure torture. She wanted him to hold her, and touch her, and kiss her again. She wanted to wrap her arms around him and be all the things he wanted in a wife. All the things she'd been so foolish to deny she could be to him.

She loved him. What if she never got the chance to tell him how she felt? She closed her eyes and pictured his face: his mahogany hair and midnight blue eyes. His high cheekbones and the rigid cut of his jaw. The strength of his muscled arms and the gentleness of his touch. His easy laughter and the—

Without warning the door swung open and Ethan burst into the cabin. She had to hold herself from rushing to him.

"Are you all right?" he asked, his chest heaving. She knew it had been a struggle to get to her.

"Yes. Are you?"

The faint curve of his lips belied the worry she saw on his face. There was a dark bruise on his right cheekbone and a deep gash above his left eyebrow. Steady rivulets of rain ran down his face, and his clothes clung to every part of his body. He'd never looked more desirable.

"I'm fine."

"I heard the crash. How bad is it?"

"There's nothing to worry about, Abby. Everything's fine."

"How bad is it?" she repeated.

Ethan breathed a deep sigh, then shook his head. "We lost the fore and main topgallant masts, and the main topsail yard."

"Are we taking on water?"

"No."

"Then we'll be all right."

She said the words even though she knew they weren't true. She knew it was only a matter of time until the wind and the waves would do more damage. She'd heard stories of ships that had been safe and sound one minute, and rubble at the bottom of the sea the next.

Ethan looked around the cabin. "Your father taught you well," he said, nodding toward the small anchored table beside the bed she'd covered with a blanket to dull the sharp corners. She'd also stored everything not fastened down behind a locked door.

Abigail nodded, then opened her arms so Mary Rose could escape. Their talking had wakened her, and upon hearing Ethan's voice, she'd dropped the cloth doll clutched in her arms and flung herself toward Ethan chattering, "Cat!"

He caught her up, then cradled her close to him and gave her a big hug. "Hi, Pud. Did that nasty storm wake you?"

He held her even closer when another violent gale struck the leeward side of the ship and threw him against the cabin wall. Then, he sat on the floor next to Abigail and nestled Mary Rose snuggly in his lap.

"Is this storm scaring you?" he asked Mary Rose

when he was settled.

Mary Rose reached out a pudgy hand and rubbed her palm against the stubble on his face, then muttered a string of inane sounds.

"So far, this has been a great adventure for her," Abigail said. The *Emerald Gold* pitched to the side, throwing all of them off balance. She righted herself. "She's not frightened in the least."

"Good," he said, tucking the blanket around the three of them. When it was securely in place, he wrapped his arm around Abigail's shoulders and pulled her close to him.

"We'll wait out the storm together," he said.

Abigail turned into him and wrapped her arm around his waist. She pressed her cheek to his chest and held tight. She knew he hadn't completed this thought. She knew he meant to say they'd wait out the storm together...or go down together. The way he held her told her as much.

. . .

The storm raged on, hour after endless hour. Wave after punishing wave crashed against the side of the ship, plunging it into deep troughs beneath the monstrous swells. The *Emerald Gold* shuddered and rocked.

More than once, Abigail was certain that each violent wave that slammed against them would be the wave that broke the ship apart. The final blow that took them to the bottom of the sea.

She held on to Ethan as the wind exploded around them. The ship lurched, then another booming sound thundered from above. It was the sound of another giant mast splintering as it fell to the deck.

She lifted her gaze and focused on the worry in Ethan's eyes. "You don't have to stay here with us," she said, although she wasn't sure she could let go of him long enough for him to leave.

"Mac ordered me below. He'll send for me if he needs me. We just have to ride out the storm the best we can."

The ship lurched again, and he held her more securely. "Close your eyes, Abby. Don't think about the storm. Tell me what you remember about the first time you went to the docks with your father."

She knew what he was trying to do, but it wouldn't work. The wind was raging all around them, threatening to shatter the *Emerald Gold* to smithereens. How did he expect her to concentrate on anything other than the thought that they might not survive this night?

"I don't remember. I can't think."

"Yes, you can. How old were you?"

"I don't know. Six perhaps. Maybe seven."

"What's the first sight you remember seeing?"

"The ships," she answered. "They were mammoth. I remember thinking that they were big enough that our town house would fit on the deck."

"Did your father take you on board?"

"Yes. That was when I fell in love with the ships."

Abigail answered his questions, then asked questions of her own. She was fascinated with his answers, with the courage that seemed to underpin each choice he'd made in his life. She had tried so long to shut out his voice, to keep some great chasm growing between them. But in this moment the divide seemed to have evaporated, swept away with the tempest, and having him close seemed to be all that mattered. There wasn't anything she wasn't eager to learn about him, and nothing he avoided telling her.

His quiet voice lulled Mary Rose to sleep and calmed Abigail's heart. His words reassured and comforted her, his arm warmed her and held her safe. And somehow, as the night raged on, slumber overtook her.

. . .

"It's over, Abby," he said from the doorway.

Abigail looked up. At first her mind didn't comprehend what he said, then surprise and disbelief rushed through her body.

She looked around the cabin, to the spot where Mary Rose lay in her little low hammock with its bumpers of thick blankets.

Stella slipped past Ethan and tiptoed to the hammock. Without waking Mary Rose, she lifted her from her bed and turned to Abigail with her hand outstretched. Abby grasped it. Their mutual smiles shared the same thought—that it was impossible to believe they'd just endured one of the worst storms imaginable. And survived it.

Ethan stepped into the room as Stella slipped out with the babe, and closed the door behind her. "It's over," he said. "The storm is over."

She looked at the relief on his face, then turned her own eyes to the window. The sky above was clear and blue, the sun shone in mocking brightness. She'd slept so soundly she hadn't noticed when the ship had stopped bucking and rolling. She hadn't noticed when the wind had stopped howling, or the thunder and lightning no longer exploded around her. She hadn't noticed when Ethan had left her and gone above to help Mac.

She looked to Ethan's face again, then brought her

trembling hands to her mouth to cover the cry that rose from the back of her throat.

"It's truly over! Oh, thank God," she cried. "Are you all right?"

"I'm fine." He helped her to her feet, then gathered her against him. Without hesitation, he brought his mouth down on hers and kissed her with a desperation that matched her own.

She could deny him nothing. He tasted of salt and rain and the elements he'd battled. He was exquisitely male and she wanted to touch and taste every part of him.

She wrapped her arms around his neck and brought him closer. They could have died. The storm could have destroyed the ship, and taken all of them to a watery grave.

She didn't want to go one more day without showing him how much she loved him, without being his wife, without giving herself to him and taking the love he'd so willingly offered before.

And pray he wouldn't realize her secret.

Abigail didn't allow herself to think what might happen if he did. She wanted him too much. Loved him too much. It was worth the risk. Loving him was worth any risk she had to take.

Ethan lifted his mouth and cupped her cheeks in his roughened palms. She cried out when he separated himself from her.

"Do you want this, Abby?"

Her hands reached inside his wet shirt, drenched and sticking to his flesh. "Oh, yes. Kiss me. Please. Want me."

"I'll not give you another chance to stop."

"I won't need one. Love me, Ethan. Make love to me. Please."

With a frantic desperation neither of them could control, she pushed the shirt from his shoulders while he undid the row of tiny buttons down her dress. He kissed her again and again, his mouth worshipping hers, while his hands worked at the clothes concealing her body. Within minutes, they both stood naked in the morning light that streamed through the tiny porthole, their hands touching and discovering and caressing every inch of each other's body.

Abigail stared into his eyes, dark with passion. She brought her hands up, threading her fingers through his thick hair, and pulled his head down to hers. She kissed him with all the emotion she'd tried to deny from the day he'd walked into her life. He kissed her back, hard and long, until neither of them could breathe. Her chest heaved as violently as his, and her lungs fought to take in enough air to breathe.

"It's too late, Abby," he whispered, picking her up and carrying her to the bed. "I need you too badly. I love you too much."

He laid her in the middle of the covers and followed her down. Oh, the beauty of it. The incredible pleasure of his body, wonderfully heavy atop her, touching her, moving against her. She thought she would die from the uncontrollable sensations surging through her.

Then he entered her.

Having him inside her was uncomfortable but didn't hurt like she thought it would.

"You're so tight," he whispered in her ear, then pulled back and thrust deep within her, breaking the thin barrier that held her secret.

He froze above her, closing his eyes as if he wanted to blot out what his mind was telling him.

Abigail felt him pull away. "Ethan. Love me. Please."

He didn't move inside her, nor did he pull away from

her. Finally, he opened his eyes and leveled her with a look that showed his confusion. His anger.

"Don't move," he said at last. "The pain will lessen soon."

It did. In only a moment, her discomfort eased.

He moved inside her, showing her the wonders of making love. Taking her to heights she'd never dreamed existed.

Higher and higher she climbed until her body could soar no higher. She cried out as his body spun through the exploding lights.

He thrust inside her one final time, then, with a shuddering cry, dropped his head back on his shoulders and closed his eyes. He fell against her and buried his face in the crook of her neck.

He didn't move.

Abigail reached out to touch him, skimming her fingers across his sweat-drenched shoulders. The muscles on his arms bunched beneath her touch, the taut flesh at his waist and back heaved with exertion.

She held him to her, touching him, caressing him, but with each passing heartbeat he pulled further away from her, distancing himself from her.

He breathed a sigh, heavy, burdensome, filled with untold bewilderment. He rolled off her, separating his body from hers. He lay on his back with one arm thrown over his eyes, as if he couldn't bear to look at her. As if he couldn't accept the secret she'd kept from him.

He knew. She'd not been able to hide her secret from him. As if she'd thought she could.

Or that it wouldn't matter when he found out.

Chapter 24

"You were a virgin," he said when he'd risen and dressed.

Abigail rose and dressed, too. She knew what was coming and didn't want to face the battle naked.

His voice was strained, his words a struggle for understanding.

She opened her mouth to speak. To deny his accusations.

He swung his hand through the air. "Don't," he hissed between clenched teeth, as if he realized her intentions. "I'm not a randy school boy, and you are far from the first woman I've made love to. Although you are the first virgin I've ever deflowered."

"And that bothers you? You're upset because your wife came to you a virgin?"

He spun to face her, his hands clenched in tight fists. "No! Not that you were a virgin. But that you didn't trust me enough to tell me you were."

"I prayed you wouldn't notice," she whispered, straightening the covers on the bed so she wouldn't have to look him in the eyes.

"Wouldn't notice? Bloody hell, woman! It was your first time. I was far from gentle."

"You didn't hurt me."

He turned back to the porthole, the bright sunlight streaming down on him, casting his features in golden magnificence. He was strong, powerful, beautiful. The most handsome man she'd ever seen.

And the angriest.

He'd washed, dressed, and shaved the two day's stubble from his face all in silence. He hadn't looked at her once. She wanted to scream her frustration. She'd known from the start he wouldn't be able to forgive her secrets.

"Who is Mary Rose's mother?"

She hesitated, knowing the time for honesty had come. "My mother died giving birth to her."

"And her father?"

"Stephen."

Ethan rubbed his fingers across his forehead in frustration. "Dammit! Why didn't you tell me?"

"Because I couldn't chance losing her! Because I didn't want you to know that I've no more right to her than you do."

He braced his hands on either side of the small opening in the cabin wall. Taut muscles bunched beneath his full-sleeved white linen shirt. His stature depicted the anger she knew she would see in his eyes.

She lowered herself to the edge of the bed and tried to think how to begin. How could she make him understand without revealing her last secret? She took a deep breath and prayed he wouldn't realize there was more.

"My mother and father hadn't lived together as husband and wife for years. Their marriage was a sham, a bitter farce. Father had always known that Mother kept lovers. It was no secret. Half of London knew she did. He no doubt had his share of lovers, too. But both of them had always been discreet. Until Stephen."

She took the corner of the cover on the bed and unconsciously worked it into a tight roll. "I don't know if Stephen's affair with my mother began before or during our engagement. It hardly matters now. The damage was done the night they were discovered together."

"Your father found them?"

A picture of her mother and Stephen wrapped in each other's arms flashed through her mind. A picture of their naked bodies joined together in lovemaking.

"No," she whispered, nearly choking on the word.

He focused on her, a look of shocked regret on his face. "Oh, hell," he hissed through clenched teeth.

Abigail spoke past the lump in her throat. "Mother and I had gone to a small dinner party hosted by the Marquis and Marchioness of Bladebury. Just before the evening's entertainment, Mother claimed she was feeling poorly and wanted to leave early. Stephen graciously offered to see her home. I remember thinking how gallant it was of him to leave my side long enough to escort my mother. He was always quite attentive."

She rose from the bed and paced the length of the room. "When Stephen didn't immediately return, I became concerned. An opportunity arose to ride home with family friends, and I took it. I went in to check on my mother and found…"

Abigail's legs trembled beneath her, and she sat down on the corner of the bed, clutching the bedclothes with her fists. Telling the story was like reliving her nightmare. Seeing the shocked looks on her mother and Stephen's faces. Hearing his footsteps as he raced out into the garden after her. Feeling his hands on her, touching her, pulling at her, hurting her. Her fingers ached from clenching them so tightly. A pain similar to the pain she'd felt just before she grabbed the rock and brought it down against Stephen's head.

The air left her body and she cried out. Ethan's soft caress pried her fingers loose from the covers. She looked into his eyes and fought against a painful pressure in her chest. "I thought my world had ended that night, but I was wrong. The worst was yet to happen."

When she could no longer hold his gaze, she closed her eyes and lowered her chin.

"Mother didn't realize she was with child, not immediately, at any rate. I think she thought it was no longer possible for her to conceive. By the time she was certain, it was too late to get rid of the child like she wanted."

"And your father," he said in a tone that did not resemble a question.

The air caught in her throat. "Father couldn't abide the sight of his wife huge with another man's child. He left Fallen Oaks and moved to London to manage his ships. He bought the new clipper and lived on the docks, drinking himself into oblivion. Fenny kept an eye on him for me. Mother stayed in seclusion at Fallen Oaks."

"And you?"

"I spent most of my time at Fallen Oaks. There was no point in going to London. Stephen's abrupt departure and my crying off had created quite a scandal. Stephen was, after all, one of the most eligible bachelors in England. The inferences your mother made as to what I had done to drive Stephen away made me the social pariah of the Season."

"You could have fought her," he said, as if that had been a possibility. "Challenged her."

"I had never enjoyed the rounds of balls and parties,

so it didn't bother me not to reside in London. Besides, Mother needed me. Her pregnancy wasn't easy. Perhaps it was her age. Perhaps it was payment for her sin."

He grasped her shoulders. "You don't believe that," he argued, his tone harsh. "God doesn't punish like that. Bringing a child into the world is a risk to a woman, at any age."

She turned her face away from him and wiped at the renegade tear that had escaped. "I knew the minute the pains started the birth would be difficult. On the second day, when the babe still showed no signs of coming, I sent a message for Father to come. The doctor held little hope for either of them."

She swallowed hard. "Mother died without ever seeing Mary Rose."

"Did your father arrive before she died?"

Abigail wrapped her arms around her middle. She remembered the pain, the fear. The cold emptiness death leaves in its wake. "I sent word to him in London of Mother's death, but he didn't arrive until two weeks later. He was a shell of the man I'd known as my father. He stayed only long enough to issue orders for Mary Rose to be taken to the convent for the sisters to raise. He left for London without ever seeing her, and circulated the story that the child had been born weak and had died."

She lifted her face, no longer caring that tears streamed down her cheeks. "If only he would have claimed Mary Rose as his own, but he couldn't bring himself to accept Stephen's child. Yet he couldn't live with himself because he'd abandoned an innocent babe.

"Every day he became more withdrawn and frail. He no longer ate or slept. I didn't think it possible for anyone to will himself to die, but I know now it is. I saw my father fade before my very eyes, until there was nothing I could do to save him."

"This is what he meant by his greatest sin?" Ethan whispered, waiting for her to reply. "Or is there more?"

Abigail's blood turned cold. "What more could there be?"

He took a step away from her. "I don't know, Abby. But there is. Isn't there?" He stared at her, his eyes like penetrating daggers, his frown an angry warning.

"Leave it be, Ethan. Please."

"I can't. There's more. It's written all over your face. You're as frightened as an animal caught in a trap. What else are you keeping from me?"

She clenched her hands into fists, the blood pounding in her head, her heart thundering in her breast.

He leaned over her, his breath a soft whisper against her neck. "Don't you see. I need you to share your secrets with me and trust that I'll understand. I need you to trust me that much. We can't survive if you don't."

She hung her head. "I can't."

She heard the long, slow hiss of his breath and watched him step away. His absence enveloped her like a cold wind wrapping around her. When he spoke, the soft edge he'd had to his voice was gone. She'd disappointed him, destroyed what he wanted there to be between them.

"What happened to Stephen after you found him with your mother? You talk as if he simply disappeared. Surely he didn't just slink away? Surely he said something to you before he left? Made some attempt to make amends? Gave some excuse for what he'd done? I know he cared for you. He would have tried to win you back."

"No. He cared nothing for me. He cared only for my dowry and the ships he knew I'd someday have." She rose and walked away from him.

Ethan crossed the cabin in long, angry strides, stopping so close she could smell the bayberry soap he'd used to bathe. His hands clamped on her shoulders, holding her steady, exhibiting the power he had over her. "All I want is for you to share your secrets. All of them. We can have no marriage with them hovering between us!"

She opened her mouth to tell him the rest, then closed it. What did she expect him to do once he knew? Forget what she'd done? Forgive her? She knew him too well. He could never do that.

"Abby, tell me," he pleaded. His voice was rife with emotion. "Something more happened the night you found Stephen with your mother. I want to know what it is. The secret can't stay between us."

Abigail breathed in a huge gasp and turned her face away from him. Her heart was breaking, yet she couldn't say the words to end her torture. With a vicious oath, Ethan released her and stepped back.

"Damn your secrets, Abby! I love you. But don't you know we can have no marriage as long as you keep secrets? Do you care that little for me? For us? For what we just shared?"

God help her, but she wanted to tell him. She wanted to unburden her soul and beg his forgiveness. She wanted there to be nothing between them except giving, and sharing, and laughter, and comfort. Nothing except the special love they had for each other and for Mary Rose.

But how could she expect there to be anything but hatred once she told him she'd murdered his brother?

Abigail clamped her hands over her mouth. Each horrid detail of that night came back in stark reality. She remembered Stephen's hands tearing at her clothes, touching her even though she did not want to be touched. Then, she remembered holding the rock in her hand—as if its falling loose was a sign for her to save herself—lifting the rock and bringing it down hard.

Stephen rolled off her, his unconscious body sprawled out on the cold ground, blood oozing from where she'd hit him. She hadn't killed him, but he was hurt. With care, he would have survived.

If only her father hadn't come home.

Her stomach still clenched and wanted to revolt. She remembered Stephen struggling to protect himself from her father's lethal blows. She could still see her father's insane anger as he hit him again and again.

Thankfully, Palmsworth came. He pulled her father away from Stephen's battered body and forced her father into the house. A short while later, the butler returned, and together they put Stephen in a carriage and took him to London.

She thought he would die before they reached the docks, but miraculously he did not. With Fenny's help, they found a ship leaving London at dawn. She knew that when Stephen died, her father would be tried for murder. Stephen was, after all, the Earl of Burnhaven. A very powerful name in London.

That had been nearly two years ago. If Stephen had lived, he would have returned long before now. The ship they'd put Stephen on returned a year later. But Stephen hadn't been aboard her. No one knew anything about him. That was because he was dead. She and her father had killed him.

Abigail looked up into Ethan's anxious face. This was the moment that would decide their future. Oh, how she loved him. She would give anything to be able to tell him what she'd done and know he would forgive her. But he wouldn't.

There was a heaviness inside her breast that wouldn't

go away. She hurt unlike she ever thought it possible to hurt, even more than when Stephen had betrayed her. She knew the look of revulsion that would appear on Ethan's face when he knew what she'd done. It would be the final image she'd be left with.

"Can't you just accept that it's better you do not know more?" she asked, her voice shaking, her lips trembling, huge tears streaming down her cheeks.

"No," he whispered. "Please, Abby. Trust me enough to forgive you anything, no matter how bad."

She stared at him, her look pleading for him to understand. "I can't," she whispered.

His gaze turned hard. With an angry sigh, he turned away from her and left the cabin.

Abigail clutched her hands to her breast. The pain inside was greater than she could bear. The sense of loss even greater. How could she go on without him?

She didn't think it was possible.

. . .

Abigail lay in Ethan's bed. The muted rays of an overcast moon streamed through the porthole above his desk, shrouding the cabin with soft gossamer filaments. It had been two days since the storm had blown them far off course. Two days since he'd held her in his arms and kissed her. Two days since he'd made her his wife.

She didn't know how she would survive one more.

The air between them sparked with a tension that made the earlier strain seem minor and inconsequential. The pull that drew them toward each other was too powerful to fight. How had she let herself fall so desperately in love with him? If only it were possible for him to forgive what she'd done.

She walked to the porthole and leaned her shoulder against the smooth oak planking on the wall. She closed her eyes and listened to the gentle waves softly slapping against the side of the *Emerald Gold*. The sound lulled her thoughts to dream of a fairy tale existence where there was no past. Only a future with Ethan, and her, and Mary Rose.

The door to the cabin opened, and she slowly turned. She knew he'd be standing there before she actually saw him. The soft light from the lantern in the corridor outlined his physique, making him appear more perfect than she remembered.

"It's late. You should be asleep." His voice was soft and husky, his tone tortured with a strange weariness.

She understood it. She felt it, too.

He stepped into the room and closed the door behind him. Her heart beat faster with each step he took closer. She opened her mouth to speak, but all that came out was a pathetically feeble excuse that explained nothing. That explained it all. "I couldn't sleep."

He stopped so close she could feel his warm breath whisper against her. "Neither could I."

He lifted his hands and let them skim ever so lightly the tender flesh at her wrists, then slowly up to the rounded curve at her shoulders. Her body sang in answer, blood rushing to her head, her breaths racing with labored urgency.

"Ethan, please," she said on a gasp. "Don't put us through such torture. Nothing has changed."

He lifted one hand and ran the back of his fingers down her cheek. "Will you answer me one question?"

She turned her face from him, afraid what he wanted to know.

"Just one, Abby. Then I'll never ask anything from you again."

She turned back to him, knowing she owed him that much. As long as he did not want to know what had happened to Stephen. She looked into his eyes, and a heavy hand pressed against her heart. "One question, Ethan."

"The truth?"

She nodded.

"Do you love me?"

The air caught in her chest. How could he ask her that? Didn't he already know?

"Do you love me?" he repeated. "I need to know."

She felt a wetness fill her eyes, then one hot tear ran down her cheek. "With all my heart."

He lowered his head. His forehead pressed against hers. His strong, sturdy fingers clasped around her neck. His thumbs wiped the wetness from her cheeks. "Then that will be enough. I can't live another day without you. I'll face whatever you've chosen to keep from me when the time comes."

She clasped her hands against his cheeks, holding him in the palms of her hands. "I wish I were stronger, but I'm too great a coward. It's easier to keep my secret and pretend I'll never lose you than to tell you my secret and know you'll be lost to me forever."

"You don't know that."

"I wish I didn't." Their eyes locked, the hunger obvious to each, their need blatant. Their desire was like a raging fire sweeping through dry brush. "Kiss me," she said, her voice husky and raw. "Love me. At least for this little while."

Abigail brought Ethan's face down to meet hers, his lips a whisper's edge above her. He kissed her lightly, then kissed her again with a desperation that matched what she felt. She moved her hands, raking her fingers through his thick, satiny hair, holding him close.

She couldn't bring him near enough.

He lifted her in his arms and carried her to the bed. He lay down atop her, and she welcomed him with open arms. For as long as she could, she would take the love he offered. Once he discovered what she'd done, she would have nothing except these memories to fill her long, lonely nights.

Chapter 25

Ethan stood at the starboard side of the *Emerald Gold* and watched as London came into view. They would stay here until Captain Parker returned with the *Abigail Rose*, then Ethan would turn over the running of Langdon Shipping to him, and he and Abby and Mary Rose would go to Windswept Manor.

He was filled with an overwhelming sense of pride each time he thought of his home. It was where he belonged. It was where he and Abby and Mary Rose would make their home.

Nowhere were the greens more vibrant, the reds more vivid, or the yellows warmer. Nowhere was the sky bluer or the clouds whiter. He would never tire of it. He was certain Abby would love it as much as he did.

He turned as Abby made her way across the deck with little Mary Rose. Abigail's face glowed with happiness, her cheeks flushed with the rosy tint of a woman well loved.

The blood raced hotter through his veins as he remembered the nights they'd spent in each other's arms. The way she gave herself to him with complete and total abandon. If Stephen had been a part of her life once, Ethan was sure he wasn't any longer. And whatever her last secret was, it couldn't be horrible enough to affect the way they felt about each other.

When they reached him, he wrapped his arm around Abigail's shoulder and pulled them close to him. He needed to touch her. Needed to have her close to him. She lifted her chin and looked at him. The unmasked adoration in her eyes was plain for him to see.

He brought his mouth down on hers and kissed her again. "I love you," he whispered.

"And I—"

"Excuse me," Mac's deep voice said from behind them. "I hate to break up such a stimulating conversation, but we're ready to dock. What are your plans?"

Ethan turned to face his longtime friend and partner. "I'm going to take Abby to Langdon House. I want you to find out what you can about the *Abigail Rose*. As soon as Captain Parker docks and the cargo of tea is unloaded, we're going take care of Langdon Shipping, then leave London for Windswept Manor."

The smile on Mac's face told Ethan his friend was as anxious to get home as he was.

"I'll find out what I can and let you know. I'll bring the bill of lading to you as soon as we get the *Emerald Gold* unloaded. I shouldn't be long. Then we can celebrate your wedding and a successful voyage properly."

Mac and Abby shared a look that told Ethan the two most important people in his life approved of—and liked—each other. He was pleased.

"We'll go now," he said, lifting Mary Rose into his arms and ushering Abby toward the gangplank. "Palmsworth and Stella will organize our things and come with you when you get the cargo unloaded."

Ethan didn't wait for an answer but ushered Abby off

the ship. He hailed a hackney, and they left for Langdon House. Ethan couldn't believe how his life had changed in little more than a week. He marveled at how content he was. And he owed it to the woman who sat beside him. He had never known he could be this happy.

The hackney stopped in front of Abby's town house, and he stepped to the ground. Mary Rose had fallen asleep before they were barely away from the docks, and he took the babe from Abby, then helped his wife step out onto the curb. They made their way up the walk, and a twinge of uneasiness passed over him.

He wasn't sure why he should feel apprehensive. Everything looked normal. There was nothing that seemed out of place. And yet...

A footman didn't come out to greet them. And Bundy didn't open the door as he'd expected him to.

"What's wrong?" Abby asked.

"Nothing, sweetheart. Why don't you take Mary Rose?"

He handed a sleeping Mary Rose over to Abby, then stretched out his arm to keep her behind him.

"Ethan?"

Ethan placed a finger against his lips and slowly opened the front door.

No one was there to greet them.

He pulled a gun from his jacket and motioned for Abby to stand against the wall inside the door.

He looked around the deserted room. The door to every room off the foyer stood ajar, the openings gaping in shadowy dimness. Ethan raised his finger to his lips and turned her in the direction of the study, swiftly moving her with him.

Before they could enter the room, something moved above them. With his gun raised, he pushed her into the study and fired one shot. Return fire splintered the wood at the corner of the frame near his head.

"Stay back, Abby. Against the wall. In the corner."

Abby ran to the corner while Ethan bolted the door. He raced across the room, locking the windows and pulling the drapery.

"Is there another gun in here?" he asked.

"In the top desk drawer on the right. There are bullets in the back."

Ethan reached in and took out the gun and the bullets. He scattered the bullets on the top of the desk and shoved them into the chambers until both weapons were loaded.

"Put Mary Rose beneath the desk," he said.

Abby put the babe on the floor and gave her a glass ball with swirling white snow to play with. She hoped it would keep her occupied so she wouldn't fuss.

"Use this if you have to," he said as he handed her the gun.

Her hands trembled when she took the gun, and he touched her cheek with the backs of his fingers. "Everything will be all right, Abby. Mac will be here soon."

She tried to smile, but her attempt was dismal. Ethan wanted to hold her, to convince her that everything would be all right. But Stafford's voice stopped him.

"Come out, Captain. I've been waiting for you. And please, bring the lovely lady with you. I have such pleasant reminders of the last time we met."

Ethan clamped his hands on either side of her face. "Stay here. No matter what happens, stay here. And use the gun if you have to."

"No, Ethan. You can't go out there."

"I don't plan to. I just need to buy time until Mac gets here." He dropped his hands from her cheeks and stepped away from her.

"I'm short on patience where you are concerned, Captain. Please join me before I send my men in to get you."

"Go to hell, Stafford."

Stafford laughed a demented cackle. "I've already been there, Cambridge. That's where you put me when you took my slaves and made me look the weak fool in front of my wife and my neighbors. And now you're going to pay for what you did."

Ethan heard the sound of heavy boots treading closer and fired a shot through the wooden door. Someone on the other side cried out in pain.

Ethan heard the scurry of retreating footsteps.

"You aren't going to get away, you bastard. You're going to suffer just as I did. You're going to watch as everything is taken away from you. *Everything!* Now come out here!"

"What kind of fool do you think I am?" Ethan said, saying anything he could to keep the conversation going. Anything to buy time until Mac arrived.

"I'll show you how foolish it is to taunt me," Stafford answered, then countered his threat with a diabolical laugh. "I think your brother should be the first to pay for your stubbornness."

It took a second or two for Stafford's words to register. *Stephen?*

What kind of trick was Stafford playing? How did he even know about Stephen?

"Come out here Cambridge, or your brother will die."

Abby sucked in a harsh breath behind him. When Ethan turned, Abby's face was a pasty white. She leaned against the desk as if her legs weren't steady enough to support her.

"Abby?" he whispered. "Sit down."

The expression on her face was one of terror. Her

wide-eyed horror frightened him. She clasped her hands over her mouth and looked to be in danger of fainting.

"Now, Cambridge! Come out now! Or your brother dies!"

Ethan took a step forward, but before he could reach the door, Abby raced to him and grabbed him by the arm.

"No, Ethan. It's a lie. Stafford doesn't have Stephen."

A thin sheen of perspiration covered her face, and tears streamed down her cheeks. Her lips trembled so violently she'd barely gotten the words from her mouth.

"What if he does, Abby?"

"He doesn't," she screamed. "Stephen's not out there. Stafford doesn't have him."

"How can you be sure?"

"Because..." She wrapped her arms around her waist as if she was in pain. "Because Stephen's dead." Tears flowed down her cheeks like a river after a thunderstorm. "Because I killed him."

Chapter 26

Time seemed to stop. The look on Ethan's face held more anger than she'd ever seen before. More revulsion and disgust than she was capable of standing up against. The ache deep inside her hurt with an unrelenting pressure, its weight an agony that increased with every breath.

He took one step away, as if he couldn't stand to be so close to her. To a murderer. To the woman who'd just announced that she'd taken his brother's life.

"What did you say?" he asked, the wide-open look of horror plain to see.

Tears ran down her face carrying the pent-up anguish she'd held inside her for almost two years. "My last secret," she whispered. "The one I'd have done anything to keep you from discovering. The secret I knew you could never forgive."

He shook his head as if a small part of his mind and heart wanted to refuse to believe such a nightmare. "How did you...? Why?"

"I didn't mean for it to happen. I'd give anything if it hadn't." Her tears were replaced by a vacant, hollow emptiness that stole every ounce of emotion. There was as much relief in giving up her secret as there had been agony in trying to keep it. Nothing was worth living with something so horrible. Nothing was worth the terror of knowing someone would eventually find out what she'd done.

Nothing had prepared her for the loss.

"Tell me what happened," Ethan demanded, his lips pressed together in a thin line, his hands doubled in fists so tight his knuckles stretched white. "How could you have killed Stephen?"

She turned away from him, unable to face the blatant disgust in his eyes. "It was the night I discovered him with my mother. I stared at the two of them wrapped in each other's arms and only wanted to escape the nightmare of the man I was to marry making love to my mother. I ran. He came after me. He intended to..."

"Intended to what!"

"He tried to force himself on me. We fought. He threw me to the ground and...I picked up a rock and hit him."

The blood roared inside her head. From the other side of the door, Stafford's angry voice shouted again for Ethan to come out or he would kill Stephen. From inside the room, Ethan's disgust loomed over her like a vile sickness that had no cure.

"I can't believe you capable of killing Stephen with a single blow. He's nearly as tall as I, and equally as broad across the shoulders. It would have taken someone much stronger than you to kill him."

"My blow merely stunned him."

"Then why do you think he's dead?"

"Before Stephen got to his feet, Father came home. When he saw Stephen on top of me, he went into a rage. He and Stephen fought, but Stephen was in no shape to defend himself against someone so insanely angry.

By the time I could stop them, Stephen was severely injured."

Abigail closed her eyes and released a breath that shuddered in the silence. "He couldn't have lived," she whispered, her voice shaky and weak. In her mind's eye, she could still see Stephen's unconscious body fighting to stay alive.

"Then what happened?"

"We took Stephen to London and put him on a ship that was sailing at dawn."

"You what!"

A startled Mary Rose whimpered from the other side of the room.

"I had to get Stephen out of London. I knew if I kept him under our roof, Father would kill him for sure. He was that angry. And I was afraid when Stephen died, Father would be tried for murder."

"Was Stephen alive when you reached London?"

"Yes, but even the doctor on the ship said he wouldn't live out the day."

"Then you can't be sure he—"

"Stop it, Ethan! Stephen is dead. If he'd lived, he would have come back. It's been nearly two years. He's dead, or he would have come back long ago."

"He left a note! A note saying he needed time to himself before he married."

Abigail hid her face from him. "I wrote the note and had it delivered to you the next day."

"You! Why didn't you tell me? All these weeks you kept this from me when you knew how desperate I was to find him. Why couldn't you trust me enough to tell me?"

"Because I didn't want to see the look I see on your face right now. At first I was just frightened of what might happen to me, that you would press charges.

Then..." She looked up at him. "I started to care for you and didn't want to lose your love. I knew you couldn't love me when you found out what I'd done."

"You couldn't have known that," he hissed, the black, angry look in his eyes glaring a fiery blaze that burned her to her very soul. "Not if you cared for me like you say you did."

"Yes. I knew," she whispered. "And I was right. The look on your face tells me so."

"Damn you, woman! How did you think we could survive this? How did you think we could have any kind of a life between us when you knew my brother was dead and didn't tell me about it?"

Her heart slammed against her ribs, causing a pain as fierce as if Ethan had struck her. "I knew we couldn't."

He braced his arm against the wall and lowered his head. His voice, when he finally spoke, was empty, lifeless, devoid of hope. "Would it have been so hard to trust me?"

She had only one answer, but when she tried to speak, her voice came out soft and fragile. "It would have been that hard to give you up."

"Cambridge! Open that door or your brother dies."

"Go to hell, Stafford. You're the one who will die when this door opens. You and as many of that little band of miscreants as I can—"

Stephen's voice stopped him cold. "Ethan?"

Every muscle in Ethan's body jerked. He spun to face her, his face taut with anger and betrayal. "That *is* Stephen! He's alive!"

Abigail staggered against the burnished leather chair, her hand reaching out to find any support that would steady her. She couldn't take in what was happening. Her mind couldn't focus on anything except the familiar voice calling from the other side of the door.

She thought he was dead. She was positive he'd died. She'd lived with the nightmare that she was a murderer, but she wasn't. Stephen was alive. That was his voice.

"Ethan," Stephen said again.

"Stephen? Are you all right?"

Ethan took a step toward the door, then stopped when Stephen's voice came at him.

"Stay where you are, Ethan! Make your fight from in there—"

The horrid sound of a fist throttling human flesh was heard from the other side of the door. Stephen's screams split the air.

"Get out here now, Cambridge! Or your brother dies!"

"No, Ethan!" Stephen called out again, his voice rasping with strain. "I'm not worth it."

There was another loud thud of flesh hitting flesh followed by a muffled cry of pain. This time the groan seemed softer, weaker.

Ethan tucked his pistol in his jacket pocket and took a step toward the door.

"No, Ethan," she cried out. "You know Stafford is no man of honor. He has no intention of letting Stephen go. He has no intention of letting any of us go."

Ethan hesitated a moment, then turned back to her. "Keep that pistol ready." He glanced at the gun on the corner of the desk. "Kill the first man who walks through that door. Mac should be here before you need to use it."

"Ethan, please. Don't go."

Her words fell on deaf ears. He looked at her as if to memorize her features, then turned and strode away from her.

Without a look back, he opened the door, then closed

it firmly behind him.

"Captain Cambridge," Stafford said from beyond the closed door. "What a pleasure to see you again. But where is your lovely wife?"

"She has nothing to do with this, Stafford. Leave her alone."

"Mrs. Cambridge," Stafford bellowed. "Come, join us. I insist. Unless you do not care to see your husband alive again."

"No, Abby. Don't come out."

The air left Abigail's body. She looked to where Mary Rose played contentedly beneath the desk. The child turned the glass ball in her pudgy hands, as if the swirling snow was the most fascinating sight in the world.

Abigail stood rooted to the floor, unable to move. She knew the wisest decision would be to stay hidden until Mac came to rescue them, but what if Stafford made a move and Ethan tried to stop him? What if Stafford killed Ethan, and she would never get to see him again? What if Ethan needed her, and she wasn't there to help him?

Without realizing she'd moved, Abigail picked up the gun from the corner of the desk and hid it in the folds of her skirt, then slowly made her way to the door.

"Tell her to come out, Captain Cambridge, or your brother will pay for your stubbornness."

Ethan's voice sounded loud and harsh. "Stay where you are, Abby."

Before she could reach for the handle, she heard the sickening thud of fists hitting flesh and knew Stephen had already paid for her refusal to come out.

Abigail turned the handle on the heavy oak door and pulled it open. Her gaze first sought Ethan. The gun he'd taken to protect himself lay on the floor in front of him.

She turned next to Stephen.

She did not know what she expected to find, what she expected to feel, but there was none of the anger and hatred she'd felt before. She was too relieved that he was alive.

Stephen stood to her left, his hands bound in front of him, the bloody results of the whip Stafford was so fond of using in evidence across his shoulders.

She looked at his face. The handsome features were still there, the strong cut of his jaw that matched Ethan's, the high cheekbones, the full lips. But there the similarities ended. Stephen's posture lacked Ethan's strength. His bearing showed only a glimmer of the unspoken authority Ethan wore like a mantle. Stephen paled in comparison to the innate pride that was Ethan's greatest asset.

His golden hair was long and unkempt, his face bruised and dirty, and he was thinner than the last time she'd seen him. But at least he was alive. She wanted to shout for joy. He was alive.

Their eyes met, his a bottomless pool of heartache and regret. She did not need words to understand what he was trying to tell her. His look alone said it all. He was begging for her forgiveness. She bit her bottom lip, wanting so terribly to let him know she forgave him everything. There was much for which she needed him to forgive her, too. She prayed he would somehow know.

He looked at her a long moment, then nodded, a sense of peace relaxing the tense muscles on his face.

He understood.

"I admit this is a lovely reunion," Stafford said, "though I didn't gather you together for your pleasure, but for mine."

"You have me, Stafford," Ethan said, stepping away from her and from Stephen. He made his way to the other side of the hall, as far from her as he could, as if the distance he was putting between them would protect her. "Let everyone else go. I'll stay."

"You don't know how tempting that is, Cambridge. But I haven't waited all these years to put you out of your misery. I prefer to create a hell from which you'll never escape."

Stafford lifted his pistol and pointed it at Ethan's chest. "I want you to live the rest of your life regretting the day you stole my slaves. Regretting the day you ruined my reputation. The day you disgraced and humiliated me in front of my wife and my neighbors. I want every day to be a living hell for you because you are alive, and everyone you ever loved is dead."

The air caught in Abigail's throat. In that second, she knew Stafford intended to kill them.

She focused on the desperate look on Ethan's face. His head moved the smallest bit toward his gun that lay on the floor. She shook her head. He'd be dead before he reached it.

Abigail clamped her fingers tighter on the gun hidden in the folds of her skirt. She knew she had no choice. Stafford's demented mind was rife with hatred, crazed with revenge. He wouldn't be satisfied until everyone Ethan cared about was dead, lost to him forever.

Stafford turned his head and smiled at her. A snide, vindictive snarl curled his lips. "I haven't forgotten what you did to me the last time we met, Mrs. Cambridge. I'm not one to forgive easily."

She would be first. She could see it in his eyes.

"Leave her alone, Stafford! This is between you and me. My wife has nothing to do with this."

Stafford preened.

"You won't get away with this," Ethan said, moving closer to Stafford, closer to his gun that lay on the floor. She knew he was trying to draw the blackguard's attention away from her. It worked for only a second.

"Won't I?" Stafford laughed, then without hesitation swung toward her with his pistol raised.

"Abby! Dear God! No!"

Everything happened at once. Ethan threw himself toward Stafford, but he was too far away to stop him from firing.

Stephen catapulted toward her, leaping in front of her to act as a shield.

Stafford pulled the trigger and fired, the loud explosion ripping through the air. The bullet intended for her slammed into Stephen, hurtling him to the floor.

Abigail wanted to scream, but she couldn't. Instead, she pulled the pistol from the folds of her skirt and answered Stafford's shot with one of her own. The bullet hit him in the center of his chest.

Stafford staggered, the shocked look on his face filled with hatred and disbelief. He looked at the growing circle of blood, then raised a second gun and pointed it at her. She tried to fire again, but her gun wouldn't fire. She had no way to protect herself.

She closed her eyes and waited to feel the pain. She heard the shot, loud and deafening, followed by a second shot. Nothing. She felt nothing.

She opened her eyes to find Stafford crumpled in a heap on the floor, his hate-filled eyes glazed even in death.

Without hesitation, Ethan swung his gun toward Stafford's men lined up against the wall. No one moved. No one lifted a weapon to continue the fight. It was as if none of them wanted a part of Stafford's revenge now that their leader was dead. Even money had not guaranteed loyalty in the men Stafford had hired to follow him. Especially when they realized their leader had been about to murder a woman in cold blood.

One by one they dropped their weapons to the floor,

surrendering even before Mac burst through the front door.

"Abby, are you all right?" Ethan said, grasping her by the shoulders and holding her. His hands touched her face and her hair and her arms, as if he needed to make sure she wasn't hurt.

She tried to stop shaking, but couldn't. "I'm fine, Ethan," she stammered, her teeth chattering uncontrollably. "But Stephen's hurt."

Ethan dropped his hands from her shoulders and bent down to Stephen lying on the floor. He didn't move.

"Hang on, Stephen. Everything will be all right. We'll get you upstairs and—"

"Ethan," Stephen whispered, his voice weak, barely loud enough to be heard.

"Don't talk, Stephen. There'll be plenty of time to talk later."

Stephen shook his head. "No. Now. There's something...you...need to...know."

"You can tell me later." Ethan looked at Mac. "Give Stafford's men four seconds to get him out of here. Shoot anyone who's still here after five seconds. Then come help me with Stephen."

Stafford's men hastily gathered up their leader's body and hurried from the house, then Mac and Ethan carried Stephen upstairs.

Abigail ran back to the study to get Mary Rose before following Ethan up the steps. When they reached the second floor, Abigail heard pounding from down the hall. She ran to the last room and turned the key in the door. Barney and the staff rushed out.

"Send someone for a doctor," Abigail ordered, and one of the footmen raced down the stairs.

"We'll need water and towels," she ordered. "And bandages."

Barney sent the staff scurrying to get what she needed. Abigail handed Mary Rose to one of the maids, then raced back to where they'd taken Stephen.

"Abigail," Stephen said when she rushed into the room.

"I'm right here." She grasped his hand and held it.

"I'm...sorry."

"Shh," she said, brushing her fingers across his forehead. "We can talk later, when you're better."

"What you saw...meant nothing."

She swallowed hard. "I know, Stephen. I know."

Stephen didn't say more. Thankfully, he closed his eyes and lost consciousness.

She raised her head and found herself staring into Ethan's questioning glare. There was still Mary Rose. The child was Stephen's.

And there was only one way Abigail could keep her.

Chapter 27

Ethan rolled his shoulders, then stretched his legs out in front of him. After three hours, it was difficult to find a more comfortable way to sit.

He looked at Stephen, peaceful in lightly sedated slumber on the bed, and felt a familiar rush of relief that his brother was improving. He would live. The doctor had declared so, yesterday morning, when he'd arrived to find Stephen standing at the side of the bed clutching the bedpost for support. Today they would take him out into the garden for a while. The sunshine would do him good.

Ethan shifted in his chair again, searching for a softer spot. The sun was just rising in the east, its hazy glow of oranges and purples and blues sifting through the open window, brightening the room. Stephen had more color in the daylight. Ethan was glad. More than once during the past three weeks, he'd feared his brother wouldn't live to see another day. From the concern he saw on Abigail's face, she didn't, either.

A knot formed in the pit of Ethan's stomach. They'd barely spoken since the day Stephen had been shot.

Both existed in a secluded shell that kept their emotions isolated and tucked safely away. He didn't have the courage to face his greatest fear—that once Stephen found out about Mary Rose, he'd refuse to give her up. And if he did, he knew what Abigail would do.

It could never be said that Abigail hoped Stephen wouldn't survive. She'd cared for Stephen, staying at his side until she was weak with exhaustion. He couldn't regret the hours she'd spent with his brother, nursing him, caring for him, even demanding that he take another breath when no one else thought he had another breath left in him.

Even though he'd been the man she'd been engaged to not that long ago, Ethan knew she no longer loved Stephen. If she ever had. The desperation in her lovemaking told him so. The way she clung to him was all the evidence he needed to know she loved him.

The tears she shed told him how frightened she was that she would have to make a choice between him and Mary Rose.

A sharp spasm of red shot through him, twisting his heart in his chest, and tearing it out by its very core. He'd even considered never telling Stephen about Mary Rose. He'd contemplated leaving with Abby and Mary Rose and not letting Stephen know he had a child.

But he knew he couldn't keep Mary Rose from him. He was her father. He and Abby could never live with such a lie between them. And yet...

He clenched his fists around the arms of the padded chair. How could he demand she stay married to him when it meant she'd lose Mary Rose? Every secret she'd kept from him had been to protect the babe and keep her safe. Abigail would sooner die than be separated from her.

Ethan bolted from the chair and walked to the

opposite side of the room. He prayed an answer to his problems would magically appear. But he knew one wouldn't.

The only solution was to give Abby up and let her make a life with Stephen and Mary Rose. But, bloody hell, he was loath to even consider that. And what if she carried his child? There was that possibility. How could he give her up if his babe was growing in her?

Ethan breathed in a deep breath that burned in his lungs. If only he didn't love her so. Then giving her up wouldn't hurt so much.

"From the look on your face, Ethan, you are in more pain than I."

Ethan looked over his shoulder to where Stephen lay on the bed. "I'm sorry. Did I wake you?"

"No. I think it's a good sign, when I no longer want to sleep away my days and nights."

Ethan smiled. "It's a very good sign. Can I get you something? Something to eat or drink?"

"No. Please, sit down. Stay with me for a while. I'd like to talk to you while Abigail isn't here. There are many things we need to discuss privately."

Ethan sat back in the chair and placed his right ankle atop his left knee. He hoped his relaxed posture made it look as though he wasn't terrified of what would result from this conversation.

Stephen leveled a penetrating gaze at Ethan. "Abigail tells me you and she are wed."

Ethan lifted his chin. "Yes. It seemed the best decision, considering..."

"Considering she'd inherited a clipper you needed desperately in order to save my inheritance," Stephen finished for him.

"You didn't leave your holdings in very stable condition, my lord."

Stephen had the good grace to look sheepish. "No, I did not." He paused. "Do I have anything to go home to?"

"Your creditors agreed to extend your credit once I announced my betrothal to Abigail. They knew about the clipper she inherited upon her father's death."

"Is that why you married her? Only to pay my debts?"

The breath caught in Ethan's lungs. "We agreed to marry because it suited us both."

"Ah, Ethan," Stephen said on a heavy sigh. "You always were better suited to be the earl than I."

Ethan gave a harsh laugh. "No. I just learned at an early age that I wouldn't be afforded the pampered life you were granted. That I'd always have to make my own way in the world and couldn't depend on Father and Mother to shower me with favors."

"And their harshness made you a better person," Stephen answered. "Their leniency spoiled me unmercifully. I've no excuses for what happened. The condition of the estates is all my fault. My only defense is that after Father died, I found that for the first time in my life I was free to make decisions of my own. There was no one looking over my shoulder, criticizing me for how I spent my money. It was a newfound freedom I had no idea how to handle. And then I met Abigail and thought if I married her, I'd have an endless supply of the riches her father's clipper ship brought in."

Stephen struggled to sit up straighter on the bed, and Ethan leaned over to put another pillow behind him. "Has Abigail told you what happened between us?" Stephen asked when he was settled.

"I know that you had an affair with her mother. That Abigail discovered the two of you together. And in her anger, she struck you, knocking you unconscious."

Stephen took in a breath that shuddered in the predawn shadows.

"She also told me her father came home and realized what had transpired between you and his wife and nearly beat you to death."

Stephen turned his head, staring at him with a very pensive look. "That was all?"

The look on Stephen's face caught Ethan's attention. It was as if another great secret lurked in the background, waiting to come out in the open. A secret that would shatter the tension already in the room. "Yes, she said you attacked her."

"I tried to rape her. I thought if I ruined her, she'd be forced to marry me. That's how desperately irrational I was. I needed her dowry. And I thought all was lost."

Ethan leaned back in his chair and contemplated what Stephen said. Stephen's words made him sick. If Stephen hadn't already come close to dying, Ethan would be tempted to kill him himself. "She thought you were dead. The doctor assured her you wouldn't survive."

For a long time, Stephen said nothing, his silence stretching between them as wide as the piece of the story that was missing. When he spoke, his voice was soft.

"And you, Ethan? Did you think I was dead? Is that why you married Abigail?"

A feeling of rage washed over him. "I was too angry with you to consider that something might have happened to you. Angry because I was forced to come back to England to get you out of another mess. Angry because you had nearly lost everything Father had worked so hard to gain. And angry because our mother couldn't see what an irresponsible wastrel you had become."

Ethan rose and paced at the foot of the bed. "I had runners looking, but they didn't discover your whereabouts until recently. What happened, Stephen? Why did it take you nearly two years to find your way back?"

Ethan didn't mean for his words to come out so harshly, still filled with such anger.

"It's a long story, Ethan. When I regained consciousness, I had no memory of who I was. I couldn't remember my name, my family, where I belonged. And I was in so much pain I thought surely I'd die. But I didn't. Each day I improved. When I was healthy enough, the captain put me to work aboard the ship." A sad smile lifted the corners of his mouth. "I developed a newfound respect for anyone sailing the sea. You are a rare breed, Ethan."

"At least you learned that much," Ethan said, although there was very little inside him that felt jovial enough to enjoy such banter. He waited for Stephen to continue.

"From the aches my body suffered at first, I knew I was not accustomed to physical labor. But each time I arrogantly insisted I couldn't be expected to do such menial work, Captain Harding found another task for me to do, worse than the one I was complaining about. In time, I learned to keep my mouth shut and do my job. By the time we rounded the Cape, I had learned to adjust. I even fit in relatively well with the rest of the crew." A small smile lifted the corners of his lips. "You would have been proud of me. I eventually turned into a fairly passable sailor."

Ethan was stunned. "But you still couldn't remember who you were?"

"No. I was known as Harry Smith." Stephen gave a hollow laugh. "As good a name as any. I lived under the guise of Mr. Smith for months. Then, slowly, small snatches of my memory returned. The tree-lined drive leading to Penhurst Manor. Recollections of dressing in evening tails and dancing with beautiful women in fancy gowns. Nothing concrete. Just enough to make my mind search for more answers.

"One morning, I woke up and remembered everything. I knew my name, where I'd come from, who my family was. And worst of all, what I'd done. I became physically ill. Everything I'd done flashed before me like a horrible nightmare. The repulsive way I'd lived my life haunted me, and tortured my every waking hour. I stood face to face with my ugly self, and I couldn't handle what stared back at me. I didn't have the courage to go home to face what I'd left behind."

"What did you do?"

"Captain Harding was making another voyage to China for tea, and I signed on with him, letting everyone still believe I was Harry Smith. I wasn't ready to come back. I didn't have the courage to face you, or Abigail. Especially Abigail. I could barely live with myself once I'd remembered what a loathsome and reprehensible person I'd been."

"How did you meet up with Stafford?" Ethan asked.

"Oh, what an ugly twist of fate." Stephen tried to sit up straighter, and Ethan moved to help him.

"I discovered a person can only ignore his mistakes so long. I tired of running. Unbelievable as it sounds, I'd changed enough that my conscience wouldn't allow me to rest until I'd made restitution."

"So you came home?" Ethan asked, remembering the message Mr. Harper had sent, telling him he had important information concerning his brother. He'd found out Stephen was in London.

"Yes. Except I didn't go right home. I spent my first evening ashore with the rest of the crew at the Keg and Barrel. While I was there, Preston Cranville, Baron Cranville's youngest son, came in. He recognized me. He was playing cards with Stafford and introduced us. The surprised look on Stafford's face should have given me warning, as well as the intent interest he showed in my family. In you. But I didn't see it until it was too late."

Stephen leaned back heavily against the propped pillows. "I left the Keg and Barrel shortly after, ready to go home. That was the last I remember. I didn't make it past the first alley before three men jumped me and hit me over the head. When I awoke, I was here. The rest you know."

Stephen turned his head to face Ethan. "The man was crazy with his hatred for you. He was still nursing a wound he said Abigail had given him, and he told me what he was going to do to make you pay for all you'd done to him. He was sick with his thoughts of revenge."

"I'm sorry you got mixed up in this, Stephen."

"I'm just glad it's over."

Ethan walked to the window. The rounded tip of the sun had just made its appearance over the horizon, a bright orange hue against the purple and blue sky. "What do you intend to do, Stephen?"

"I've changed, Ethan. I'm not the same man I was when I left nearly two years ago. I intend to take my place as the sixth Earl of Burnhaven. I've done much for which I must make restitution. Especially to you. You'll never have to be responsible for me again. I'm going to be a son Father would have been proud to claim."

There was a noise in the doorway, and Abigail stood there with Mary Rose in her arms and tears streaming down her cheeks.

Chapter 28

Ethan went to stand beside Abby, then walked with her to the bed, so Stephen could get a clear look at Mary Rose.

Stephen's eyes widened. An expression that contained a mixture of disbelief and incredulity covered his face.

"Is the babe...yours?" he asked Abby.

Ethan placed his arm around Abby's shoulders and held her more securely. She turned her head until her tear-filled eyes were locked with his.

He knew she wanted an answer from him. An indication of how she should answer. He knew, though, that the answer had to be hers. That the decision that would affect the rest of their lives was hers to make.

She pressed a kiss to Mary Rose's forehead, then slowly shifted her gaze to where Stephen lay and shook her head. "Her name is Mary Rose," Abby answered in a broken voice. "My mother died giving birth to her."

The sound that came from Stephen echoed in the room. It resembled the keening moan of an animal in pain. Or the cry of a wounded seaman injured in battle.

"She is mine?" he said, more as a statement than a question.

Abby didn't answer him, and neither did Ethan.

"Did your father claim her as his own?"

Abby shook her head.

Stephen's face paled. He took in several harsh breaths, then looked from Abigail to Ethan. "Is this why you married? To give my daughter a name?"

Ethan dropped his arm from around Abby's shoulder and stepped to the bed. When he was close enough, he grabbed Stephen's nightshirt and pulled him toward him. "How dare you! There is only one reason I married Abigail. That's because I love her! As I do Mary Rose."

"Ethan," Abby said, placing a calming hand on his arm. "This will get us nowhere."

Ethan released Stephen and let him fall back to the pillows.

"You have my apology," Stephen said when he'd recovered. "That was uncalled for. I never deserved Abigail. Especially as the person I was before. But I've changed, and I intend to show you that I'm not the worthless no-good I used to be."

"Then you will do what is best for the child?"

"Yes. I have a daughter now. I intend to be her father."

The air froze in Ethan's lungs. Stephen's words struck him with the thrust of a battering ram. Abby staggered beside him, and he reached out an arm to steady her.

"I'll not turn my back on what is mine ever again, Ethan. You have been my keeper long enough. You've taken care of all my mistakes as if you made them. You've taken the brunt of my punishment as if the errors were your own. If I've learned anything these past two years, it's that I alone am responsible for my actions. Mary Rose is mine. I'll not turn my back on her."

"You can't mean that Stephen," Ethan argued. Black spots of fear nearly blinded him.

"But I do. Mary Rose's mother would want her daughter to have all the benefits I can provide her. She would want her to be raised in London, to learn the social graces she can learn nowhere else in the world. She would want Mary Rose to take her rightful place in Society."

Ethan stared at his brother with an anger he could contain no longer. "Mary Rose's mother is dead! If you took her to London, she would always be branded a bastard."

Stephen shook his head. "I'm the Earl of Burnhaven. Once the size of my daughter's dowry is known, the circumstances surrounding her birth won't be important."

"Enough!" Abigail shouted loud enough to startle them. "Do I get a say in what will be best for me? And for Mary Rose? Or do only you two intend to decide what I'll do?"

Stephen answered, his voice as steady and sure as if he already knew what she would decide. "Yes. Of course you'll have a say in your future. And that of Mary Rose. The choice will be yours. You can make a life for yourself with Ethan and raise a family of your own, or you can come with Mary Rose and me."

Abigail didn't react. Ethan thought he saw a slight lift to her chin, and recognized a more determined look on her face, but her thoughts were hidden from him.

"There's no need to make your decision now, Abigail," Stephen added, his voice teaming with consideration. "You may have all the time you want. There's no need to make a decision until I am healthy enough to return to Society."

Abigail didn't look at Ethan but kept her eyes riveted on Stephen, the man she'd once agreed to marry.

Ethan's heart threatened to stop beating. His world tipped on its axis. He was in jeopardy of losing everything. He was in jeopardy of losing Abigail. And Mary Rose.

He couldn't let it end like this. "Abigail?"

She didn't look at him. Didn't twitch a muscle or lift a brow. Or clench her fists in indecision. "I'm the only mother Mary Rose has ever known. I'll never be separated from her," she said without hesitation. "Never."

Ethan digested what she said as if each word was a bullet fired at him from close range. The heavy weight inside his chest ached with a force he could barely stand up against.

On legs that felt inhumanly wooden, he made his way to the door. He struggled to take in enough air to sustain him until he made it through the opening. Then he closed the door behind him.

She had made her choice.

Dear God in Heaven. How could he live with what she'd decided?

Chapter 29

Ethan pulled harder on the fallen yardarm, the hot sun beating down on his bare back, the muscles across his shoulders straining under the weight of the heavy wood that had trapped the knotted rigging he endeavored to untangle.

Another set of helping hands would have made the job much easier, but there wasn't a sailor aboard the *Emerald Gold* foolish enough to come within fifty feet of him. Mac included.

He'd been doing the work of three men ever since he'd left Abigail nearly six hours earlier, working out his anger and frustration as if eventually the pain of losing her wouldn't hurt quite so much. Ethan sucked in another heavy breath, the burning in his chest razor sharp and biting. What if this hurt never went away?

He heaved another piece of timber that should have taken two men to lift. *Bloody hell!* She hadn't even hesitated when she'd made her declaration to stay with Mary Rose.

I'll never be separated from Mary Rose. Never.

How had he been so foolish as to think she would

choose him? How could she have given herself to him with such total and complete abandon all those weeks on the ship when she could make the decision to leave him so easily? How could he have given her his heart without realizing he was at risk of losing it?

He straightened his stance, his feet braced wide, his arms stretched out, his hands gripping two taut lines of rigging. A breeze washed over him, soothing the burning muscles across his shoulders. If only the wind could ease the hurt inside his chest, the ache that threatened to take him to his knees.

A cruel desperation consumed every part of him, especially the part that knew he wouldn't survive when she left.

He dropped his head back on his shoulders and closed his eyes, letting the bright sunshine bathe him. How could he ever give her up?

How could he force her to stay with him if it meant she'd lose Mary Rose?

His fingers tightened around the rigging that spiraled high above him. If he closed his eyes, he could still see the glazed look of passion in her eyes the last time they'd made love. Hear her loud cries of fulfillment when she found her release. Feel the desperation in her kisses, the frantic clutching of her hands as she'd pulled him to her and held him close. How could he survive without ever loving her again.

"Ethan."

Every muscle in his body froze. Her voice reached out to him, attacking him with a fresh wave of pain and loss and regret. He lifted his chin and stared out at the long line of ships anchored in the delta.

He fixed his gaze further into the distance. In the direction they would sail from London.

He couldn't look at her yet. Couldn't glimpse the face

that bewitched his every waking hour. That haunted his dreams and kept him awake. That drove him insane with wanting to hold her, to be with her, to bury himself deep within her. That didn't want to ever let her go. That sure as hell didn't want to hear her say goodbye.

"Go back, Abby. Stephen might need you."

"We need to talk."

"Not now. Maybe later."

"No. Now."

The challenge in her voice cut through the air like a sharpened sword slashing through satin.

He turned to face her. His heart twisted in his chest when he saw the determined look on her face. Her beauty stole his breath. She had such strength. Such daunting courage. She'd struggled to keep Mary Rose a secret, offering to give up her father's ships, even though losing them would cost her everything she owned.

She'd yielded to him when he'd forced her to marry him.

She'd faced Stafford not once, but twice, and had come out the victor both times.

She'd struggled so hard to keep her secrets, and as he discovered them, she'd acquiesced, giving over another part of herself, even though it cost her much to do it.

She deserved to be with Mary Rose and make a life where she would be happy. He owed her as much.

"Very well. Perhaps it's best to get this over."

She nodded. "I'll wait for you in your cabin." She walked to the stairway that led to the cabin where they'd first made love.

He thought of that first night and all the nights they'd spent together after. That seemed so long ago. Nearly three weeks. Could she know yet?

"Abby?"

She paused and looked over her shoulder. She wore a questioning look on her face.

"Is there any chance you are with child?"

He saw that his words took her aback. Her chin lifted just enough to show her surprise. An expression he couldn't read covered her face, then she slowly shook her head. "No, Ethan," she whispered, before turning away and making her way to the stairs.

A knot tightened in the pit of his stomach. Her denial sealed their fate. He would release her from her vows. He owed it to her. He loved her too much to keep her bound to him.

He breathed in a deep breath and followed her down the familiar six stairs, through the narrow corridor, and into the cabin. She stood in the center of the room, her hands clasped in front of her, her shoulders braced with regal stiffness. Her chin held high.

"I'll not force you to stay with me," he said, walking into the room and standing beside the window next to the desk. "And I'll not fight to keep you as my wife. I want you to go to Sydney. He will help you obtain an annulment. You may use whatever excuse you want to have our marriage dissolved. The reason matters very little." His words burned as he said them, and he extended his arm and braced it against the wall, thankful for something solid to hold him. "I'll sign the papers before I leave."

"How generous of you," she said, unable to hide the sting in her voice. "Does that mean you no longer want me?" She paused. "Or that you never did."

He turned his head until he could see her. "You know better than that. I was not the one who chose to stay with Mary Rose."

"No. You were not. You were the one who refused to

fight to keep me."

Her words cut him to the quick, and he closed his eyes to block out the pain. He heard her emerald-green satin skirts swish as she walked across the room, then heard the door close, the hollow thud of her leaving landing yet another painful punch low in his gut.

He thought she was gone but turned at the next sound he heard. The sound of the key turning in the lock.

"What are you doing?"

"I've locked the door."

He stared at her, at the calm look on her face, at the brave and defiant glimmer in her eyes as she faced him. She was like a woman possessed. A woman with a purpose.

"Why?"

"Because you have left me no choice." She dangled the key from her fingers, then dropped it to the cabin floor in front of the door. "Because in that noble, irritating, self-sacrificing habit of yours, you have made the biggest mistake of your life. I'll not allow it. One of us has to fight."

With a graceful swish of her foot, she kicked the key with her soft kid slipper and sent it flying beneath the door out into the corridor.

"That was the only key I had," he said, his mind struggling to make sense of what she'd just done.

"Really?"

Even though he knew it was futile, he couldn't resist reaching out to test the door. "We're locked in here."

She ignored his warning and walked past him with a haughty swish of her satin skirts.

He stared at her with a look of incredulity as she made her way to the tall clothes chest in the corner and swung open the door. Without hesitation, she undid each of the small ivory buttons on the bodice of her dress. When her gown gaped open to below her waist, she pushed it from her shoulders and let it puddle at her feet on the floor. The creamy white of her shoulders glistened in the bright sunlight. The soft rise of her generous breasts bubbled above her lace-edged undergarment. A knot tightened low in his stomach.

"What are you doing?"

"I'm getting undressed." She hung her gown on a hook inside the closet.

Every inch of his flesh warmed at the sight of her. "I can see that. But why?"

He could almost remember the feel of her satiny skin beneath his roving fingertips. Feel the warmth of her naked flesh moving beneath him. Feel the welcoming openness in her embrace.

She looked at him with a glint in her eyes and a seductive smile on her face he was not used to seeing. She pulled at the satin ribbon that laced her chemise and let it gape open. "The door is locked and we have no way of getting out until someone comes to rescue us. Which I can assure you will not happen anytime soon. Perhaps days. Surely, husband, you can think of something for us to do to occupy our time until we are interrupted."

With that, she unfastened the tabs to her petticoats and let them fall. His mouth went dry, his body hardened in anticipation.

"What about Stephen?"

She stopped and pierced him with an intense look, then kicked off her slippers. "What about him?"

"He intends to take Mary Rose back with him and be a father to her."

Clad only in a calico chemise and white stockings, she walked over to where he stood and touched a finger to his naked chest. "I've convinced him that taking Mary Rose to London wouldn't be in her best interest. Or his own."

All she'd done was touch him, but his skin burned hotter than if she'd bathed him in fire. When he spoke, his voice came out rough and dry. "How did you do that?"

"It was simple." She ran her nails across his shoulders, then teased her fingers across his chest. He thought he would die.

"I simply told him that if he tried to take Mary Rose away from us, I'd tell the world that you were her father and I was her mother."

"But that's not true," he whispered. His breathing came in heavy gasps. "No one would believe you."

"Of course they would," she said, then lifted her hand and brushed his hair from his forehead. "Society is always eager for a new scandal."

Before he could recover, she leaned forward and kissed his skin, her hands working their way down his torso. He fisted his hands at his side while every muscle in his body screamed in response.

"Especially when I tell them the reason Stephen left all those months ago was because he discovered us in bed together and couldn't stand the humiliation."

"But you would be ruined," he said. He had to touch her. He skimmed his hands over her flesh, letting his callused fingertips appreciate her softness.

"No. My life would be ruined if I were separated from you. My life would be nothing if I couldn't spend every day until I die being your wife." She leaned up and kissed him. "Oh, Ethan. Don't you know? I love you. I've loved you for so long, but was afraid. Afraid to trust you enough to tell you my secrets. Afraid you could never forgive what I'd done. Afraid that I'd lose you when you found out. Please, tell me you still love me. Please."

He pulled her close to him and held her in his arms, fearful that he'd lose her if he let her go. "I do, Abby. I love you more than life itself. I'd have died if you had left me."

"Kiss me, Ethan. Now."

He lowered his head and pressed his mouth against hers. All the pent-up need and hunger and desire he'd felt for her took form in the melding of their lips, in the frantic desperation of their kiss.

He tipped her head to the side, deepening his kiss, satisfying the craving he'd thought would never be sated again. He opened his mouth atop hers, demanding submission.

She yielded. Her mouth opened to grant him admittance, her tongue eagerly awaiting, anticipating his assault, his dominance.

He kissed her again. And again. He couldn't take in enough of her, couldn't touch enough of her with his hands. He scooped her into his arms and carried her to the bed.

His breathing came in ragged gulps, his lungs fighting to fill with air, his hands trembling with desire. He wanted her so desperately he couldn't wait to lie beside her and take her in his arms. He put his weight on the bed, then stopped. "We're moving," he said, then leaned down to kiss her again.

"I know," she answered between kisses.

"Where are we going?"

"I didn't ask. But Mac promised he wouldn't bring us back until I told him to."

He lay down with her on the bed. "And when will that be?" he asked, kissing her again.

"It's a secret."

His head came away from hers. "No. There will be no more secrets between us. Do you hear?"

"Oh, yes," she said, pulling his mouth back to hers. He kissed her deeply.

"So when will we be coming back?"

"Not for a long time, husband. A very long time. Not until I'm certain you never doubt how much I love you ever again."

He lowered his head and kissed her again, then worked his way down her neck and lower. "I think you should begin convincing me right now, love."

"Oh, yes," she gasped, holding him to her. "A task I intend to continue for the rest of our lives."

"I love you," he whispered, and matched her wave for wave as the sea they both loved carried them gently into the life they'd made in one another.

About
Laura Landon

Laura Landon enjoyed ten years as a high school teacher and nine years making sundaes and malts in her very own ice cream shop, but once she penned her first novel, she closed up shop to spend every free minute writing. Now she enjoys creating her very own heroes and heroines, and making sure they find their happily ever after.

A vital member of her rural community, Laura directed the town's Quasquicentennial celebration, organized funding for an exercise center for the town, and serves on the hospital board.

Laura lives in the Midwest, surrounded by her family and friends. She has written nearly two dozen Victorian historicals, all of which are selling worldwide in English, and several which are currently printed in Japanese, German, Turkish and Russian. She is a Prairie Muse Platinum and Amazon Montlake author.

Visit Laura at
www.lauralandon.com

Also from Laura Landon
by Prairie Muse Publishing

SHATTERED DREAMS
WHEN LOVE IS ENOUGH
BROKEN PROMISE
A MATTER OF CHOICE
MORE THAN WILLING
NOT MINE TO GIVE
TANGLED: Boxed Set
LOVE UNBIDDEN
THE DARK DUKE
CAST IN SHADOWS
CAST IN RUIN
CAST IN ICE

From Laura Landon
by Montlake Romance

SILENT REVENGE
INTIMATE SURRENDER
INTIMATE DECEPTION
THE MOST TO LOSE
A RISK WORTH TAKING
BETRAYED BY YOUR KISS
WHERE THE WOMAN BELONGS novella

From Kindle Press
THE SECRET ROSE new in 2016

LAURA LANDON IS A PRAIRIE MUSE PLATINUM
AMAZON MONTLAKE AND KINDLE PRESS AUTHOR

WWW.LAURALANDON.COM

CPSIA information can be obtained at www.ICGtesting.com
Printed in the USA
BVOW02s0742310716

457429BV00001B/36/P

9 781937 216689